W9-AER-490

JOSEPH IN EGYPT

THOMAS MANN

JOSEPH IN EGYPT

[VOLUME TWO]

Translated from the German for the first time by H. T. Lowe-Porter

NEW YORK · ALFRED · A · KNOPF

1938

CONTENTS

VOLUME TWO

21512

JOSEPH IN EGYPT

�֍

THE SMITTEN ONE

THE WORD OF MISTAKING

AND it came to pass after these things that his master's wife cast her eyes upon Joseph; and she said —

All the world knows what Mut-em-enet, Potiphar's chief wife, is supposed to have said when she cast her eyes upon Joseph, her husband's young steward, and I will not and dare not deny that at last, one day, in her extremity, in the fever of her despair she did actually so speak, did make use of the frightfully direct and frank expression which tradition puts in her mouth. So direct, indeed, so frank, that it sounds like a lewd proposal coming from a woman who made it quite naturally and at small cost to herself, instead of being the final outcry of her utter agony of spirit and flesh. To tell the truth, I am horrified at the briefness and curtness of the original account, which does so little justice to life's bitter circumstantiality. Seldom have I felt more acutely than in this connection the harm done to truth by abbreviation and compression. Yet let no one think that I am deaf to the reproach — whether expressed or, out of politeness, not expressed — which hangs over my account, my entire exposition: to the effect that the laconic terseness of the original text cannot be surpassed, and that my whole enterprise, which is already of such long continuance, is so much labour lost. But since when, may I ask, does a commentator set himself up in competition with his text? And besides, is there not as much dignity and importance attached to the discussion of the " how " as to the transmission of the " what "? Yes, does not life first fulfill itself in the " how "? Let us remind ourselves once again that before the story was first told, it had to tell itself — with an exactitude of which life alone is master, and to attain which a narrator has no hope or prospect at all. He can only approach it by serving the " how " of life more faithfully than the lapidary spirit of the " what " condescended to do. But if ever the fidelity of a commentator can justify itself, then surely it does in the story of Potiphar's wife and of just what, according to the tradition, she is supposed to have said.

For the picture which one inevitably makes, or is irresistibly tempted to make, of Joseph's mistress; the picture, I fear, which most people make of her, is so false that one does a service to the original in correcting it in the way of truth — if we understand by original the first written, or better yet the story as life first told it. This deceptive picture of unbridled lust and shameless allurement does not, at least, agree with what we overheard, when we were with Joseph in the garden-house, from the lips of dignified old Tuia about her daughter-in-law. It was there that we began to learn with a little more particularity of the life of the house. Petepre's mother called her " proud," after declaring that it was impossible to accuse her of being a goose. Haughty she said she was, reserved, a moon-nun, a nature with the bitter fragrance of the myrtle leaf. Does such a one speak as tradition

makes her speak? Yet she did so speak, literally and re-
peatedly, as her pride broke under the assaults of passion.
We are agreed upon that. But the tradition neglects to
state how much time passed during which she would have
bitten out her tongue rather than have so spoken. It neglects to say that sitting in solitude she actually, literally,
and physically bit her tongue so that she stammered for
pain when first she uttered the words that for all time
have stamped her for a seductress. A seductress? A
woman, overcome as she was, is of course seductive —
seductiveness is the exterior and physical shape taken by
her affliction; it is nature makes her eyes sparkle more
sweetly than any drops the toilette-table can supply;
heightens more alluringly the red of her lips than rouge
can do it, and pouts them in a soulful, suggestive smile;
makes her dress and adorn herself with innocently abandoned calculation; gives her movements and all her body
a purposeful grace, lending to it, as far as physical constitution permits, and even a little further, an expression
of blissful promise. And all that fundamentally means
nothing else than what Joseph's mistress finally said to
him. But is she to whom it happens so to speak from
within to be made responsible? Does she do it out of
deviltry? Does she even know of it — otherwise than
through her torturing pangs which express themselves in
outward charm? In short, if she is made seductive, is she
then a seductress?

In the first place we must examine the nature and form
of the seduction in the light of the birth and upbringing
of the smitten one. Against the assumption that Mut-em-
enet, familiarly called Eni or even Enti, behaved herself
in her afflicted state like a common prostitute must be set

her whole nurture, which was aristocratic to an unimaginable degree. It is but just that we should — as we did in the case of Mont-kaw — consider briefly the origins of the woman who exerted upon Joseph's destiny an influence so very different from that of our honest steward.

It will surprise nobody to hear that the wife of Petepre the fan-bearer was no daughter of an innkeeper or quarry labourer. Her stock was no more and no less than that of the old princes of the nome, though it had been long ago that her forbears had lived like patriarchal kings on their extended property in one of the districts of Middle Egypt. Foreign sovereigns of Asiatic shepherd blood had then lived in the north and worn the double crown, and the princes of Wese, in the south, had for centuries been subject to these invaders. But there had arisen men of might, Sekenenre and his son Kamose, who rebelled against the shepherd kings and fought them stoutly, finding their foreign blood an effective stimulant to their own ambitions. Yes, Ahmoses, the dauntless brother of Kamose, had laid siege to the invaders' fortified royal seat, Avaris, had taken it and driven the kings from the country, setting it free, in the sense that he and his house took it for their own and substituted their domination for the foreign one. Not all of the nome princes had been at once willing to regard the hero Ahmoses as their deliverer or his sovereignty over them as freedom. Some of them had on whatever grounds adhered to the foreigners in Avaris, preferring to remain their vassals rather than be freed by somebody else. Even after their old overlords had been entirely ejected some of these petty kings, unambitious for freedom, mutinied against their deliverer and, as the sources say, " gathered the rebels against him " so that he had first to defeat them in open battle before freedom was established. It goes without saying that these rebels forfeited their estates. It was the method of the Theban deliverers to keep for themselves what they had taken from the foreigner; so that a process now began which at the time of our tale was already far advanced though only entirely consummated in the course of it: that is to say, the dispossession of the princes and the confiscation of their property in favour of the Theban crown. The latter gradually became the owner of all the lands and let them out or presented them to favourites or religious houses — as, for instance, Pharaoh had presented the island in the river to Petepre. But the old princes of the nome became a new class of officials and nobility, who owed allegiance to Pharaoh and occupied commanding posts in his army and administration.

From such as these, then, Mut had come. Joseph's mistress descended directly from a nome prince called Teti-'an, who in his time had " gathered the rebels " and had to be defeated in battle before he admitted that he was free. But Pharaoh did not lay that up against Teti-'an's grandchildren and great-grandchildren. Their clan had remained great and aristocratic, it gave to the state commanders of troops, heads of cabinets, and administrators of the treasury, to the court high stewards, first charioteers and overseers of the royal bath-house; some of them, for instance the administrative heads of large cities, like Menfe or Tine, even kept their old princely titles. Eni's father, Mi-Sakhme, held the high office of a city prince of Wese — one of two; for there

was one for the city of the living and one for the city of
the dead in the West, and Mi-Sakhme was prince of the
Western city. As such, to use Joseph's language, he lived
as one of high rank and might certainly anoint himself
with the oil of gladness — he and his, including Eni, his
fine-limbed child, even though she was no longer a landed
princess but the daughter of a modern office-holder. In
the destiny which her parents chose for her one can read
the changes that had taken place in the ways of thinking
of the clan since the days of the fathers. They gained
great advantage at court when they gave their beloved
child in her tender age to the son of Tuia and Huia, Petepre, the man-made courtier; yet in doing so they proved
that the instinct for fruitfulness possessed by their land-
owning, soil-attached forbears had been greatly weak-
ened by modern ideas.

Mut was a child when her parents disposed of her
destiny in the same way that Potiphar's parents had disposed of their unsteady little son when they speculated
in the hereafter and made him a courtier of light. The
claims of sex which Mut's parents passed over, claims
symbolized by the water-darkened earth, the moon-egg,
the origin of all material life, were still but a germ, still
slumbering within her; she was unconscious of them, she
made not the least objection to the loving, life-denying
deed. She was blithe, merry, untroubled, free. She was
like a water-flower swimming upon a glassy pool, smiling
beneath the kisses of the sun, untouched by the knowledge
that its long stem is rooted in the black slime of the
depths. The conflict between her eyes and her mouth
had not existed in those days, rather a childish inexpres-
sive harmony, and her pert, little-girl glance was undark-

ened by any harshness. The peculiar serpentine shape of
the mouth, with its deep corners, had not been nearly
so pronounced. The discord between them had come
about gradually in the course of years during her life as
moon-nun and titular consort of the sun-chamberlain —
in token, obviously, that the mouth is a tool and image
more closely allied to the nether powers than is the eye.

As for her body, everybody knew its shape and loveliness, for the " woven air," that luxurious silken fabric like
a zephyr's breath which she wore in compliance with the
custom of the land, revealed its every line to the admiring
eye. And one might say that it was more in harmony
with her mouth than with her eyes. Its honourable rank
had not checked its ripening or its bloom. The small firm
breasts, the fine line of neck and back, the tender shoulders and perfect statuesque arms, the high-flanked legs
expanding into the splendidly feminine haunches and
pelvis — all these composed a form admitted far and
wide to be the most beautiful of its sex. Wese knew none
more worthy of praise; and as men's nature was, the sight
of it stirred in them old lovely fantasies, pictures of beginnings and pre-beginnings, pictures that had to do with
the moon-egg and the origin of things: the picture of a
glorious virgin, which, at bottom — right at the bottom,
in the moist earth — was the goose of love itself in the
shape of a virgin, and in its lap, with spread wings flap-
ping, nestled a splendid specimen of a swan, a strong
and tender snowy-feathered god, fluttering his love-sick
work upon her, honourably surprised, that she might bear
the egg.

Such pictures of aforetime did indeed light up in the
inmost depths of Wese's folk, where they had lain in

darkness, at sight of Mut-em-enet's translucent form, although they knew the moon-chaste honourable state in which she lived and which could be read from the stern look in her eyes. They knew that those eyes gave a truer measure of her essence and activities than did the mouth, which said far other things and which might well have looked down smiling if protesting upon the activities of a royal bird. They were aware that this body knew its greatest moments, its highest satisfaction and fulfilment, not in receiving such royal visits, but only on the feast-days when she shook her rattle and danced the cult-dance before Amun-Re. They did not gossip about her; no evil rumours went round in the sense of Mut-em-enet's mouth, to which her eyes would have given the lie. They were sharp-tongued enough about others, who were more truly married than Teti-'an's grandchild and yet played fast and loose in the point of morals: ladies of the order, harem women of the god. Renenutet, for instance, wife of the overseer of bulls: things were known of her which Amun's overseer wotted not of. Plenty was known, jokes enough were made behind her car or her carrying-chair — hers and others' too. But of Petepre's chief and, so to speak, true wife nothing was known in Thebes, and folk were convinced that there was nothing to know. They took her for a saint, reserved and apart, in Petepre's house and court as well as abroad; and that was signifi-cant, considering the love of joking inborn among the people.

Whatever my readers may think, I do not consider it to be my task to inquire into the habits of Mizraim and in particular of No-Amun's feminine world. I mean such habits as long ago we heard condemned in old Jacob's forthright way. His knowledge of the world had a strongly emotional tinge, a mythical reference, which we must realize in order not to exaggerate. Yet his lofty condemnation was not without grounds. Among a people who have neither word nor understanding for sin, and who go about in garments made of woven air, people whose attitude toward death and worship of animals betokens and induces a certain fleshliness, one must assume — even without knowledge or experience — the existence of a light moral attitude. And Jacob, making this assumption, couched it in poetic, high-sounding words. Experience, then, bore out the assumption — I say it less in malice than in satisfaction of the claims of logic. But to confirm the assumption by prying into the daily lives of the wives of Wese would be beneath our dignity. Much can be pardoned, little disputed. We should need only to intercept a few glances between Renenutet, wife of the overseer of bulls, and a certain very smart lieutenant of the royal bodyguard, or between the same exalted lady and a young shiny-pated temple-treader of Khonsu, to realize that things went on which to some extent justified Jacob's picturesque language. It is not our affair to sit in judgment on the morals of Wese — that great city of more than a hundred thousand people. We must, where we cannot sustain a position, abandon it. But I would put my hand in the fire and swear, staking the whole of my reputation as a story-teller, that one of those led a blameless life, up to a certain time, when the gods made of her a reeling mænad: I mean the daughter of Mi-Sakhme, prince of the nome, Mut-em-enet, Potiphar's wife. To see her as a natural prostitute, upon whose lips those words we know for ever trembled and were lightly released, is so false that truth demands its complete refutation. When she did, biting her tongue, utter them, she knew herself no more; she was beside herself, her reason dethroned by agony, a sacrifice to the scourge-swinging, avenging lust of powers to which she was committed by her mouth, while the eyes had thought to treat them with detachment and contempt.

THE OPENING OF THE EYES

WE know that Mut's well-intentioned parents had betrothed and married her to the son of Huia and Tuia when she was still a child. We need to remember this; for it followed that she had got accustomed to the formal nature of her married life, while the moment when she might have realized its actual character still lay in fluid darkness. Thus she had nominally lost her maiden state at too early an age — but there it stopped. Hardly yet even a maiden, rather a half-grown girl, she found herself a spoilt darling, head of an aristocratic " house of women," in command of every luxury, every flattery, surrounded by the half-savage servility of naked Moorish women and kneeling eunuchs; first and titular wife and chief over fifteen other idle, passive, and voluptuous females chosen for their beauty, of very varied origins, and themselves the empty and honorary apanage of a courtier who could not enjoy them. Of these dreamy-eyed, chattering females she was the queen; they hung on her words, were plunged in melancholy when she was sad, and burst into delighted cackles when she was merry. They quarrelled addle-patedly over Petepre's favours when he came to the women's house to play a game at draughts with Mut-em-enet, while amber brandy and sweets were handed round. So then she was the star of the harem, and at the same time the female head of the whole establishment, Potiphar's wife in a higher and more special sense than the concubines; the real mistress and — under other circumstances — the mother of his children. She occupied when she chose quarters of her own, separated from her husband's by the northern columned hall where Joseph performed his reading service. And she was hostess and housewife at those exclusive entertainments and musicales given by Petepre, the friend of Pharaoh, to the high society of Thebes — in return for which they were entertained at similar functions in aristocratic houses in the city.

It was a nervous life, full of elegant obligations — superfluous ones if you like, but no less consuming to the energies for all that. We know that in every civilization that ever existed the demands of social life, of culture itself, tend to choke with luxuriant detail the overburdened forces of the upper-class woman; so that the life of her soul and her senses is submerged in conventional circumstance and she never actually gets round to it at all. A cool, unoccupied heart, not troubled because unaware of a lack, and thus not even pathetic, becomes a habitual state of existence. In all times and regions these worldly women, possessing no temperament, have existed in high society. One may go so far as to say that it matters little whether the husband of such a one is a captain of troops in an actual or only in an honorary sense. The ritual of the toilette is equally important whether its aim is to preserve desire in the breast of a husband or is practised as an end in itself and as a social duty. Mut, like other ladies of her station, devoted hours to it daily. There was the painfully elaborated care of her finger- and toe-nails, until they shone like enamel; the perfumed baths, the depilatories, the massage to which she sub- jected her beautiful body. There was the critical busi- ness of applying drops and paint to her eyes — beautiful enough already, with their irises of metallic blue and their practised and sparkling glances, they became veri- table jewels through the artful application of rouge, pencil, and other sweet enhancements. There was the care of her hair; her own was a half-length mass of shining black locks, which she liked to dust with gold or blue powder — and besides that the wigs, in various colours, braided, plaited, in tresses, and with pearl fringes. There was the fastidious adjustment of the snowy garments to the embroidered sashes pressed by the iron into lyre-shape and the little shoulder-capes moulded into tiny pleats; the choice of ornaments for head, neck, and arms, presented by kneeling slaves. And throughout all this nobody must so much as smile: the nude Moorish girls, the sewing-women, the barber eunuchs preserved their solemnity nor did Mut herself smile, for the slight- est carelessness or neglect in these high matters would have called down the reproach of the great world and made a scandal at court.

Then there were the visits in her carrying-chair to friends of like station; and the receiving of them at home. And Mut was lady-in-waiting to Tiy, the wife of the god; she must attend at the palace Merimat and like her husband carry the fan. Also she was summoned to the evening water-parties which the consort of Amun held on the artificial lake called into being by Pharaoh's com-

mand in the royal gardens, where torches of the recently
invented coloured fire steeped the water in sparkling hues.
And then — as we are reminded by our mention of the
mother of the god — there were the famous honorary
religious duties, functions combining the social with the
priestly, and responsible more than anything else for the
stern and haughty expression of Mut's eyes. These duties
arose out of her membership of the order of Hathor and
her capacity of wife to Amun; they fell to her as wearer
of the cow's horns with the sun's disk between; in short,
as " goddess in her time." It is strange how much this
side of Eni's life contributed to heighten her cool world-
liness as a great lady and to keep her heart empty of
softer dreams. It did so in connection with the titular
character of her marriage — though there was no necessary connection between them. Amun's house of women
was in no sense a place of the *intactæ*. Restraint of the
flesh was far from being an attribute of the great mother
as whose representatives Mut and her fellow-members
performed their feasts. The queen, the god's bedfellow
and mother of the coming sun, was the protectress of the
order. Its head, as I have already more than once mentioned, was a married woman, wife of Amun's prepotent
high priest; and married women preponderated among
its members — such as Renenutet, wife of the overseer of
bulls (we pass over further comment on the state of her
morals). In fact, Mut's temple office had to do with her
marriage only in so far as she owed, socially speaking,
the one to the other. But in her own mind, privately, she
did what Huia the hoarse had done in his conversation
with his old bed-sister: she connected her priestly office
with the singularity of her marriage and, without putting

the thing into words, found it suitable, indeed quite the proper thing, for a wife of the god to have an earthly husband made like Petepre. And she knew how to convey this conception to her social circle, so that they sustained her in it and thought of her membership in the order of Hathor as that of a being set apart and religiously chaste. And all this contributed even more than Mut's lovely voice and the elegance of her dancing to the pre-eminence of her position in the order — almost equal indeed to the lofty station of its head. In this way did Mut's will-power mould outward conditions and create for her those super-compensations of which the mute depths of her being so painfully stood in need.

Was she a nymphomaniac? A loose woman? The idea is absurd. Mut-em-enet was a saint, a chaste moon-nun of high social position, whose strength was consumed partly in the demands of her highly cultured life, but partly, so to speak, was temple property and transmuted into spiritual pride. Thus had she lived: as Potiphar's first and titular wife, petted and indulged, carried in the arms of subordinates, knelt to and bowed to from all sides. Her compensations were so superior that not even in dreams was she confronted by images from that sphere so well represented by her sinuous mouth. By goose-wishes, to put it arrestingly! For it is false to regard the dream as a free and savage domain where all that is forbidden to the waking thought may come out and revel unashamed. What the waking state definitely does not know, what is simply shut off from it, the dream does not know either. The border between the two is fluid, it permits of interpenetration; there is but one space, through which the soul hesitantly moves, and that it is one, indivisible for the conscience and the pride, is proved by Mut's bewilderment, the panic shame she suffered not only in her waking hours but when she for the first time dreamed of Joseph.

When did that happen? In her world, the world of our narration, they were careless about counting the years; and we are somewhat conditioned by their habit. We must estimate as best we can. Eni was certainly several years younger than her husband, whom we have seen as a man at the end of the thirties when Joseph was sold to him. In the meantime he had added seven years to his age. She, then, was not like him in the middle of her forties, but several years less; certainly, however, a mature woman, much older than Joseph. Just how much older I am reluctant to ask; my reluctance is justifiable, springing as it does from a profound respect for the feminine cult of the toilette-table, which can go far to annihilate the years, and in its results upon the senses surely possesses a higher veracity than mere reckoning with a pencil can have. Since the day when Joseph first saw his mistress, as she swayed past him in her golden chair, he had increased his charms for the feminine eye. But she had not increased hers — at least not for one who saw her uninterruptedly. Woe to the preparers of creams and the massage-eunuchs if those years had been able to show any change to her disadvantage! But her face, with its saddle-nose and strange shadowy hollows in the cheeks, though it had never been actually beautiful, still preserved its mixture of conformity and caprice, of fashionable convention and anomalous charm, which it had always had; though the disturbing contradiction between the eyes and the sinuous mouth had probably been accentuated. To one inclined to be attracted by the disturbing — and there are such people — she had probably only grown more lovely.

The beauty of Joseph, on the other hand, had probably outgrown the stage of youthful charm for which it had always been so bepraised. At four-and-twenty he was still — perhaps only then entirely — a figure to marvel at. But his beauty had ripened beyond that equivocalness of his youth while preserving its general effectiveness; and specifically in that it made a much more direct appeal to the feminine emotions. It had been ennobled, because it had become more manly. His face was no longer that of the Bedouin boy, insidiously seductive — though still reminiscent of it at times, as when — though not at all short-sighted — he narrowed his eyes and veiled them in the way that Rachel had done. But it was fuller and more serious, and darkened by Egypt's sun; its features too had grown more regular and refined. I have referred already to the changes in his figure, his movements, and the sound of his voice — due, these last, to the tasks he had performed. We must add, in order to get a true picture of him as he now was, that his whole appearance had become more refined, being worked upon by the cultural influences of the land. We must think of him arrayed in the white linen of the Egyptian upper classes; transparent, so that the under-garments showed through; with short sleeves, revealing the forearms adorned with enamel rings. His head was bare, dressed in its own smooth hair, save on formal occasions, when he wore a light wig of the best sheep's-wool, something between a head-cloth and a peruke, fitting the top of his head with thick, fine, even strands like ribbed silk. Along a diagonal line it changed into small overlapping curls, like tiles on a roof, which came down on neck and shoulders. Round his neck besides the gaily coloured collar he wore a flat chain made of reed and gold beads, with a scarab amulet. His face had slightly changed its expression; it had a hieratic cast, due to his make-up; for he accentuated the line of the brows and lengthened the eyes evenly toward the temples. Thus he looked as he went about, setting his long staff before him, among the work-people, the steward's first " mouth." Thus he went to market, or stood behind Petepre's chair and beckoned to the waiters. Thus the mistress saw him, in the dining-room or the house of women, when he came before her, submissive in posture and speech, to deal with some household matter. And thus it was she actually first saw him; for previously her eyes never dwelt on the purchased slave, not even at the time when first he had known how to warm the heart of Potiphar. Even while he lived and waxed as by a spring, it had needed Dudu's complainings to open her eyes to the slave's appearance.

And even after her eyes had been opened, Dudu's tongue playing the part of calf's foot, she was far from properly seeing him. When after hearing of his offensive advancement in the house she had had to look at him, it was solely with stern-eyed curiosity that she gazed. The element of danger (we must put it like that, if we are concerned for her pride or her peace of mind) consisted in that it was Joseph on whom her eyes fell, Joseph whose eyes met hers at seconds of time. It was a circumstance big with fate; and big enough too that little Bes, in his dwarfish wisdom, had perceived in it a hidden and fearful danger. He saw that Dudu's malice was bringing about a situation more destructive than anything he had dreamed of or could dream of, and that the opening of the eyes might be even all too wide. Inborn fear and dread of powers which he saw in the image of the fire-breathing bull made him prone to such intuitions. But Joseph, with culpable lightness — in this point I am not inclined to spare him — had affected not to understand, and assumed that Bes was dreaming, though probably in his heart he was of the same mind. For he too laid stress on the moments in the dining-room — less for what they meant than for the fact that they actually happened; in his folly he was glad that he was no longer empty air for the mistress, but that her look rested on him as on a human being, no matter how angry her gaze. And our Eni?

Well, Eni was no wiser than Joseph. She too had affected to misunderstand the dwarf. That she looked angrily at Joseph excused her in her own mind for looking at him at all. And this was a mistake from the very beginning; pardonable before she realized whom she saw when she looked, but after that less excusable and more culpable every time. The unhappy creature refused to see that the stern-eyed curiosity with which she regarded her husband's body-servant was losing its sternness, leaving the curiosity deserving of another and less orthodox name. She supposed herself to share in Dudu's indignation; she felt bound, indeed, to share in it on religious grounds, or — which was the same thing — on political and partisan ones: on the grounds of her relation with Amun, who could not fail to see in the preponderance of a Shabirite slave in Petepre's house an insult to himself and a surrender to the Asiatic tendencies of

Atum-Re. She had to make the anger last in order to justify the pleasure she felt in entertaining it; so she called it righteous anger and zeal for her cause. Our capacity for self-deception is amazing. When Mut had an hour free from her social duties — a short summer hour or a longer winter one — she would lie stretched out on her couch at the edge of the square basin let into the pavement of the open columned hall in the house of women. And lying there, watching the bright fish, seeing the floating lotus blossoms, she would muse to the accompaniment of soft stringed music played by an oily-locked little Nubian girl crouching at the back of the hall. And she was quite convinced of the tenor of her musings: she was considering the problem how, despite the obstinacy of her husband and Beknechons's statesmanlike vagueness, she could prevent this evil thing, that a slave from Zahi-land, one of the Ibrim, waxed great in the house. And so considering she omitted to notice how much pleasure it gave her to think about it. Though surely she knew that her pleasure had no other source than the intent to think about Joseph. Had we no pity for her we might be angered at such blindness. She even did not notice that she had begun to look forward to the meal-hour in the dining-room, when she might see him. She fancied that her pleasure sprang from her purpose to dart angry looks at him; it is pathetic, but she never dreamed that her sinuous lips curved in a self-forgotten smile, remembering how at her stern fixed gaze his startled, humble one would be swiftly hidden beneath his lowered lids. It was enough, she thought, if at such times she frowned her indignation at the affront to her house. Had the dwarf's little wisdom sought to warn her too, if it had spoken of the fire-breathing bull or hinted that the artificial fabric of her life was already shaken and threatened to totter to its fall, perhaps her face, too, might have got red. But she would have said that she blushed for anger at such nonsensical babble; she would have outdone herself in extravagant, hypocritical merriment and in deliberate misunderstanding of such misgivings. Who would be deceived by these exaggerated disclaimers? Certainly not he who sought to dissuade her. For they were but meant to dissemble the path of adventure which the deluded soul is bent on treading. To delude oneself, up to the point where it is too late to turn back — that one must do at all costs. To be awaked, warned, called back to oneself before it is too late: there lies the danger which is at all costs to be avoided. Then let the kind-hearted observer beware of making himself absurd with unwarranted sympathy. Let him not benevolently assume that the human being's deepest concern is for peace, tranquillity, the preservation of the carefully erected structure of his life from shattering and collapse. For, to put it mildly, the assumption is unwarranted. Too much evidence goes to show that he is headed straight for ecstasy and ruin — and thanks nobody in the very least who would hold him back. In that case — what use?

As for Enti, the kind-hearted observer must — not without some bitterness — take it for granted that she was brilliantly successful in gliding over the moment when it was not yet too late and she was not yet quite lost. A moment of terrifying rapture and realization came to her with the dream I spoke of, which she dreamed about Joseph. Then truly she was aghast and shook in all her limbs. She remembered that she was a being endowed with reason, and she behaved accordingly. That is to say, she imitated the conduct of a reasonable being; mechanically she behaved like one, but not actually as one. She took steps, for the success of which she could no longer sincerely wish — confused, unworthy steps, before which the well-wishing friend must simply hide his head and take care lest he feel an unseasonable pity.

It is almost impossible to put a dream into words and relate it. For in a dream little importance attaches to the actual matter and everything to the aura and atmosphere, the incommunicable sense of horror or of blessedness, or both, which wraps it and which often till long afterwards engrosses the soul of the dreamer. In this tale of ours dreams play a decisive rôle; its hero dreams greatly and childishly; and there will be others in it who will dream. But how hard would all of them find it even to approach the inwardness of what they dream, how unsatisfactory would they find every effort to do so! We have only to recall Joseph's dream of the sun, moon, and stars, and the helpless insufficiency with which he told it. I may then be forgiven if in relating Mut's dream I fail quite to convey the impression it made upon the dreamer, both when she dreamed it and afterwards. But having said so much, I may not withhold an accounting of it.

She dreamed, then, that she sat at table in the hall with the blue columns; in her chair on the dais, beside old Huia, and ate her dinner in the tactful silence which always prevailed. But this time the silence was particularly forbearing and profound; the four companions not only refrained from speech but were even noiseless in all their motions, so that in the stillness one could hear the breathing of the servants as they passed to and fro —

so distinctly indeed that they seemed not to be breathing
so much as panting and would have been audible even
were the silence less profound. The quick, soft sounds
were disquieting; perhaps because Mut was listening,
perhaps for some other reason, she lost sight of what she
was doing and gave herself a wound. She was cutting a
pomegranate with a sharp little bronze knife, when it
slipped and went into her hand, making rather a deep
gash in the soft flesh between the thumb and the four
fingers, so that it bled. There was a good deal of blood,
ruby red like the juice of the pomegranate; she saw it
flowing with distress and shame. Yes, she felt ashamed,
despite the beautiful ruby colour; partly of course because it stained the pure white of her garment, but also
aside from and beyond this she felt disproportionately
ashamed and sought to hide the blood from those about
her. Successfully as it seemed, or as they wanted it to
seem, for they assiduously behaved — with more or less
ease and convincingness — as though they saw nothing at
all. None of them troubled themselves over her distress,
which distressed her the more. She did not want to betray
that she was bleeding, she was ashamed; at the same time
she was indignant that nobody cared to see it, nobody
lifted a finger, but by common consent left her to herself. Her waitress, the affected damsel in the spider-web
garment, bent over the little one-legged table absorbed in
putting things on it to rights; old Huia at her side, his
head waggling, chewed away toothlessly at a gilt thigh-
bone whereon were stuck pieces of cake soaked in wine.
He held it by one end in his hand and acted as though he
were entirely consumed in chewing. Petepre, the master,
raised his cup behind him over his shoulder, for his

Syrian cup-bearer to fill it. And his mother, old Tuia, was cheerfully nodding her great pale face with the blind slits of eyes in the direction of the distracted Mut; though it was hard to say whether she even saw her daughter-in-law's predicament. And Mut, in her dream, went on bleeding, staining her white frock and feeling silent bitterness at the general indifference to her plight; also a distress which had nothing to do with that, but with the bright crimson blood itself. She rued indescribably the seeping and spouting flow; it was such a pity, such a pity! She felt so sorry for it, so sorry — she felt a deep, unspeakable anguish in her soul, not about herself and her plight, but about the sweet blood that was flowing away. She gave a short dry sob. Then she realized that in her trouble she had forgotten her duty to Amun, the obligation to look angrily at that offence to her house, the Canaanite slave, and do her part in discountenancing his advancement. So she darkened her brows and looked fiercely across at him where he stood behind Petepre's chair: young Osarsiph. Then he, as though summoned by her look, left his place and office and came toward her. And was near to her, so that she felt his nearness. But he had come near to her to quench the flowing of her blood. For he took her injured hand and carried it to his mouth, so that the fingers lay on his one cheek and the thumb on the other, the wound on the lips between. Then her blood stood still with ecstasy and was stanched. But in the hall, while she was being healed, there was unpleasant and disquieting bustle. All the servants there ran about distraught; light-footed, indeed, but panting in confused chorus. Petepre, the master, had veiled his face, his mother was touching the bowed and covered head with her outspread hands, desperately groping for him with her blind, upturned gaze. But Huia — Eni saw him get up and threaten her with his gold thigh-bone, from which all the cake had been munched. He scolded her soundlessly and his sorry little beard wagged up and down. The gods knew what abuse he was shaping with his toothless mouth and busy tongue! Perhaps its tenor was the same as what the servants were saying as they panted. For loud whispers formed themselves out of the panting and came to her ears: " To the fire, to the flood, to the dogs, to the crocodile! " They said it over and over. She had that awful whispering chant still in her ear when she emerged from her dream; cold with horror, then hot with ecstasy of her healing; and aware that life's rod had been laid about her shoulders.

HUSBAND AND WIFE

Now that her eyes were open, Mut resolved to behave like a reasonable human being and take a step worthy to stand before reason's throne. Its clear and unequivocal intent was to put Joseph out of her sight. She would lay the case for his departure before Petepre, her husband, with all the powers she had at command.

She had spent the next day after her dream alone, withdrawn from her sister wives and receiving no visits. She had sat beside the basin in the court and watched the darting fish; concentrating, as we say of a person whose gaze passes over the objects in its path and fixes itself on space. But all at once in the midst of this staring her eyes widened in alarm, opened wider and wider as though with horror while still staring at nothing; she opened her mouth and drew in a gasping breath. Then the eyes retracted; the corners of her mouth deepened and the lips relaxed in an unconscious smile beneath the dreaming gaze. For a whole minute she knew not that she smiled; with a start she pressed her hand upon those errant lips, the thumb on one cheek, the four fingers on the other. " Ye gods! " she murmured. Then it began anew: the dreamy stare, the gasp, the unconscious smiling, and the shocked recall — until at last the conclusion came: she must make an end to it all.

Toward sunset she inquired and learned that Petepre was in the house, and summoned her maids to dress her, that she might visit him.

Petepre was in his western hall, which looked out on the orchard and the little summerhouse on the mound. The sunset light, falling through the gay outer columns, began to fill the room and enrich the pale colours on the walls, the floor, and the ceiling, where pictures flung with careless ease by an artist hand adorned the stucco facing: a swamp with hovering birds; calves jumping; ponds with ducks; a herd of bulls being driven across a ford while a crocodile leered at them out of the water. The rear wall, between the doors which led into the dining-room, displayed pictures of the master of the house in his habit as he lived, and showed him returning home attended by assiduous servants. The doors were framed in glazed tiles covered with picture-writing in blue, red, and green on a dun-coloured background: sayings from ancient authors and lines from hymns to the gods. Along the wall between the doors ran a sort of raised ledge with a back, both of clay, covered with white stucco and with coloured picture-writing on the front. This ledge or bench

served as a stand for works of art, the presents in which
Petepre's house abounded. But you could also sit on it;
and there now he sat, the man full of honours, in the
middle, on a cushion, his feet together on a footstool,
while on both sides of him extended in a row the
most lovely objects: animals, images of the gods, royal
sphinxes, all made of gold, malachite, and ivory, and behind him the falcons, owls, ducks, wavy lines, and other
symbols of the inscriptions. He had made himself com-
fortable by taking off all his clothes down to the knee-
length skirt of strong white linen with a wide starched
draw-string. His upper garment, and his staff with his
sandals tied to it, lay on a lion-footed chair near one of
the doors. Yet there was no relaxation in his posture;
he sat up perfectly straight, his little hands stretched out
in his lap. They looked tiny compared with the massive-
ness of his body, as did his finely shaped, severely erect
head with its aristocratically hooked nose and well-cut
mouth. He sat there, a well-composed seated statue of
a fat yet dignified man. His powerful legs were like
straight columns, his arms like those of a fat woman; his
fat-upholstered chest was thrust out. His mild long-
lashed brown eyes looked straight before him through the
hall into the red evening light. In all his fatness he had no
belly, being narrow round the hips. His navel was striking: very large and horizontal, so that it looked like a
mouth.

He had sat there a long time thus motionless, in an idleness ennobled by the man's natural dignity. In the tomb
which awaited him a life-size counterfeit would stand in
a false door, in darkness, in the same immovable calm
which he now displayed in life, and gaze out of brown

glass eyes at paintings on the wall, where his household surroundings were depicted, for purposes of magic, that he might have them with him to all eternity. This statue would be the same precisely as he was — he anticipated the identity with it as he sat here now and made himself eternal. At his back and on the ledge close to his feet the picture-writings, red, blue, and green, expressed their meaning; on either side of him extended Pharaoh's gifts in long rows; most consonant with the Egyptian sense of form were the painted columns between which he gazed into the evening glow. To be surrounded by possessions favours immobility. One's possessions shall endure, and oneself endure in their midst, one's limbs composed to quiet. For others movement: for those who face the world, who sow, who give out and, giving, expend themselves in their seed. But not for one constituted and made like Petepre, in the inviolability of his being. Composed, symmetrical, he sat there, without access to the world, inaccessible to the death of begetting; eternal, a god in his chapel.

A black shadow glided between the pillars, sidewise to the direction of his eyes, an outline against the red glow. It entered crouching and so remained, silent, its brow between its hands, upon the floor. He slowly turned his eyeballs toward it. It was one of Mut's naked Moorish handmaids, animal-like. He blinked and roused himself. Then he raised one hand, from the wrist only, and commanded:

" Speak! "

She jerked her forehead up from the floor, rolled her eyes, and answered in a husky, barbaric voice:

" The mistress is at hand and would approach the master."

He bethought himself again. Then he replied:

" It is granted."

The little animal disappeared backwards over the threshold. Petepre sat with lifted brows. After a few moments Mut appeared on the spot where the slave had crouched. With her elbows at her sides she extended toward him both palms like an offerant. He saw that she was heavily clad, in a long, full, pleated mantle above her narrow ankle-length under-garment. Her shadowy cheeks were framed in a dark-blue head-cloth like a wig which fell on shoulders and neck and was confined by an embroidered band. On top of it stood a cone of ointment, with a hole through which the stem of a lotus was drawn, curving down parallel with the line of the head so that the blossom swayed above her brow. The stones in her necklace and arm-bands glittered darkly.

Petepre lifted his small hands likewise in greeting and carried the back of one of them to his mouth to kiss.

" Flower of the lands! " he said in a tone of surprise. " Lovely of face, having a place in the house of Amun! Pure-handed loveliness, alone among those that bear the sistrum, and with voice of beauty when she sings! " He continued on a note of joyous surprise as he rapidly repeated the stilted phrases. " You that fill the house with beauty, charming one to whom all pay homage, familiar of the queen — you can read my heart, since you fulfil its every wish ere it be spoken, and fulfil them all by your coming. — Here is a cushion," he went on in an ordinary tone, as he drew one from behind his back and placed it on the lower ledge at his feet. " Would the gods," he resumed the courtly key, " you had come with a plea, that the greater it were, with the more joy could I grant it."

He had ground for curiosity. For her visit was quite out of the usual order and tactful routine and therefore disturbed him. He divined some special reason for it and felt a certain uneasy joy. But for the moment she uttered only fulsome phrases.

"What wish, as your sister, could I still cherish, my master and friend? " she said in her soft voice, a sonorous alto which betrayed cultivation. " For I have breath only through you, yet, thanks to your greatness, all is vouchsafed me. That I have a place in the temple is due to your eminence among the great of the land. That I am called friend to the queen, is solely because you are Pharaoh's friend and gilded with the favour of the sun since your rising. Without you I were dark. As yours I have a fullness of light."

" It were useless to gainsay you, if such is your belief," he said with a smile. " At least let us take care that your fullness of light be not darkened where we stand." He clapped his hands. " Make light! " he ordered the slave who appeared from the dining-room.

Eni demurred. " Not yet, my husband," said she. " It is hardly dusk. You were sitting to enjoy the beautiful twilight hour; I have no wish to regret that I disturbed you."

" Nay, I insist," he answered her. " Receive it as evidence of that for which they blame me: that my will is like black granite from the quarries of the Retenu. I cannot change it, I am too old to alter. For to do that would be to show myself ungrateful to my dearest and best, who has guessed the secretest wish of my heart with this wish, and shall I receive her in darkness and gloom? Is it not a feast-day when you come, and shall I leave the feast unillumined? All four lights! " he said to the two servants bearing torches, with which they hastened to light the candelabra standing on columns in the four corners of the hall. " Let them burn up bright! "

" As you will," said she with an admiring, submissive shrug. " Truly I know the firmness of your resolution, and may the blame rest on those who strike against it! Women cannot but esteem inflexibility in a man. Shall I say why? "

" I would gladly hear."

" Because only that can give worth to surrender and make of it something of which we may be proud when we receive it."

" Most charming," said he, and blinked. Partly because of the brightness, for the hall now lay in the light of twenty lamp-wicks stuck in blazing wax, that sent up thick glaring flames till the hall became a sea of mingled milk and blood from the white light and the sunset glow. But partly too he blinked reflectively at the meaning her words might bear. Obviously she had a request, he thought, and no small one, otherwise she would not so carefully lead up to it. " It is not her way, for she knows full well my honourable peculiarities and how much it means to me to be left in peace and take nothing upon myself. And she is usually too proud to ask anything; her pride and my convenience thus coincide. Yet it would be good, and elevate my spirits, to do her a favour and show my power. I am curious, and concerned, to hear what she would have. The best would be if it seemed to her great yet was not so for me, so that I may do her pleasure without too great cost to my comfort. Lo, there is a conflict in my breast: it rises from my justified self-esteem, that flows from my peculiar and consecrated state and makes me find it hateful when I am approached too closely and my rest disturbed; and on the other hand from my desire to show myself loving and strong to this woman. She is lovely in her heavy robe, which she wears in my presence for the same reason that made me command the lights to be brought — lovely with her eyes like precious stones and her shadowy cheeks. I love her, in so far as my justified self-esteem permits; but here is the actual contradiction, for I hate her too, I always hate her, because of the claim which of course she does not make upon me but which is taken for granted in a marriage. Yet I do not like to hate her, rather I would that I could love her without hate. Were she to give me good occasion to show myself strong and loving, the hatred might be taken from my love and I might be happy. Therefore am I so curious to know what she would have, if also a little disturbed on account of my comfort."

Such were Petepre's thoughts as he blinked, while the slaves finished lighting the lamps and with silent haste withdrew, the torches held in their crossed arms.

" You permit me to sit beside you? " he heard Eni ask with a little laugh; starting from his thoughts, he bent once more to arrange the cushion as he expressed his pleasure. She sat down at his feet on the inscribed ledge.

" Truly," she said, " it happens too seldom that we are together like this for an hour, enjoying each other's presence without other purpose than to talk — of no matter what; for with an object in view we must talk, whereas without one talk is the pleasanter for being superfluous. Do you not agree? "

He nodded assent, sitting with his big feminine-looking arms stretched out along the back-rest of the ledge. He thought: " Seldom happens? It never happens; for we members of this noble and exalted family, parents and children, lead our lives apart, each in his own place; we avoid each other out of delicacy save when we break bread. That it happens today must have a reason, and I am full of curiosity and misgiving. Am I wrong? Is she here simply to see me, to be with me at this hour because her nature demands it? I do not know what to wish. For I could wish that she should have a need provided it be not too inconvenient to me; yet that she came for the sake of my presence solely I could wish even more — almost." He was thinking this as he said:

" I quite agree. It is a poor and narrow mind that uses speech merely as a tool for practical understandings. Whereas the rich and noble require beauty and superfluity in everything, speech as well. For beauty and superfluity are the same thing. How strange it is about words, and the dignity of them: that they can lift themselves out of their bald sufficience to the whole height of their significance! The word ' superfluous,' for instance, often carries with it a contemptuous meaning; yet it can rise to a royal height, beyond the reach of contempt and in itself actually signify the name and nature of beauty. I often think of the mystery of words when I sit alone, and amuse my mind with such charming and idle occupation."

" Thanks to my lord that he lets me share his thought,"

answered she. " Your mind is clear, like the lamps you have had lighted for our meeting. If you were not Pharaoh's chamberlain, you might well be one of the learned scribes of the god, who walk in the temple courts and ponder words of wisdom."

" Very likely," said he. " For a man might be many other things than precisely that which it is his lot to be or to represent. He may often marvel at the absurd play-acting he has to do in his allotted rôle; he feels stifled in the mask life has put on him, as the priests may at times feel stifled in the mask of the god. Do you agree? "

" Quite."

" Yet perhaps not quite," he said insinuatingly. " Probably women have less understanding of such a feeling. For the Great Mother has granted them a more general sense in respect of their being more women and image of the Mother, and less this or that individual woman. For instance as though you were less bound to be Mut-em-enet than I am to be Petepre because I am conditioned by the sterner father-spirit. Do you agree? "

" It is so very bright in this hall," said she, with her head bowed, " from the flames that blaze by virtue of your masculine will. Such thoughts, it seems to me, are better pursued by softer light; it would be easier for me in the twilight to consider this matter of being more a woman and image of the Mother than just plain Mut-em-enet."

" Pardon me," he hastened to reply; " it was untactful of me not to adapt our delightfully idle conversation to the light which befits this joyous hour. I will give it a turn more suited to the festal illumination I have seen fit to make. Nothing could be easier. I will pass over the things of the mind and speak of matters of the tangible daylight world. But before I make that easy transition let me have my pleasure in the pretty mystery which consists in the fact that the world of tangible things is also the intelligible world. For what one can actually grasp with the hand is intelligible to the mind of women, children, and the common folk; whereas the intangible is intelligible only to the sterner mind of the male. The word ' comprehend ' is figurative, the word ' tangible ' is literal — though the latter may easily become figurative as well: we even say of an easily comprehensible thing that we can actually grasp it with our senses."

" Your observations and idle thoughts are most charming, my husband," said she, " and I cannot express the refreshment this connubial conversation gives me. Do not think I am in haste to pass over from the intangible things to the tangible. On the contrary, I would gladly linger with you in the realm of your idle thoughts, and counter them in the measure of my powers as a woman or a child. I had no meaning in my words save that a less glaring light suits better for the exchange of intimate thoughts."

He did not answer at once, being annoyed. But presently, in a chiding tone and shaking his head:

" The mistress of the house keeps coming back to the point in which things went not according to her will but to that of the stronger. That is not quite fine, the less so that it is the way of women to cling to and dissect such occasions. Permit me the suggestion that in this one respect my Eni should try to be more Mut the exceptional woman and less the ordinary one."

" I hear and repent," she murmured.

" If we were bent on mutual reproach," he continued,

giving his irritation further vent, " how easily might I express my regret that you come to me at this hour, my friend, clad in so thick a mantle; for surely it is the joy and desire of your friend to follow the lines of your swanlike form through the kind transparency of a linen garment."

" Woe is me indeed! " she said, and drooped her head with a blush. " It would be better for me to die rather than learn that I have come before my lord in an unpleasing garb. I swear that I thought to give you special pleasure in this dress. For it is more costly and full of art than most of mine. My sewing-woman Heti worked with sleepless industry to make it and I shared her care that I might find favour in your eyes. But a care shared is not a care halved."

" No matter, my dear," he answered. " Let it pass. I did not say that I wished to complain, only that I could do it if you so desired. But I will not take for granted that you do. Let us go on with our idle conversation, as though the question of blame had never crept into it, like a false note. For now I will pass over to the things of the tangible world and say how I rejoice that my task in life is stamped with the seal of superfluity and not of need. I used the word ' royal ' to characterize the superfluous; and indeed it is in its right place at court and in the palace Merimat; as ornament, as form for form's sake, as the elegantly turned phrase with which one greets the god. All these are the affair of the courtier; so that one may say in a way that the mask is less stifling than to him who is hemmed in by the objective fact and stands closer to the feminine because it is granted him to be less individual. It is true, I am not among those whom Pha-

raoh summons for advice about boring a well on the road
through the desert to the sea, or the erection of a monu-
ment, or how many men it takes to wash a load of gold-
dust out of the mines of the wretched Kush; and it may
be that it detracts from my satisfaction and I am angry
with the man Hor-em-heb, who commands the household
troops and holds the head office among the executioners,
almost without asking my advice, although I bear the
title of the office. But always I have overcome these at-
tacks of annoyance. For after all I am different from
Hor-em-heb, as the possessor of the title is different from
the necessary but unimportant official who actually holds
the fan over Pharaoh when he drives out. People like that
are beneath me. For mine it is to stand before Pharaoh
at his levee with the other title-bearers and dignitaries of
the court and repeat the hymn of salutation to the majesty
of this god: ' Thou art like Re,' with our adoring voices;
and to expend myself in utterly ornamental flourishes
such as: ' A scale is thy tongue, O Neb-mat-Re, and thy
lips are more just than the little tongue on the scale of
Thoth '; or extravagant protestations like: ' Speakest thou
to the ocean and sayest: " Rise up to the mountain! " lo,
the waters come up, even as thou hast spoken.' So must
I speak, in beautiful, objectless form, far from the com-
pulsions of ordinary life. For pure form, adornment
without purpose, is my honour and my task, as it is the
task of royalty to be royal. And all this is an aid to my
self-esteem."

"Splendid and fitting it is too," she answered, " if also
the truth be honoured and receive support, as is doubtless
the case in your words, my husband. Yet it seems to me
that the beautiful superfluities of the court and the ex-

travagances at the levee serve to clothe with honour and
dread the material cares of the god, such as wells and
buildings and gold-mines, for the sake of their importance
to the land; and that concern for these things is the most
royal thing about royalty."

Petepre again closed his lips and refrained from any
answer, playing with the draw-string of his skirt.

" I should be untruthful," he said at last with a little
sigh, " were I to say that your share in our pleasant conversation is conducted with great tact. I made a skilful
transition to the more worldly and material things of life,
bringing the subject round to Pharaoh and the court. I
expected you to return the ball by asking me some question, such as for instance whose ear-lobe Pharaoh tweaked
in token of his favour when we went out of the hall of the
canopy after the levee; but instead you turned aside into
observations about such irritating matters as mines and
desert wells, about which, truly, my love, you must certainly understand even less than I."

" You are right," she replied, shaking her head over
her blunder. " Forgive me. My eagerness to know whose
ear-lobe Pharaoh tweaked today was only too great. I
dissembled it by small talk. Pray understand me: I
thought to put off the question, feeling that a slow lead-
ing up to the important subject is the finest and most important feature of elegant conversation. Only the clumsy
blunder in their approach by precipitation, betraying at
once the whole content of their minds. But now that you
have permitted me the question: Was it not yourself, my
husband, whom the god distinguished? "

" No," said Petepre, " it was not I. It often has been,
but not today. But your words betrayed — I know not

how, yet it appeared as though you inclined to the view that Hor-em-heb, the acting captain of the guard, is greater at court and in the lands than I — "

" The gods forbid, my husband! In the name of the Hidden One! " she cried in alarm, laying her beringed hand on his knee. He looked at it as though a bird had alighted there. " I should need to be weak-minded indeed, past hope of betterment, if for a single moment — "

" Your words made it seem so," he asseverated, with a regretful shrug, " though of course contrary to any such intent. It was almost as though you would say — what example shall I give? As though in your mind a baker of Pharaoh's bakery, who actually bakes the bread for the god and his house and sticks his head in the oven is greater than the great overseer of the royal bakery, Pharaoh's chief baker, whose title is prince of Menfe. Or as though I, who of course take nothing upon myself, were of less importance here in the house than Mont-kaw, my steward, or even than his youthful ' mouth,' the Syrian Osarsiph who oversees the workshops. Those are striking instances — "

Mut had shrunk back.

" They strike me indeed, so that I quail beneath them," said she. " You see my confusion and in your great-heartedness will let the punishment rest at that. I see now how I have disarranged our dialogue with my proneness to delay. But gratify my curiosity, which I hoped to conceal, and quench it as one quenches blood: let me hear who it was that received the caress of favour in the throne-room today."

" It was Nofer-rohu, chief of the anointers from the treasury of the king," answered he.

" So it was that prince," she said. " Did they surround him? "

" They did, according to the custom, and congratulated him," he answered. " He is at the moment very much in the forefront of attention; it would be well that he should be seen at the entertainment we purpose giving at the next quarter of the moon. It would add to the lustre of the occasion and to that of our house."

" Certainly," she agreed; " you must invite him in a beautiful letter in which he will take pleasure because of the elegance of the phrases, such as: ' Beloved of his master! ' or ' Rewarded and distinguished by his lord '; and you must send him a present to his house besides, by special messenger. Then it would be most unlikely that Nofer-rohu would decline."

" I think so too," said Petepre. " And the present must be something very choice, of course. I will have various things brought before me to choose from and this evening I will write an invitation which he will really enjoy reading. My child," he went on, " I should like this entertainment to be particularly choice, so that it will be talked of in the city and the report of it reach other distant ones. With some seventy guests, and rich in unguents, flowers, musicians, food, and wine. I have purchased a very good figure of a mummy to be carried about, a good piece, an ell and a half long — I will show it to you beforehand if you like: the case is gold, the body of ebony, with ' Celebrate the joyful day ' written on the forehead. Have you heard of the Babylonian dancers? "

" Which dancers, my husband? "

" There is a travelling company of foreign dancers in the city. I have had presents sent to them, that they may come to my entertainment. From all that I hear, they are of exotic beauty and accompany their performance with bells and sounding tambourines. They are said to know some new and striking poses, and to have a strange fire of fury in their eyes as they dance, as well as in their caresses. I promise myself a sensation, and for our party great success from their presence."

Eni looked down, she seemed to reflect.

" Do you intend," she said after a pause, " to invite Beknechons, first priest of Amun, to your party? "

" Of course, naturally," he answered. " Beknechons? It goes without saying. Why do you ask? "

" His presence seems important to you? "

" Why not? Beknechons is a great man."

" More important than that of the Babylonian maidens? "

" What sort of comparisons are these, my love? What choice are you putting before me? "

" The two are not reconcilable, my husband. I must make it clear to you that you must choose between them. For if the Babylonian maidens dance before Amun's high priest at your feast, it may be that the strange fire of fury in their eyes would not equal that in Beknechons's heart and that he would rise and summon his servants and leave your house."

" Impossible! "

" Even probable, my friend. He would not suffer the Hidden One to be affronted before his eyes."

" By a dance? "

" By a dance danced by foreign dancers — when, after all, Egypt is full of beauty of this kind and even sends its dancers abroad."

" So much the better may Egypt allow itself the pleasure of the novel and unknown."

" That is not Beknechons's view. His objection to what
is foreign is very strong."

" But I hope that it is your view."

" My view is that of my master and friend," said she,
" for how can that go against the honour of our gods? "

" The honour of the gods, the honour of the gods," he
repeated, shrugging his shoulders. " I must confess that
my mood and spirit begin to be clouded by our talk —
which is quite contrary to the purpose of elegant conversation."

" I should be alarmed," she replied, " if that were the
result of my care for your peace of mind. For how would
it stand with that if Beknechons in anger called his servants and left the feast so that there would be talk of his
rebuff in both the lands? "

" He would not be so petty as to feel offence at an elegant diversion nor so bold as to offer an indignity to the
friend of Pharaoh."

" He is great enough that his thoughts travel easily
from small affairs to large and he would give offence to
Pharaoh's friend sooner than to Pharaoh, in the sense of
a warning to the latter. Amun hates the laxity of foreign
ways and the disregard of pious old custom, because it
enervates the land and weakens the authority of the kingdom. That is what Amun hates, as we both know; for he
wishes the fibre of moral discipline to be strong in the
land, as it always has been in Kemt, and to have its children walk in the path of patriotic tradition. But you
know, as well as I, that down there " — Mut pointed west-
ward, toward the Nile and beyond it to the palace —

" another sun-sense rules and is lightly favoured among Pharaoh's wise men: the sense of On at the apex of the Delta; the mobile sense of Aton-Re, inclined to broadness and conciliation — they call it Aton, with I know not what weakening effect. Must not Beknechons be angered for Amun if his son in the body favours this laxness and permits his thinkers and seekers to weaken the marrow of the land by toying with foreign ways? He may not blame Pharaoh. But he will blame him in you, and make demonstration for Amun by raging like a leopard of Egypt when he sees the Babylonian maidens, and will spring up to summon his servants."

" I hear you speak," he retorted, " like the clapper-bird of Punt with tongue like a rattle, who hears and repeats what is not in its head. The marrow of the lands, and the good old ways, and the laxity of foreign ones — all that is Beknechons, those are his disagreeable and crafty words, and it upsets me to have you repeat them; for your coming gave me hope of familiar converse with yourself, not with him."

" I only remind you, my friend," she answered, " of his views, which you know, in order to protect you from serious unpleasantness. I say not that Beknechons's thoughts are mine."

" But they are," he retorted. " I hear his voice in yours; but you do not utter his thoughts as something foreign in which you have no share, but rather you have made them yours and are of one mind with him, the shiny-pated priest, against me — and that is what I cannot bear. Do I not know that he goes in and out in our house, visiting you each quarter of the moon or even oftener? And always to my unspoken distress, for he is not my friend,

I cannot bear him or his guile and bad manners. My nature and temperament demand a mild, refined, and tolerant sun-sense; thus in my heart I am for Atum-Re, the tolerant god; but especially because I belong to Pharaoh and am his courtier, for he permits the experimental thought of his wise men to dwell upon the benign and universal sun-sense of this glorious god. But you, my consort and sister before gods and men, where do you stand in these matters? Do you hold, not with me — in other words, with Pharaoh and the tendencies of the court — but rather with Amun the inflexible, the brazen-browed; do you lean to his party against me and are of one house with the chief shiny-pate of the ungracious god, not realizing how offensive it is to infringe upon my dignity or show me disloyalty? "

" You use comparisons, my lord," said she, in a voice thin and pinched with anger, " lacking in good taste, which is strange considering the reading you do. For it is without taste, or in poor taste, to say that I am of one house with the prophet and therefore disloyal to you. That is a lame and distorted comparison. I must remind you that Pharaoh is Amun's son, according to the teaching of the fathers and the people's ancient belief, and therefore you would do no violence to your duty as courtier by paying heed to the sacred sun-sense of Amun, however ill-mannered you find him, and by bringing him the light sacrifice of your own and your guests' curiosity in respect of a paltry dance, however striking. So much with respect to yourself. As for me, I am utterly and entirely Amun's, in piety and devotion, for I am the bride of his temple and of his house of women, Hathor am I, and dance before him in the garment of the goddess, that is all my honour and my desire and further have I none, this honourable rank is my life's sole content. And you would quarrel with me because I keep faith with the lord my god and unearthly spouse, and make comparisons against me that cry to heaven with their falseness." And she lifted up a fold of her mantle and, bending over, shrouded her face with it.

The captain of the guard was more than distressed. He shuddered, he even felt cold all over; for it seemed to him that intimate matters, always most tactfully passed over in silence, threatened to come to speech in the most shocking and destructive way. He leaned, with his arms spread out along the back of his seat, still farther away from her; and sat numbly, looking down, indignant, guilty, and bewildered, to where she wept. " What is this? " he thought. " It is all quite wild and unheard-of, it threatens danger to my peace of mind. I went too far. I brought my justified self-interest into the field, but she struck it down with her own; it is not only our talk; for my heart is pierced by her words so that pity and pain are mingled with my dread of her tears. Yes, I love her; I know it by my dread of her tears; and would like to let her know it by what I say." He raised his arms and bent over her, yet not touching her, as he said, not without painful hesitation:

" You see, dear flower, indeed your own words make it clear, that you did not speak solely to warn me of Bekne-chons's churlish state of mind, but because you share it, because his ideas are yours and your heart is of his party against me. You have said it plain and clear in my face: ' I am utterly and entirely Amun's ' — those were your words. Was then my comparison so false and can I help it that the taste of it is bitter to me, your husband? "

She took the mantle from her face and looked at him.

" Are you jealous of god, the Hidden One? " she asked. Her mouth was wry, scorn and weeping mingled in the jewelled eyes so close to his that he started and bent back again. " I must retreat," he thought. " I have gone too far, and must by some means or other withdraw, for my own peace and for the peace of the house. For both stand in sudden and horrible danger. How can it have happened that they are both so threatened, and that this woman's eyes are all at once so terrible? Everything seemed so safe and plain." And he recalled many a home-coming, from a journey or from the court, when his first question to his steward was always: " Is all well with the household? Is the mistress happy? " For there abode in his inmost mind a secret misgiving about the peace of the house, its dignity and security — a dim consciousness that its footing was weak and imperilled. And now, by the look in Eni's angry eyes, by her tears, he knew that he had been right and that his secret dread threatened to fulfil itself.

" No," said he, " far from it. The idea that I could be jealous of Amun, the god, that I repudiate. Well I know how to make distinction between what is due from you to the Hidden One and what to your spouse. And if, as I think, the expression was displeasing to you, which I used to characterize your familiar intercourse with Beknechons, I am at all times ready and even seek occasion to give you pleasure, and will do so by withdrawing the comparison about being of one house — it shall be as though I had not said it and that it be erased from the record of my words. Are you content? "

Mut let her wet eyes dry of themselves, as though she were unconscious of the tears that stood in them. Her husband had expected gratitude for his complaisance, but she showed none.

"That is but a small matter," she said, shaking her head.

"She sees that I shrink, in respect of my fear for the peace of my house," he thought; "and she will use her advantage, as is a woman's way. She is more a female than she is an individual and my wife. I may not be surprised, though it is always a little painful to see the eternal feminine displaying its wiles in one's own wife. It would make one laugh ruefully, it has indeed an irritating effect upon me, to perceive that a person thinks to deal according to his individual mind, when all he really does is to repeat the general pattern — mortifying indeed it is! But what use are such thoughts? I can only think, not say them. What I must say is this." And he went on:

"Probably not of the smallest, indeed, but still the least of what I would say. For I did not think to end with it, but rather to increase your relief by saying that while we have been speaking I have reconsidered my idea of inviting the Babylonian dancers. I have no wish to anger a highly placed man to whom you stand in close relations, by seeming to offend what may seem to me his prejudices but which I have even so no desire to attack. Our entertainment will be brilliant enough without the foreigners."

"That too, Petepre, is most unimportant," she said. She called him by his name, he noted it with mounting apprehension.

"What do you mean?" he asked. "Still unimportant?

Most unimportant of what? And compared to what? "

"To that which is desirable. To that which is needful," answered she with an intake of breath. "There should be changes, there must be changes here in this house, my husband, that it may not become a house of offending to the pious, but instead a place of good example. You are the master; who does not bow before you? Who would not grant you the mild refinement of the tolerant sun-sense, by which you order your life and which you prac-tise in all your ways? I see well that one cannot at the same time be for the kingdom and for the stern old ways, for out of the second came the first, and life now in the richness of the kingdom must be otherwise than in the simplicity of the old times. You must not say that I have no understanding of life and its changes. But there must be measure in all things; a remnant of the ancient disci-pline, out of which sprang the kingdom and the riches of it, must be preserved and held in honour, that the lands become not shamefully corrupt and the sceptre fall from their hands. Would you deny this truth, or would Pha-raoh's wise men deny it, they who occupy themselves with the mobile sun-sense of Atum-Re? "

"Nobody," responded the fan-bearer, "denies the truth. It might be dearer than even the sceptre. You speak of destiny. We are children of our age, and it seems to me it is always better to live by the truth of the time wherein we are born than to try to guide ourselves by the immemorial past and the stern maxims of antiquity and so doing to deny our own souls. Pharaoh has many mercenaries — Asiatic, Libyan, Nubian, even native. They will guard the realm so long as destiny permits. But we must live in sincerity."

" Sincerity," said she, " is easy, and therefore it is not lofty. What would become of men if each would live only in the sincerity of his own desires, claiming for them the dignity of truth and unwilling to be strict with himself to his own improvement? The thief too is sincere, and the drunkard in the gutter, and likewise the adulterer. But shall we by reason of its sincerity pass over their conduct? You wish to live in sincerity, my husband, as a child of your time, and not according to the ancient precepts. But that is barbaric antiquity, where each lives according to his lust; a more advanced age demands the limitation of the personal for the sake of higher considerations."

" Wherein would you have me alter myself? " he said in some panic.

" In nothing, my husband. You are unchangeable, and far be it from me to shake the sacred moveless calm of your being. Far, too, any reproach because you make nothing your affair in the household or elsewhere in the world but to eat and drink. For if this were not a consequence of your nature, it would be of your rank. Your servants' hands do all for you as they will do in your tomb. Your part is but to command, or not even this, for you command only one, him who is set over all to direct the house in your name, in the sense that it is the house of a great man of Egypt. Only this, this alone is your affair; a thing of the utmost ease, yet of the last importance: that you should not err nor point wrongly with your finger. Upon that all depends."

" For years which I no longer count," said he, " Mont-kaw has been my steward. A worthy soul, who loves me as he should, and is sensitive for all that could give me offense. Never so far as I could tell has he betrayed me in great matters, or hardly in small, and he has administered the household nobly, and fittingly to my state. Has he the misfortune to incur your displeasure? "

She smiled contemptuously at his evasion.

" You know," she answered, " as well as I and all of Wese that Mont-kaw is dying of his kidneys and for some time has had as little charge of affairs as you yourself. Another rules in his place, whom they call his mouth; and the advancement of this youth in your household must be seen to be believed. But that is not all; for it is said that after Mont-kaw's expected death this so-called mouth shall step into his place and all that you have shall fall into his hands. You praise your steward for his loyalty to your interest — but in this matter I seek in vain for evidence of it."

" You are thinking of Osarsiph? "

She bowed her head.

" It is a strange way of putting it," she said, " to say that I am thinking of him. Might the Hidden One grant there were no ground to think of him! Instead of which one is driven to do so, by this blunder of your steward, and in a way most mortifying to our pride. This ailing man bought him you speak of as a boy, from some travelling pedlars; then, instead of treating him as befitted his base blood and origins, he advanced him and let him take the upper hand in the house; he put all the household under him, my servants as well as yours, till you yourself, my lord, speak of him, a slave, with a readiness most painful to me, which rouses up my anger. For if you had stopped to think and then said: 'Do you mean the Syrian, the Hebrew lad from the wretched Retenu? '

that would have been natural and fitting. But things have gone very far, your own words betray it, for you spoke as though he were your cousin, naming him familiarly by name and asking: ' Are you thinking of Osarsiph? ' "

Thus then she too uttered the name, bringing it over herself with a secret ecstasy and blissful satisfaction. She spoke the mystic syllables, with their echo of death and divinity, syllables conveying to her fate's utmost sweetness in their sound, with a sob. But she pretended that it was a sob of outraged dignity and once more she hid her face in her mantle.

For the second time Petepre was sincerely alarmed.

" What is it, what is it, my love? " he said, stretching out his hands above her head. " More tears? Let me understand why. I spoke of the slave by his name, as he calls himself and is known to all. Is not a name the quickest way to indicate one's meaning? And I see that I was correct. You did have in mind that Canaanitish youth who serves me as cup-bearer and reader — to my great satisfaction, I deny it not. Should that not be a ground for you to think favourably of him? I had no part in his purchase. Mont-kaw, who has power to buy and to sell, took him years ago from some honest traders. But it came about that I had speech with him to try him, when he was putting date blossoms to ride in my orchard, and found him exceedingly pleasing, gifted by the gods with graces of body and mind most unusually mingled. For his looks seem but the natural expression of the charm of his spirit, and in turn his mental parts are in invisible correspondence with the outward grace; so that you will, I hope, permit me to call him remarkable, for it is the due and proper word. His origins are not of the best;

indeed, one might, if one chose, call his birth virgin; but at least he who begot him was undoubtedly a prince of a sort, a prince of God and king over his flocks, and the boy led a princely life and was favoured with the gifts of favour, where he grew up amongst his father's flocks. After that, indeed, affliction was his portion, and there were those who set snares for his feet and he walked into them. But even the tale of his sufferings is remarkable; it has spirit and sense, it holds together, as one may say, and in it there rules that same combination which makes his inward and outward parts seem one and the same thing. For it has its own reality, but also seemingly a higher reference as well, and both so related that one is mirrored in the other, which only adds to the youth's mysterious charm. When he had not ill sustained the test I gave him, he was appointed my cup-bearer and reader — without my stir, out of love of me, of course — and I confess that in this capacity he has become indispensable. But again, he has grown up, without any motion of mine, to have oversight of all the things of the household, and it has proved that the Hidden One grants success through him, in all that he does — I cannot put it otherwise. And now that he has become indispensable to me and to the house, what would you have me do with him? "

Truly, what was there to wish or to do, when he had finished speaking? When he stopped, he looked round with a satisfied smile. He had secured himself strongly against attack and stamped the threatened demand as monstrous, as an unloving offence against himself, which no one could think of inflicting upon him. He could not have dreamed that the woman before him paid no heed to this interpretation. Sitting crouched under her cloak, she had greedily sucked in the honey of his words; her tense excitement had let no syllable escape of all that he said in Joseph's praise; which greatly diminished its intended effect. Yet, strange to say, Mut remained honourably true to the strict and reasonable dictates which had given rise to this visit to Potiphar. She sat up erect and said:

"I will assume, my husband, that what you have said in favour of the slave is the uttermost that can be justly said. And it is not enough, it is untenable before Egypt's gods. All this that you have been so good as to tell me, of the wonderful combination of qualities in your servant, and of his mysterious charm — all that counts as nothing in face of Amun's just demand through my mouth. For I too am a mouthpiece — not alone he whom you say is indispensable to your house — clearly without due reflection, for how can a chance stranger be indispensable in the land of men and in Petepre's house, which was a house of blessing before this outlander began to wax strong within it? That should never have come to pass. If the lad was once bought, he should have been sent to labour in the fields instead of keeping him in the courtyard and even entrusting him with your cup and lending your ear to his reading because of his insinuating gifts. The talents are not the man; one must make a distinction. For it is so much the worse when a base man has gifts which can make one finally forget his natural baseness. What are those gifts which can justify the elevation of the base? Mont-kaw, your steward, should have asked himself that, who without your orders, as you say, made this lowly slave flourish like a weed in your house, to the shame of all the pious. Will you permit him, now that he is dying, to defy the gods and point with his finger at the Shabirite as his successor, so shaming your house before the world and humbling your own people beneath his foot, so that they gnash their teeth? "

" My dear one," said the chamberlain, " how you deceive yourself! You are not well informed, to judge from your words, for there is no thought of teeth-gnashing. All the other servants love Osarsiph, from high to low, from the scribe of the buffet to the kennel-boys and to the least of your handmaidens, and take no shame to do his will. I know not whence this report, that folk gnash their teeth at his advancement, for it is quite false. On the contrary, they all seek his glance and gladly vie to do each his best when he comes amongst them; they hang joyously upon his lips when he gives them orders. Yes, even those who had to step aside from their office to make way for him, even they do not look askance, but straight in his eye, for his gifts are irresistible. And why? Because he is not what you say, nor are his gifts a lying appendage to his person, and to be distinguished from it. For they are mingled together and are one, the gifts of one blest with the blessing, so that you might say he deserves them, if that again were not an untenable division between the person and his gifts, or if you can speak at all of merit in connection with natural gifts. But it has come about that on the land-ways and the water-ways folk recognize him from afar, they nudge each other and say: ' There is Osarsiph, Petepre's body-servant and mouth to Mont-kaw, an excellent youth, going about the business of his lord, which he will perform to advantage as is his way.' Moreover, though men look him in the eye, it is said that women avoid it, but give him sidling glances, which is as good a sign. And when he shows himself in the streets of the city and in the bazaar, it often happens that the maidens mount on the house-tops and fling down gold rings upon him from their fingers, that he may look up at them. But he never does."

Eni listened, in speechless ecstasy. This glorification of Joseph, the description of his popularity, intoxicated her beyond words. Bliss ran like fire through her veins, made her bosom rise and fall and her breath come sobbingly in gasps; her very ears grew red — only with the greatest difficulty could she prevent her lips from curving in a beatific smile as she listened. A benevolent onlooker must have shaken his head at the deluded creature. This praise of Joseph must have confirmed her in her weakness — if we may so express it — for the foreign slave; it must have justified this weakness in the face of her own pride, plunged her still deeper in, made her still less capable of carrying out her purpose of saving her own life. Was that a ground for joy? No, not for joy, but for ecstasy — a distinction which the well-wishing friend, though shaking his head, is bound to make. She suffered, too — that goes without saying. What Petepre said about the women: how they looked, how they cast down their rings, that confirmed her again in her weakness and filled her at the same time with scorching jealousy and with hatred for those whose feelings were her own. It consoled her a little to hear that Joseph did not look at them; and it helped her to persevere in her project of behaving like a reasonable being. She said:

" I will pass over, my friend, your lack of delicacy in entertaining me with the ill behaviour of the women of

Wese, be there much or little truth in such reports — for they may have their source in the conceited youth himself or in such as he has bribed with promises." It cost her less than one would think, to speak thus of the object of her already hopeless love. She did it mechanically, making herself speak like another than herself; her musical voice took on a hollow tone corresponding to the fixity of her features and the vacancy of her gaze. The whole made up a picture of deliberate guile. " It is more important to point out that when you say I am falsely informed as to the situation in the house, your charge is unfounded and falls to the ground. It would be much better if you had not made it. Your habit of taking nothing upon yourself, but of seeing all with distant and detached eye, should make you doubt whether you are yourself so well informed. The truth is that the forwardness of this youth has become a subject for violent anger and widespread disaffection in the house. Dudu, the guardian of your jewel-caskets, has more than once, yes, very often, taken occasion to speak before me, uttering bitter complaints of the offence to the pious in making them suffer the domination of impure stock — "

Petepre laughed. " You have found a wonderful witness, my blossom — take it not ill of me that I say so! Dudu is a pompous puffed-up toad, a quarter-size man and made to be laughed at. How in the world could he be taken seriously in this or any other matter? "

" The size of his person," she retorted, " is not to the purpose. But if his view is so contemptible, his judgment so worthless, how then is it that he was chosen guardian of your wardrobe? "

" It was a joke," said Petepre. " Only in jest could one give such a man an office. The other clown, his little mate, they even call vizier, but certainly they are not serious when they do it."

" I need not call your attention to the difference between them," she answered. " You know it well enough, though at this moment you would deny it. But it is sad that I must defend your most loyal and worthy servant against your ingratitude. Aside from his small stature Dudu is a serious and dignified man, who in no way deserves the name of clown, and whose judgment is valuable in affairs of the house and of his own honour."

" He reaches up to here on me," remarked the captain of the guard, making a line on his shin with the edge of his hand.

Mut was silent for a while.

" You know, my husband," she said then, with self-control, " that you are uncommon in height and strength, so that Dudu's size must seem smaller to you than to most other men — or for instance to Djeset, his wife, my woman, and to his children, who are of ordinary size and look up to their father with loving respect."

" They look up — ha ha ! "

" I use the word advisedly, in a higher, poetic sense."

" So you express yourself even poetically about your Dudu," Petepre mocked her. " Since you have complained of my bad taste in choice of subjects, I may remind you that you have dwelt overlong upon this conceited fool."

" We may well leave the subject," she said compliantly, " if it displeases you. I do not need his evidence or support in the matter of our discussion, since the request I would make is thrice justified of itself; his evidence is not needed to prove that you must grant it."

" You have a request? " he asked. (" So, then," he said to himself, rather bitterly, " it is true that she came with some purpose of a more or less troublesome nature. My hope is vain that her visit was simply for the sake of my presence. It cannot make me well-disposed toward her request.") — He asked:

" And what request? "

"This, my husband: that you should send away the foreign slave, whose name I will not again speak, from your house and courtyard, where he has sprung up like a weed, by dint of culpable negligence and lying favour, so that he has made it a house of offence instead of an example to the lands."

" Osarsiph — from house and courtyard? What are you thinking of? "

"I think, my husband, of right and justice. I think of the honour of your house, of the gods of Egypt and what you owe to them. Not alone to them, but to yourself and me, your sister-wife, who shakes the sistrum before Amun in the adornment of the Mother, consecrate and set apart. I think of these things and am certain beyond any doubt that I need only remind you of them for your thoughts to unite with mine and for you to grant my request without delay."

" By sending Osarsiph. . . . My dear, it may not be. Put it out of your mind, it is in vain, it is a whim which I cannot entertain, for it is a stranger to my mind, and all my thoughts rise up against it."

" So there we have it," he said to himself, in anger and

bewilderment. "That is the request, and that is why she came to me at this hour and seemed to come that we might talk together. I saw it coming, yet on my side would not see it, so offensive it is to my justified self-interest. I would have granted something small, wishing to seem great to her; but unhappily this that she thinks small and simple to grant is for me inconvenient in the extreme. Not without justification did I feel the approach of a disturbance to my peace. Yet what a pity that she has offered me no occasion to rejoice her heart, for I am reluctant to hate her."

"Your prejudice, my little flower," said he, "against the person of this youth, so great as to make you launch so foolish a request, is very sad. Clearly you know nothing of him save for the complaints and curses of mis-shapen and misbegotten persons and have no direct knowledge of his excellent gifts, which, young as he is, could in my opinion exalt him much further than even the stewardship of my house. You call him barbarian and slave — and literally you are right — but is that right enough, if it denies the spirit? Is it the custom and way of our land to esteem a man accordingly as he is free or unfree, native or foreign, and not rather according to his spirit whether it is dark and undisciplined or enlightened through the word and ennobled by the magic of its eloquence? What is our practice in Egypt? For the youth has a blithe and lucid manner of speech, with well-chosen words and charming intonation, writes a decorative hand, and reads aloud from my books as though he spoke himself by the motion of his own spirit, so that all their wit and wisdom seem to come from him and belong to him and one can only wonder.

I could wish you to take notice of his parts, to talk graciously with him and win his friendship, which would be much more pleasing to you than that of yon arrogant toad. . . ."

" I will neither take notice of him nor have speech with him," she said frigidly. " I see that I was mistaken when I thought you had exhausted your praise. You had still something to add. But now I await your word and the granting of my well-justified, my pious request."

" No such word," he replied, " can I utter, in response to a request so signally mistaken. It cannot be granted, and for more than one reason; the only question is whether I can make this clear to you. If not, alas, it will not be the more easily granted. I have told you that Osarsiph is not an ordinary slave. He brings increase to our house, he serves it incredibly; who could bring himself to send such a person away? It would be to rob the household; and to him gross injustice for he is free from error and a youth of the finest fibre, so that it would be a rarely unpleasant business simply to send him away without cause, and no one would be prepared to do it."

" You fear the slave? "

" I fear the gods who are with him, who make everything that is put in his hands succeed, and give him charm in the eyes of all the world. What gods they are is beyond my judgment, but they show themselves powerful in him, beyond a doubt. You would quickly forget such ideas — for instance, of burying him in field labour or selling him, if you would once forget your refusal to know him better. Very soon, I assure you, your heart would feel sympathy and softening toward the youth, for there is more than one point of contact between your life and his; and if I love to have him about me, believe me that it is because often he reminds me of you."

" Petepre! "

" I say what I say, and what I think is by no means meaningless. Are you not dedicate and set apart for the god, before whom you dance as his bride, and do you not wear your sacrificial adornments before men? Well, then, I have it from the youth himself that he, too, wears such an adornment, invisible, like your own. One must imagine a sort of evergreen, which is a symbol of consecrated youth and bears the significant name of touch-me-not. All this he has told me and I listened not without amazement, for he spoke of strange things. I knew of the gods of Asia, Atys and Ashrat, and the Baals of the growth. But he and his live under a god strange to me, and of amazing jealousy. For this unique god is solitary and feels a great need of loyalty, and he has betrothed himself to them as a bridegroom. It is all strange enough. In principle they each wear the evergreen and are set apart to their god like a bride. But one among them he chooses as a whole sacrifice, and that one must wear it with a difference and as one specially dedicate to the jealous god. And such a one is Osarsiph! They know a thing, he says, which is called sin, and the garden of sin, and have imagined beasts which leer from among the branches in the garden, ugly beyond conception. There are three of these and they are called ' Shame,' ' Guilt,' and ' Mocking Laughter.' But now I will ask you two questions: First, can one have a better servant and steward than one born to loyalty, and fearing sin in his very bones? And second, was it too much to say when I spoke of a point of contact between you and this youth? "

Ah, how Mut's heart contracted at her husband's words! Agony had consumed it when he spoke of the maidens who threw down their rings; but that had been nothing compared with the icy sword which pierced it when she understood why the daughters of Wese had not succeeded in drawing his gaze upon them. A frightful anguish, a presentiment of all she was to bear, came over her and painted itself openly on the pale agonized face turned up to Petepre. If we try to put ourselves in her place we shall see that the situation did not lack an element of absurdity. For why was she struggling and wrestling with her husband's obstinacy, if he was speaking the truth? If the healing and revealing dream which had brought her hither was but a lying dream? If he from whom she would save her own life and her husband's was a whole sacrifice, already promised, devoted, and set apart? What an involvement was this, in which she had feared to involve herself? She had not strength, she dared not attempt to cover her eyes with her hand; they stared into space, where she seemed to see the three beasts in the garden: Shame, Guilt, and Mocking Laughter, of whom the last whined like a hyena. It was unbearable. She was overwhelmed. Only away with him, more than ever now, since those healing dreams had been all a lie — thrice shameless dreams, since it would be quite vain were she even to throw down to him the rings from her fingers! " Yes, I must fight," she thought, " more than ever now, if this be true! But do I believe it? Or do I not rather cherish a secret hope that my dreams will prove stronger than his bond, will overpower it so that he will return my gaze and still my blood? Do I not hope and fear with a force which in

my soul I believe to be irresistible? And seeing that
clearly, once for all, must he not away, out of my sight,
out of this house, that my life may be saved? There sits
my fat-armed husband, like a tower of strength; Dudu,
who can beget children, reaches up to his shin. He commands the troops. From him and his cherishing have I
to hope healing and saving, from his alone." — It was
this thought of taking refuge in her husband, her nearest,
of trying on him the power of her craving for help, that
spoke when she said in a clear ringing voice:

" I will not enter further upon your words, my friend,
nor try by contending to refute them. It would be idle.
For what you say is not to the point of our dispute, there is
no need for you to say it; you need only speak the words:
' I will not.' For all the rest is but the cloak for your inflexible will; it is the iron firmness of your resolve, the
granite determination which informs all that you say.
Should I then enter into unavailing and ungrateful strife,
since after all as a woman I must rather admire and love
your strength? It is rather something else for which I
wait — something which without that iron resolve would
mean little or nothing, but with it is rich and glorious:
I mean your gracious granting of this boon for which I
plead. This hour is not like other hours; it is for us two
alone, and full of the expectancy in which I came to it —
came to beg that your strong will should incline to me and
give me my desire, saying: ' This offence shall be removed from the house, and Osarsiph shall be deprived
of his office and sold and sent away.' Shall I hear those
words, my husband and lord? "

"You have heard, my dear, that you cannot hear them,
not with the best of goodwill on my part. I cannot sell

Osarsiph and send him away, I cannot desire to, the will is lacking."

" You cannot will it? Then your will is your master, and not you master of your will? "

" My child, these are hair-splittings. Is there a difference between me and my will, one being servant and the other master and one lording it over the other? Master your own will, and will what is repugnant, what is entirely repulsive to yourself! "

" I am ready to do so," said she, and flung back her head, " when higher things come into play, such as honour, pride, and the kingdom."

" But nothing of that sort is involved here," he replied, " or rather what is involved is respect for sound sense, the pride of wisdom, and the kingdom of moderation."

" Think not of these, Petepre! " she begged in her ringing voice. " Think alone of this hour, this single hour, and its expectancy, and my coming to you unannounced to disturb your rest. Lo, I put my arms about your knee and implore you to grant me this favour, my husband, and to send me away in peace."

" It is pleasant to me," he responded, " to feel your lovely arms about my knee; yet however pleasant, they cannot make me yield; it is but due to their softness that my reproach is so gentle for the disturbing of my repose and the heedlessness toward my well-being. For that you have no concern; yet even so I will speak of it and tell you something in this hour when we are alone together. Know then," he said with a certain mysterious solemnity, " that I must keep Osarsiph, not alone for the good of the house, to which he gives such increase, or because he reads my books in praise of wisdom as no other can. For another reason he is supremely important to my well-being. In saying that he gives me a feeling of self-confidence I do not say it all; it is even more indispensable than that. His mind is fertile in invention of easements of every sort; but of these the chief is that by day and hour he speaks to me of myself in a favouring light, almost divine, and strengthens my heart in my own regard, so that I feel — "

" Let me wrestle with him," she said, holding his knee in a closer embrace, " let me defeat him, who only knows words to strengthen your heart and your confidence in yourself. I can do it better. I will give you power to strengthen your own heart in deeds, through yourself, in fulfilling the expectation of this hour and giving back the boy to the desert whence he came! For how greatly, my husband, will you feel yourself when you have consoled me and I go from you in peace! "

" Do you think so? " he asked, blinking. " Then hearken: I will command that when my steward Montkaw departs this life, for he is near his end, Osarsiph shall not be head in his place, but another, perhaps Khamat, the scribe of the buffet. But Osarsiph shall remain in the house."

She shook her head.

" Therewith, my friend, is my need not served, nor will any increase of strength or knowledge come to you. For my wish would be but half or partly granted and no satisfaction be given to my expectation. Osarsiph must go from the house."

" Then," said he quickly, " if that is not enough, then I withdraw what I said, and the youth shall come to the headship of the house."

She relaxed her arms.

"I hear your final word?"

"Another, alas, I have not to give."

"Then I will go," she breathed, and stood up.

"Yes," he acquiesced. "But after all, it was a charming hour. I will send presents after you to rejoice you: an ointment-dish of ivory, carven with eyes and fish and mice."

She turned her back and moved toward the columned archway. There for a moment she paused, supporting one hand, still holding her garment's folds, upon a column, and leaning her forehead against it so that her face was shrouded. No one has ever known how it looked in that hidden face.

Then she clapped her hands and went out.

THREEFOLD EXCHANGE

WITH the recording of the above conversation we have got so far into our story that we can now link it on to a remark which I made somewhat earlier and only in passing. I referred, that is, to the strange constellation, the pattern into which life's kaleidoscope here fell. I have said that about this time, when the mistress was making apparently sincere efforts to have Joseph removed, there came a change in the attitude of Dudu, the married dwarf. For whereas formerly his efforts had all been in the same direction, he now began to ply Joseph with sweet words and to behave like his devoted friend; not only to Joseph himself but also in conversation with the mistress, praising him in all possible keys. And in saying this I said not a word too much. But the reason was that Dudu perceived Mut-em-enet's state, and the ground of her desire to have Joseph put away from the sight of her eyes. He had divined it, by virtue of the sun-property of his dwarfish wisdom; a gift which, however surprisingly it sat upon him, he yet cultivated with assiduity. Actually he was expert and connoisseur in the field, with sharpened senses for all its manifestations — though in other respects his dwarfish wisdom might sorely suffer from the gift.

It was not long, then, before he saw what he had brought about — or at least fostered — by his patriotic indignation at Joseph's growth in the house. He saw it actually much sooner than she did herself, being guided by her proud self-unconsciousness which would take no thought of the need for caution. Then, when her eyes were open, he profited by the usual incapacity of the deluded and stricken heart to conceal its state from the eyes of men. Dudu perceived that the mistress was on the verge of falling in love, headlong, calamitously, and with all the seriousness of her nature, with the foreign body-servant of her spouse. He rubbed his hands. He had not expected this, but shrewdly surmised that by its means a deeper pit would be digged for the interloper than could have been prepared for him in any other way. He changed his face from one day to the next, assuming a rôle which many people have played since his day, though he was himself scarcely the first to play it, being relatively late in time. Little as we know of his predecessors, we cannot doubt that he walked in the footsteps of others as he played his part. He began, that is, to instigate mischief by acting as go-between, to and fro between Joseph and Mut-em-enet.

In talk with her he skilfully changed his tune, speaking tentatively at first, but more boldly as he felt more certain of the state of her heart. For now she sent for him, where before he had urged the matter upon her; and of her own accord began to discuss the affront to the household. At first he took this as a sign that he had won her over to his own hatred and made her active in its service. But soon he scented a different posture of affairs in the strangeness of the language she used.

" Steward," said she (to his joy she called him so, though in fact his office was an inferior one), " steward, I have summoned you through one of the gate-keepers of the house of women, to whom I sent one of my Nubian slaves. For I waited in vain for your appearance to continue our necessary conference in that affair which I so call because it is an affair of yours and it is you who have brought it to my attention. I would reproach you, though but gently, in consideration on the one hand of your merits and on the other of your size, that you have not before now come to me of your own accord, but let me suffer torture by neglect. For waiting is in any case a torture, always unfitting to a woman of my station and so for me even worse. My heart is on fire with this disgrace, this foreign youth of whose name I have been obliged to take note, since I hear that he has become steward in the household in the place of the Osiris Mont-kaw, and walks in his beauty through the establishment and oversees all, to the rapture of most of you. This shame, I say, burns in my heart; the which, dwarf, should rejoice yours since you were the first to arouse me to it by your complaints, without which I might have rested in peace, whereas now it is before me day and night. And

then after making the thing a concern of mine you came
no more to speak with me of it, as is needful, but left me
alone in my anger until I was driven to send for you before my face to discuss what must be done; for nothing
is more painful than to be left hanging in such a matter.
This you should know of yourself, for what can you do
alone and without me as ally, against the object of our
hate, he being so powerful that by comparison your
hatred is impotent, however much I approve it. He sits
unshakable in the favour of the master, who cannot abide
you; and has known by means of cleverness and magic
spells to make himself prized, also because his gods make
all to succeed that is put into his hands. How can they do
this? I cannot think them so powerful, certainly not here
in the lands where they are strange and without honour,
as to achieve all that he has achieved since he came
amongst us. The gifts must lie in himself, for without
them could no one rise from the base position of a chattel
to the overseer of all the household. It is plain that you
can compare with him in shrewdness as little as in outward favour, dwarf. For his wisdom and his way seem
to appeal to everybody, little as you and I can understand the fact. They love him and seek his glance; not
only the people of the house but also in the city and on the
land- and water-ways. Yes, I have heard that when he
appears the women mount the house-tops to stare down
upon him and throw down their rings in token of their
desire. This, then, is the height of the abomination; and
for this reason I was impatient to see you, steward, and
hear your advice or give you mine, to the end that this
shameless situation be ended. For last night when sleep
fled my couch, I pondered whether we might not send

archers with him to the city, who should shoot their arrows into the faces of these women, directly into their faces, who so conduct themselves. I considered and found that we should do this thing; and now you are at last come, I charge you with it, upon my responsibility. Yet you are not to name me in the business, but make it seem as though the idea were yours and plume yourself with it. Only to Osarsiph you will say that I, the mistress, would have it so, and have the bowmen shoot in the women's faces, and you must listen to what he says to this my order. Afterwards you will tell me what he said, coming of yourself and at once to make report, that I need not send and command your coming, having first suffered the torments of waiting and the pain of being left alone in so weighty a matter. For it seems to me you have grown careless, steward, while I give myself trouble and pain for Amun. His Grace Beknechons and you have advised that I embrace the knees of my husband Petepre, captain of the king's bodyguard; and I have wrestled with him half the night for the ending of this annoyance, making myself a burden to him and a humiliation to myself, and all in vain, for his granite will was not broken and I went forth alone and unconsoled. And messenger after messenger had I to send, only that you should come and make report of the infamous youth who grows rank in the house: how he spreads himself in the honours for which he has schemed, and what he utters about masters and servants, but especially about me, its mistress — how he may chance to express himself about me. For if I am to meet him and oppose him, I must know him and his way of speech and thought about myself. Your negligence leaves me uninformed. You could, if you were

active and ingenious, move him to approach me and seek
my favour. Then might I test him and find out the magic
by means of which he besots the hearts of men and draws
them to his side. For that must be a mystery, and the
ways of it past finding out. Or can you, O guardian of
the robes, see and say what all the world sees in him?
It is for this I have summoned you, for you know the ways
of the world; had you come sooner, I would have asked
you before now. Is he then so unsurpassed in figure and
stature? By no means, he is as many others are, in the
measure of a man, of course not so small as you are, yet
far from the towering height of my husband, Petepre.
One might say he is of just the right height — but would
that be so everwhelming? Or is he so strong that he can
carry five bushels or more of seed-corn out of the granary,
amazing the men and bewitching the women? No, for
his strength is but average, it is again just the right
strength. If he bend his arm, the virile muscle stands out
not grossly and boastfully, but only with moderate and
graceful power, which one might call human, or one
might also call divine. For so it is, my friend. But
thousands of such are there in the world, and how little
it justifies his triumphs! It is the head and face that impart meaning and dignity to a man; and let us admit in
fairness that his eyes are lovely in their darkness beneath
the arch of the brows; lovely in their clear open gaze and
also when it pleases him to veil them in a dreamy and
artful way which you have doubtless observed. But what
sort of mouth has he, that he can bewitch mankind, so that
they actually call him, as I have heard, the mouth of the
house? It is incomprehensible, it is not to be fathomed;
for his lips are too thick, and the smile with which he

knows how to grace them, with his teeth shining as they part, can but little explain the delusion, even considering the felicity of his words. I incline to the view that good part of the mystery lies in this same mouth; at that door must one listen would one trap the adventurer in his own snare. If my servants will not betray me or leave me to wait in torment for their aid, I will take it on myself to ensnare him and bring him to a fall. But if he resist me, know then, dwarf, that I will order the bowmen to turn their weapons and shoot their arrows into his face, into the night of his eyes and the fatal sweetness of his mouth! "

To this extraordinary speech from his mistress Dudu listened with great dignity, the thatch of his upper lip shoved out over the lower one; his hand curved round his ear in token of an attention not at all feigned. Being past master in a certain field, he was in a position to interpret her words. So, understanding how things stood, he changed his tune; not too abruptly, but by degrees gliding from one position to another. On the morrow he spoke differently of Joseph, yet as though his words of yesterday had been uttered in the same sense, though in fact they had been much more derogatory. And in general he sought to turn gall into honey and all that he had previously uttered into its opposite. Such gross inconsistency must have angered any reasonable person, for it insulted the human understanding. But Dudu was instructed by his prowess in a certain field; he knew how much people in Mut-em-enet's state can be made to believe and he took no shame to himself for urging her on. And she — she was far too bemused to take offence at the insolence; she was even grateful to the dwarf for his complaisance.

" Noble lady," he said, " if your servant appeared not yesterday before you to discuss ways and means in our affair — for the day before I was here, as you will re- call when I remind you, and only your great zeal magni- fies the term of my absence — the cause was but the press- ing claims of my office; yet could not even so my mind be distracted from the problem which lies next to your heart and mine, touching Osarsiph, the new steward. The duties of my office are none the less dear to me, for the which you will not chide me; they are precious, and have become so by inclination, whereas at first they were a burden — as will often come to pass. For the same is true of that problem and occupation concerning which your servant is privileged to take frequent counsel with you. How could one but take that duty to his heart which permitted him daily or almost daily to exchange speech with his mistress, whether summoned or unsummoned? It is even true and natural that my gratitude for the great privilege be extended to the subject of our discourse, so that I must needs take him to my heart who was the cause of my advancement in being the cause of your con- cern. It could scarcely be otherwise; and indeed I am re- minded to my satisfaction that I have never thought of the subject of our discourse, the person in question, otherwise than as one worthy of your concern. It were unjust to Dudu to suppose that he has neglected for an hour the elegant duties of the wardrobe, even to be active in the business which his lady grants him to share with her. One must do the one without neglecting the other, that was always my motto, in earthly as also in heavenly things. Amun is a great god, there can be no greater. But shall one therefore neglect to worship and cherish the other gods of the land — even such as are so near to him as almost to be the same and have named him their name, as for instance Atum-Re-Horakhte at On in Lower Egypt? Even when it was vouchsafed me to speak with you last time, I sought to explain, albeit clumsily and with unsuccess, that I found him a god great, wise, and mild, pre-eminent for such inventions as the clock and almanac, without which we were as the beasts. From my youth up I have asked myself privily, but now aloud, if Amun in his chapel could find it amiss were we to take account in our hearts of the mild and magnanimous thoughts of that majestic being with whose name he has united his own. Is not His Grace Beknechons the first prophet of one as well as the other? When my lady shakes her loud rattle in the dance before Amun as his bride in the feast, then her name is not Mut as on other days, but Hathor, the sister-bride of Atum-Re, with disk and horns — not the bride of Amun. In the light of these things, your faithful servant has not failed to take trouble in the matter close to our hearts; but has approached nearer to the seed of Asia, that youth who flourishes so exceedingly in the house that he is now steward and the object of your concern. I have sought to search him to the end that I might speak with more knowledge before you than was last time possible despite all my effort. All in all I found him charming — within the limits set by the natural order for a man like me. The feelings of the women on the roofs are different, of course. But I found that the youth would have little or no objection to letting the bowmen shoot at them, and in this respect there would be no ground at all for turning the bows in the other direction. For he seemed to say that but one had the right to look upon him and fix him with her eye — whereat he darted me a glance with his great eyes like night, at first large and shining, but then veiled and artful, in the interesting way he has. His words might have been an indication of his feeling for you; but I did not let it stop there. For I am used to weigh and estimate men according to their attitude toward you. So I led the talk round to feminine charm and asked him, as one man another, whom he found the most beautiful of all that he knew. ' Our mistress, Mut-em-enet,' he said, ' is the most beautiful here and in all the region round. One could cross seven mountains and not find one more full of charm.' And there came an Atum-redness in his cheek, which I can but compare with that which now colours yours — the source of which, I may hope, is your satisfaction over my zeal in our cause. And not stopping at that, I furthered your desire that the young steward should wait often upon you and put himself to proof before you that you might come upon the sources of his magic and the secret of his mouth — for to that I feel myself by my nature uncalled. Urgently I pressed him and chid his timidity, counselling him to approach you, O my lady, the more assiduously the better, kissing with his mouth the ground before you, the which may suffer it. He made no reply. But the blush which had gone from his cheek swiftly returned, which I took for a sign of his fear to betray himself to you and reveal his secret. Yet I am convinced that he will follow my advice. True, he has risen above me in this house, by whatever means, and is at its head; but I am the older in years and office, so that I can speak to such a youth as a plain, forthright man, which I am, and as which I commend myself to my lady's favour."

And Dudu bowed very correctly as he took leave, his stumpy little arms dangling from his shoulders. He went straight to Joseph, whom he greeted with the words:

" My respects to you, mouthpiece of the house! "

" So, Dudu," answered Joseph, " you come to pay me your valued respects? But how is this? For only a little while since you would not eat with me, but showed in word and deed that your friendliness was not great."

" Friendliness? " repeated the husband of Djeset, tilting back his head to look into Joseph's face. " It was always greater than that of many who have behaved more like it these seven years, while I had it but did not show it. I am a cautious, reserved man, who grants not all at once his respect and devotion to a man for the sake of his beautiful eyes, but lets it ripen in silence even for seven years. But let it once be mature, then is all trust and dependence to be placed upon it, as he who has been tested soon can test."

" Very good," answered Joseph. " I rejoice to have won your favour without having put myself to great charge thereby."

" Charge or no," answered the manikin, suppressing his anger, " you may at all times count on my zeal from now on, which springs above all from the fact that the gods are with you. I am a religious man, with respect for the voice of the gods, and I esteem a man's virtue according to his good fortune. The favour of the gods brings conviction. Who would be so obstinate as to oppose his own opinion in their face? So stupid and so stubborn Dudu is not; and hence am I become your man to the last gasp."

" I am gratified to hear it," said Joseph, " and congratulate you on your mingled piety and wisdom. On which note I might perhaps take leave, for my affairs call me."

" It is my impression," persisted Dudu, " that our young steward has not understood how to esteem my overtures — which amount to a formal offer — at quite their true worth. Else you would not make to leave me without seeking to understand their extent and the advantages they hold out. For you may trust me and avail yourself of my loyalty and initiative in all your affairs: in the business of the household as well as in reference to your personal happiness. I have thorough knowledge of the ways of the world, on which you may build; versed am I in walking hidden ways, in spying and eavesdropping, carrying messages, and my secrecy is like nothing on earth, so subtle is it and so inviolable. I hope that your eyes are beginning to open upon the meaning of my offers."

" They were never closed," Joseph assured him. " You have mistaken me quite, to think that I undervalue the advantages of your friendliness."

" Your words reassure me," said the dwarf, " if not quite the tone of your voice. If my ear deceives me not, it expresses a certain reluctance, which in my eyes belongs to past time, and for which there should be no more room between you and me, since for my part I have abandoned it utterly. From you it pains me as an injustice, for you have had as long time as I in which your trust in me might ripen — namely, seven years. Trust for trust. But I see that I must do yet more to take you into my confidence that you may give me yours without reserve. Know then, Osarsiph," he said, and sank his voice to a whisper, " that my resolve to love you and give myself to your service utterly comes not alone from my reverence for the gods. It was the wish and the desire of an earthly person, if one very near the gods, which was as I now confess the decisive motive — " He paused, blinking his eyes.

" Who, then? " Joseph could not refrain from asking.

" You ask? " Dudu replied. " Good, then; with my answer I give such proof of my confidence that you must needs return it." He stood on his tiptoes, put his hand over his mouth, and whispered:

" It was the mistress."

" The mistress! " Joseph made answer — far too quickly and far too low, as he bent down. It was true, alas: the dwarf had known what to say to arouse the other's immediate curiosity. Joseph's heart — that heart which Jacob, far away, believed long stilled in death, whereas here it was in Egypt, ticking on and exposed to all the perils of life — that heart stood a moment still, then, as a heart does, throbbed the faster in order to overtake its lost beats.

He stood up erect again at once, and commanded:

" Take your hand from your mouth! Speak low if you must, but take your hollowed hand away! "

He said this that no one might suppose him to have secrets with the dwarf. He was ready to have them, but rebelled against their outward signs.

Dudu obeyed.

" It was Mut, our lady," he asseverated, " the chief and true wife. She summoned me before her to speak of you and addressed me thus: 'Steward' (pardon, but so did she speak, with gracious flattery, whereas I know that you alone are steward since Mont-kaw's death, and occupy the special room of trust, whereas the title was and is mine in but a limited sense), 'Steward,' said she, 'to come back to the youth Osarsiph, about whom we have before now taken counsel together; the moment, so it seems to me, has come for you to lay aside the reserve and dignity which you have practised toward him these past years, some seven years, perhaps, and to lend yourself frankly to his service. For in your heart you have long yearned to do so. I have considered the misgivings which you have now and then expressed before me concerning his precipitate advancement in the house; but I have at length rejected them, on the ground of his obvious virtues. This was the easier because you yourself have gradually lost sight of your objections and finally could no longer conceal your increasing goodwill. It is my wish that you will no longer put this constraint upon yourself, but rather serve him with fervent love and loyal heart, for this indeed is the heart's wish of your mistress. What could be dearer to her than that the best servants of the house be friendly with each other and enter into a bond for its welfare? Such a pact, Dudu, you will make with the young steward; and as the older and more experienced, give him aid and counsel and be his messenger and guide. For it lies near to my heart. He is shrewd, and in what he does the gods mostly grant success through him. Yet in some things is his youth a hindrance and a peril. The peril rises from his youth, that being united with great measure of beauty, the beauty of his years and growth as well as of his swiftly veiled glance and his

ripe lips — one might climb seven mountains without
finding a stripling of such pleasing exterior. What I
enjoin upon you is that you shall protect his person
against offensive curiosity, giving him a troop of bowmen when he goes into the cities, who shall shoot their
arrows to rescue him from the peril of things thrown down
upon him from roofs and walls. But I have said that his
youth is also a hindrance to him; for he is timorous,
and I would have you extend your aid to overcome it and
give him confidence. For instance, all too seldom or almost never does he come before me, the mistress, to
speak concerning the affairs of the house. I am loth to
miss it, being not like unto Petepre, my husband, who on
principle takes nothing on himself. For I as mistress
take lively interest in the economy of the household and
have ever regretted that the departed Mont-kaw — from
too great ambition or exaggerated respect, I know not
which — excluded me from these affairs. I have promised myself some improvement from the change, and appoint you, my friend, to ply between me and our young
steward, subtly, as you know how, and to teach him how
timidity may be overcome; that he may appear often
before me for converse about this and that. This indeed
you may regard as the chief aim of the pact you make
with him even as I, Mut-em-enet, make one with you.
For thus I bind you in allegiance to him and in obedience
to a bond between him, yourself, and me.' These," concluded Dudu, " were my mistress's words; in repeating
which I give you intimate confidence, that you may return it. For now you can better understand the meaning
of my offers, whereby I give myself blindly to your serv-

THE SMITTEN ONE 449

ice, and am prepared to walk all sorts of secret ways for
the sake of our threefold bond."

" Very good," Joseph answered. He forced himself
to be calm and his voice was low. " I have listened to
you, overseer of the wardrobe, out of respect for our
mistress, whose words spoke from your mouth, as you
would have me believe; also in respect of yourself, the
man of the world — for it would be unfitting for me to
meet you with a coolness and polish inferior to your own.
For I have not much faith in your recent conversion, taking it to be worldly wisdom instead, sharp practice, if I
may speak frankly without offence. Nor is my love for
you without limits; indeed, like my feeling for your
person, it hath rather the opposite quality. But I seek
to show you that I am not less man of the world than you,
and equally master of my feelings; for I am capable
quite in their despite of cold-blooded wisdom. A man
like me cannot always walk the straightest path. He must
not fear to take a crooked one. And such a man can use
not only the honest for friends; he needs eavesdroppers
and clever rogues and must prize their services. Therefore, Master Dudu, I will not reject your offer, but readily accept your service and duty. There shall be no talk
of a bond between us — such a vow would not be to my
taste, even were the mistress included in it. But what
gossip you hear in house or city, that bring always to me
and I will seek to make it avail."

" If you but trust me," responded the little man, " I
care not whether you think me worldly or sincere. I need
no love from the world, having it ever in my home from
Djeset, my wife, and from the sons I have begotten, Esesi

and Ebebi. But my glorious mistress has set her heart upon this bond between you and me; and that I shall be aid and counsel to your youth, messenger and guide; to this I cling, for my own part, and shall be satisfied if you will trust me, whether with your heart or your understanding matters not to me. Only forget not what I whispered you, of the mistress's desire to be initiated into the affairs of the household, more intimately than in the time of Mont-kaw; and that she will often have speech with you. Have you perhaps a message to give me for her in return?"

"Nothing that I can think of," replied Joseph. "Let it content you that you have delivered hers, and leave it to me to consider it."

"As you will," said the dwarf. "But I can add still a little. For the mistress let fall that she would walk today at sunset in the garden for the comfort of her lovely spirit and mount the slope into the secluded gardenhouse, there to commune with her thoughts. If there were someone who would have speech with her to make a report or prefer a request he should take advantage of the rare opportunity to present himself for audience."

This was simply a lie on Dudu's part. The mistress had said nothing of the sort. But if Joseph fell into the snare he would lure her to the summerhouse by turning the tale the other way about, thus contriving a rendezvous between them. And though Joseph did not rise to his hint, yet the dwarf did not relinquish his purpose.

Joseph, indeed, made no sign of intending to avail himself of the suggestion he had heard, simply turning his back on the guardian of the wardrobe without more ado. His heart beat high, though not so quickly as it had before, having by now caught up with itself; and it would be idle to deny that he was glad almost to rapture at what he had heard about the mistress, as likewise at the opportunity which awaited him at the setting of the sun. We may guess that an insistent inner voice warned him not to go; nor need it surprise us that presently an outward whisper, like a cricket's chirp, reinforced the inward one. For when after leaving Dudu he had made for the house to consider these matters in the special room of trust, it was Sa'ankh-Wen-nofer-and-so-on, it was Shepses-Bes in his wrinkled finery, who slipped in with him and murmured:

" Osarsiph, do not that which the wicked advise you, do it not now or ever."

" What, little friend, are you there? " he asked, rather confused. And asked him in what crack or cranny he had crept that he could know what Dudu said.

" In none at all," responded the little man. " But my dwarf eyes are sharp, and from afar I saw you bend down to him, after you had chidden him for the hand over his mouth. Then knew I whose name he had whispered."

" A wizard you are, indeed! " answered Joseph. " And are now slipped hither to congratulate me on the turn affairs have taken; for here was my enemy, who has so long complained of me to the mistress, and she sends him to me with the plain meaning that I have at last found favour in her eyes and she covets to speak with me about the affairs of the household! Confess now that it is a marvellous turn, and rejoice with me that I may if I choose have audience with her today in the garden-house at sunset — for I myself rejoice beyond all words. Mind, I do not say that I purpose to go — I am far from having made up my mind. But that I may go, that the choice rests with me to go or stay, that rejoices me unspeakably, and you too, thumbling, shall wish me joy! "

" Ah, Osarsiph," sighed the little man, " if you had in mind not to go your joy would be less; that, to my little wisdom, is a sign that you will go. Shall the dwarf rejoice with you over that? "

" Small wisdom is it, as you say," scolded Joseph; " and in this case your piping and plaining serve me not at all. Can you not grant it to a son of man to be glad of his free choice, in such a matter that he had no thought ever to be able to rejoice at it? Only think back with me to the time, the day and the hour, when the man who is now departed bought me for the master, and the bargaining was done by the scribe Khamat with my father of the well, the old man from Midian, and we stood thereafter alone in the courtyard: I, you and your ape, do you recall? Then did you whisper to me as I stood there dazed and said: ' Fling yourself on your face! ' Then my unknown mistress rode past, lifted high and proud on the shoulders of rubber-eaters, the mistress of the house into which I was sold, and her lily-white arm hung down from the chair, as I saw from between my fingers. She looked upon me with contemptuous seeing, as though I were not a man but a thing, while I, a boy, gazed up as though at a goddess, blinded with awe. But God brought it about by His will that I grew up in this house and flourished as by a spring, for these seven years long, till I fell heir to the office of the ailing man and came to the headship. So the Lord my God glorified Himself in me. There was but one cloud in the mirror of my fortune, and in one part dross mingled with its bronze: the mistress was against me, with Beknechons, the priest of Amun, and Dudu, the married dwarf. I must rejoice when she frowned upon me, for black looks are better than none. But now, lo: is it not the consummation of my good fortune, is it not now for the first time free from dross, that her brow has lightened and she sends me word of her relenting and even of her desire for speech with me in special audience? Who could have dreamed, at the hour when you whispered to the boy: ' Fling yourself on your face! ' that one day it would lie with him to choose or not to choose to have speech with her? Then take it not amiss of me, my friend, if I rejoice! "

" Ah, Osarsiph, be glad, but after you have resolved not to see her, not before! "

" Begin not each sentence with ' Ah ' and ' Alas,' little wizened one, instead of with ' Oh,' as in wonder and rejoicing! Why do you croak like a raven and spin gloomy fancies? I told you that I was more inclined not to go to the summerhouse. But even so, it must be thought of. For after all it is the mistress who has sent; or rather one might say that in the first place it is she, and that makes it important. In my place a man must keep his head and be cool and worldly. Such a man must be mindful of his advantage and not fear to take opportunity by the forelock that he may strengthen himself. Consider how much a bond with the mistress and a nearness to her person can advance me and be a prop to me in the house; but on top of that, tell me, who am I to pass judgment on the mistress's wish and command? True, I am set over the house, but I belong to the house, I am the bought servant of it. Whereas she is the chief and true wife, lady of the house, and I owe to her obedience. There could be nobody, among the living or the dead, to blame me were I

to fulfil her bidding in blind loyalty; even the dead and
living might blame me did I otherwise. For plainly I
had risen too early to command, had I not first learned
to obey. So I begin to ask myself whether you were not
right to chide me for my joy in the free choice. For perhaps I have no such, and no other course is left me but to
go."

"Ah, Osarsiph," came the whispering little voice,
"how can I answer aught but 'Ah' and 'Alas' when I
hear you speak and utter such quibbling with your
tongue! You were good, you were lovely and wise, when
you came to us, O seventh gift! And I spoke for you and
your purchase against the evil old gossip because with
my unclouded little wisdom I saw at first glance the
power and the blessing. Beautiful you are still, and good
at heart; but of the other — better be silent. Is it not a
calamity to hear you, thinking on past times? Wise you
were till now, unerring in shrewdness, your thoughts went
like the arrow, your head was blithely erect as you
walked in the service of your mind. Then came the fiery
bull, which I fear more than aught else in the world, and
breathed one breath in your face. And you are grown
foolish that God may pity you, and like an ass which one
drives round the town with cudgellings, for your thoughts
go on all fours, while your tongue hangs out, serviceable
no longer to your mind, but to your evil proneness. Ah,
alas, and woe to your ignominy! For all that you say is
but beating the air, it is but crooked conclusions and sub-
terfuge, betraying the bondage of your mind to the yearning to go on all fours! Even would you pull the wool over
the eyes of your little faithful here, saying that he was
right to rebuke you for your joy in free choice, because

in fact you have none — as though it is not just therein you should find your true joy! What a shame is that, what a boundless shame and mortification! " Here the dwarf put his two little hands before his wrinkled face and began to weep.

" Nay, nay, little gnomeling! " said Joseph in distress. " Take heart, weep no more! It goes to my heart to see you so low — and all because of some false conclusions that have crept into our talk. You may well find it an easy thing to draw the right ones and guide yourself by the spirit; yet you must not suffer such pathetic distress over one whose mind is somewhat clouded by the proneness to err."

"Now you are good again," said the little man, still sobbing. He dried his eyes on his crumpled batiste skirt. " You pity my tears. Alas, that you have no pity on yourself, to hold upright your reason with all your strength that it fail you not when you have most need! Lo, from the beginning have I seen it come, when you would not understand and pretended ignorance when I whispered. I saw that much worse could unfold itself from the complaints of that evil man when he complained before Mut, the mistress — something much more dangerous than that danger. For thinking to do you ill, he did more ill than he knew, opening her eyes to you, you good and lovely one! And you, will you now close your own eyes before the opening pit, that is deeper far than the other of your tale, whereinto you were thrown after your envious brethren had snatched your wreath and veil? No Ishmaelite from Midian will there be to draw you up from this pit which the bad man digged when he opened the eyes of the mistress to your beauty! Now she, the exalted one, makes eyes at you, and you return her glances, and they are the terrible glances of the fiery bull that lays waste the fields, and after them comes naught but ashes and darkness!"

"Fearful are you by nature, dear manling," Joseph answered him, "and you torture your small soul with dwarfish imaginings. But tell me what it is you see in your weakness only because our lady has let her eyes rest upon me. When I was a little lad I thought that everyone who saw me must love me more than himself — so foolish was I. It brought me to the pit, but I have climbed out of the pit and overcome my folly. Yet that folly, methinks, has descended upon you and whispers fears. As yet the mistress has looked but sternly upon me, nor I upon her save with reverence. If she will speak with me and hear reports upon the business of the house, shall I interpret that according to your conceit of me? Not flattering is that conceit, for it assumes that I am lost, were the mistress but to hold out her little finger to me. I myself have no such fear, nor think to come again so swiftly to the pit. If now I would challenge your fiery bull, do you think I am so ill armed and cannot take him by the horns? Verily you imagine me to be of great frailty! Comfort yourself; go to the house of women and cheer them with dance and song. It is most likely I shall not present myself for audience in the little house. But I must ponder these things alone, and as a grown man come to some compromise with my thoughts: how to reconcile one wisdom with the other, neither offending the mistress nor yet being disloyal to either the living or the dead or . . . But that you cannot understand; for to you children here below, the third is contained in the

second. Your dead are gods, and your gods are dead, and
you know not what that is: the living God."

Thus Joseph, condescendingly, to the wizened little
man. Yet knew he not that he, Joseph, was dead and
deified, Osarsiph, in other words? It was to ponder all
these things that he would be alone; alone too with a
thought inevitably bound up with them: the thought
of the god in deathly readiness, rigidly awaiting the
vulture-woman.

IN THE TOILS

How narrow is the span when we look back upon our own
lives; how vast when we contemplate the world's abysmal
past! And yet we lose ourselves as easily, as dreamily,
in the one as in the other; by virtue of our perception
of a unity between the two. As little in the small sphere
as in the large can we go back to the time of our birth
and the beginning of our days, to say nothing of further
back. It lies in darkness before the beginnings of the
dawn of consciousness or memory. But with our earliest
mental life, when we first enter — as primitive man once
entered — into civilization, giving and receiving our first
little contributions, we are aware of a sympathy, we feel
ourselves recognize that abiding unity; with pleased surprise we acclaim our kinship with the larger whole. And
the content of the kinship is always the same: it is the
idea of a catastrophe, the invasion of destructive and
wanton forces into an ordered scheme and a life bent
upon self-control and a happiness conditioned by it. The
saga of peace wrung from conflict and seemingly assured; of life laughingly sweeping away the structure of

art; of mastery and overpowering, and the coming of the stranger god — all that was there from the beginning, as it was in the middle. And in a late age which is aware of its affinity with human beginnings, we find ourselves still united with them in that bond of sympathy.

For Mut-em-enet, Potiphar's wife, the sweet singer, that far-away form, which the epic spirit grants us to see as though close at hand — she too was one afflicted and overpowered, a bacchantic sacrifice to the stranger god, the careful structure of her life no less than wrecked by the nether powers which in her ignorance she had thought to mock, whereas they alone it was who made mock of all her compensations and super-compensations. Old Huia might well have told her not to be a goose — not a bird of the black water-logged depths, whom the swan visiteth and covereth. Not a goose, but a moon-chaste priestess, yet not the less feminine for that. He himself, old Huia, had dwelt in the marshy, murky brother-sister darkness, yet felt strange and awkward stirrings of conscience and intuitions that new things were come to pass in the world. He had mutilated his little son that he might be a courtier of light, sapped his son's virile powers and made him a human nonentity, and then given him in the stern bond of marriage to the woman who bore the ancient name of mother. Now might they see themselves prop up each other's dignity by dint of tact and mutual consideration! It is undeniable that human dignity realizes itself in the two sexes, male and female; so that when one is neither one nor the other, one stands outside the human pale — and whence then can human dignity come? Efforts to sustain it are worthy of respect, for they deal with the spiritual, and thus, let us admit in honour, with the pre-eminently human. But truth demands the hard confession that thought and the spirit come badly off, in the long run, against nature. How little can the precepts of civilization avail against the dark, deep, silent knowledge of the flesh! How little it lets itself be taken in by the spirit! All this we saw in the early days of our story, in connection with the bewilderment of Rachel. And now Rachel's sister here below, Mut, once princess of the nome, by virtue of her relation with the sun-chamberlain was just as remote from the female side of human life as he was from the male. As a woman, she led a life as hollow, as dishonouring to the flesh as did he; nor were her compensations, and the Amun-honour in which she thought to veil her dim perceptions from herself, any less frail a support, though a support to the spirit, than those props to the amour-propre of her fat husband when he posed as a horse-tamer and hippopotamus-hunter and urged himself on to feats of valour. Joseph had known how to flatter his master by making these exploits appear as the essence of masculinity; but actually they were sicklied and forced, and when Petepre went hunting in the swamps he was always yearning for the peace and quiet of his library — in other words, for the life of the mind, pure and simple and quite unapplied.

However, we are not now thinking of Petepre, but of his Eni, the priestess of Amun, and of the anguishing dilemma of her position between the honour of the spirit and the honour of the flesh. Two dark eyes had done this to her, the eyes of a beloved one who had lived far away and been all too extravagantly loved; her surrender to them was by its nature nothing else than a violent, terrified outburst concerned to save, in the last or almost the last moment, her fleshly honour and her human womanhood — to save, or rather to secure it, though it meant the abandonment and sacrifice of her spiritual and religious honour, of everything in the realm of the idea on which her life was based.

Let us pause here to look at her situation — look at it with the eyes of this woman who thought of nothing else by day and night, in a torture of mounting desire. Was it a genuine dilemma, does that sacrifice always and everywhere dishonour and desecrate? That was the question. Does dedication amount to chastity? Yes, and no. For her state of bridehood involved certain contradictions which cancelled each other out; the veil, the token of the goddess of love, is also the token of its sacrifice, the sign at once of the nun and of the courtesan. The spirit of her time and her temple recognized the consecrated and immaculate, the *kedesha,* who was an " enticer "; that is to say, a street prostitute. Theirs was the veil; these *kadishtu* were immaculate, as is an animal, which precisely because of its immaculateness is destined for a sacrifice to god in the feast. Consecrated? One asks: to whom, and why? If one is consecrated to Ishtar, then chastity is only a phase of the sacrifice, a veil destined to be rent.

Such were Mut's lovelorn thoughts as she wrestled; and if the little dwarf had heard them, he would, in his fear of sex, his remoteness from all such ideas, have wept at the insidiousness of her thoughts, so little serviceable to reason, so prone to go on all fours. It would have been easy for him to weep, knowing, as he did, nothing of human dignity, being but a little dancing dervish of a man. But to Mut, the mistress, it was a matter of the honour of her flesh, and she sought out thoughts by which she might reconcile it with her religious honour. So we owe her consideration and sympathy, however much she rationalized; for thoughts are seldom present for their own sake only. She had hard work with hers; for her awakening to her womanhood from that sleep of the senses in which she had rested as aristocrat, lady, and priestess was nothing like the traditional one of the daughter of the king summoned by the sight of the majesty of the prince of heaven from the peace of childhood to endure the torment and desire of consuming love. She had not the fatal happiness of loving so exaltedly above her station (which condemns one in the end to accept the extremest pangs of jealousy and even to be turned into a cow); no, her misfortune lay — in her mind — in the fact that she loved so far below it: a nameless slave, a bought chattel and Asiatic house-servant. That was bitterer to her dainty pride than anything we have had so far to tell. It long prevented her from admitting her feelings even to herself, and when she finally did so, there mingled in the bliss which love always brings us an element of humiliation which, rising from the deepest depths of cruelty, can arm desire with its sharpest thorn. The rationalization which she sought to apply to these humbling thoughts centred in the fact that the *kedesha* and temple maiden cannot seek out her own lover either, her caresses being the property of him who throws the price in her lap. But how unavailing the justification, what violence it did to herself in allotting her so passive a rôle! For surely hers was the active, wooing, choosing part — though even so she had not been quite independ

ent, her choice having been guided by Dudu's complaints.
But her station and years entitled her to the position of
attack and challenge; it could never have been possible
that the slave of his own motion and will had lifted up
his eyes to her or that she could have been the submissive
recipient of his desire. Never! In this affair her pride
decisively laid claim to the masculine rôle; and yet in
the depths of her being, the rôle did not suit. For however one might try to twist the fact, it remained true that
this young servant, consciously and wilfully or not, had
been, by virtue of his existence, the awakener of her
womanhood from its enchanted sleep, and had therewith
made himself the master of his mistress, so that she
served him in her thoughts and hung upon his eyes, in
panic lest he see that she would be his, yet trembling
for fear lest he might requite her incommunicable longings. All in all, it was a humility pervaded by a frightful sweetness. Yet she sought to lessen it, as passion will
do. For while not at all actuated by considerations of
worth or dignity, it will always seek to seem so, and to
justify itself in all possible ways for its choice. Thus she
contrived to raise the boy whose mistress she would be,
out of his lowly condition; adducing his bearing, his
cleverness, his position in the house. She even, taking a
leaf from Dudu's book, called in religion to justify her
" proneness to all fours," as the mock-vizier would have
said: in other words, she brought into the field Atum-
Re of On, the complaisant god, friendly to foreigners,
against stern old Amun, her former lord, and enlisted
the court, the royal power itself, in support of her love.
Which for her subtilizing conscience had the further advantage that she came closer in spirit to her husband,

Pharaoh's friend, and won him in a certain sense as a party to her own burning wish to betray him!

Thus Mut-em-enet, twisting and turning in the toils of her own desire — as in the coils of a serpent sent by a god to embrace and strangle her — so that she gasped for breath. And she wrestled alone; she had no one to talk to, save Dudu, with whom she never got beyond veiled allusion — at least not in the beginning, for later she lost all restraint and made her whole entourage partakers of her frenzy. Remember further that the urge of her blood had lighted upon a zealot, one devoted to higher purposes, wearing the rue in token of his loyalty and proud devotion; in other words, one set apart, who might not and would not yield to her allure. Remember, finally, that her torture lasted three years, from the seventh to the tenth of Joseph's sojourn in Potiphar's house, and then was not satisfied, but only slain. And remembering all this, shall we not concede that the lot of Potiphar's wife, lewd wanton as she was in the popular legend, was a tragic one? Shall we not bestow upon her at least the pity born of the perception that the instruments of such a trial bear their punishment in themselves and have it in fuller measure than they deserve, considering the inevitability of their function?

THE FIRST YEAR

THREE years: in the first she tried to conceal her love from him; in the second she let him see it; in the third she offered it to him.

Three years: and she must or might see him every day, for they lived as members of one family, and there was daily fuel for her folly, great encouragement and also great torment. For with love we cannot speak of must and may as Joseph had spoken to Mont-kaw about sleep, saying soothingly not that he must sleep but that he might. For in love there is a painful, involved, and bewildering struggle; it splits the soul with half-wishing, half-unwishing, so that the lover curses the must-see with as good will as he would blissfully welcome the may-see. And the more violent his anguish from the last time of seeing, the more passionately he strives for the next opportunity to aggravate his disease. This most of all when the patient had ground to rejoice that the pain was growing less! For it can actually happen that a meeting can tarnish the brilliance of the desired object and bring about a certain disappointment, cooling, and detachment. That should be the more welcome to the lover since with the diminishing of his own infatuation, thanks to desire, he has a growing power of self-conquest and of inflicting on another what he suffers himself. Such would be the result were one lord and master of one's passion instead of its victim; for the chances of winning the other are greatly improved by the cooling of one's own feeling. But the lover will listen to nothing of all this; the advantages of returning sanity, coolness, and boldness — for they are advantages, in pursuit of a goal which is the highest he knows — he reckons as nothing compared with the loss he imagines that he will suffer by the diminution of his feeling. He declines upon a state of desolation and emptiness comparable to that of a drug-taker deprived of his drug, and strains every muscle to regain his former state of infatuation by fresh doses of re-infecting impressions.

Thus it is with must and may in the field of love's folly — which of all follies is the greatest, so that in it one may best study the nature of folly and its effect on its victim. For he, however much he may groan under the lash of his passion, is not only incapable of wishing to be free, he is even incapable of wanting to wish it. He probably knows that if he did not see the object of his passion for a certain time — quite an absurdly short time, perhaps — he would be free. But it is just forgetting of which he is more afraid than of anything else; indeed, every pain at parting rests upon a secret dread of the inevitable forgetting. When it has happened, one can grieve no more — and therefore one grieves in advance. No one saw Mut-em-enet's face when she hid it against the pillar, after wrestling in vain with Petepre, her husband, for the sending away of Joseph. But there is much, there is everything, in favour of the guess that it was radiant with joy, because now she must see every day him who had awaked her love, and so would not be able to forget him.

It must have been all-important, for her especially, and particularly strong, her dread of the parting and the inevitably ensuing forgetting, the dying down of her passion. For women of her age, when their blood has been late stirred, and perhaps without extraordinary provocation never would have been stirred, yield themselves with more than common abandon to their feelings, which are their first and may be their last, and would rather die than exchange this new life of blissful anguish for the old peace of mind which they now find so empty. It was then the more meritorious in Mut that in all seriousness and reasonableness she did what she could to

persuade her indolent husband to withdraw from her
eyes the object of her longing. If his nature could have
brought him to grant her the favour, she would have
sacrificed her feelings. But to move and arouse him was
simply not possible, he being a proper captain of the
guard; and the real truth is that Eni had secretly known
that and counted on it; in other words, her struggle with
her husband had been a device by which his refusal
should set her free for her passion and her fate.

For free she might in fact consider herself after the
evening in the hall at sunset. If she bridled her passions
for such a long time afterwards the reason was less duty
than pride. Her carriage was lofty indeed, and only the
very keenest eye could have seen any trace of weakness
or tenderness shining through, when at sunset on the day
of the three conversations she went to meet Joseph in the
garden, at the foot of the little summerhouse. Dudu had
carried out his plan with the utmost slyness and shrewdness. From Joseph he had returned to the mistress and
told her that the new steward rejoiced in the opportunity
of giving account of the business of the household and
laid stress on their meeting for this purpose alone and
undisturbed, at whatever hour and place it pleased the
mistress to appoint. He would, he had said, be visiting
the little house in the garden at sunset that day, to inspect its furnishings and the condition of the frescoes.
Dudu had given this second piece of information inde-
pendently from the first, sandwiched in between other
matters, delicately leaving it to the mistress to draw her
own conclusions. But his manœuvres had not quite succeeded, for both parties had contented themselves with
half-measures: Joseph had found a middle way between

his two choices and without mounting up to the summer-house had merely walked round its base, as he might or should have done in any case, to inspect the trees and flower-beds in this part of the garden. Neither had Mut, the mistress, been minded to climb the mound. But she had seen no reason why she need be prevented by what the dwarf had happened to murmur in her ear from carrying out what she remembered to have intended from the beginning: namely, to linger awhile in the garden at sunset and watch the beautiful fiery sky as it mirrored itself in the duck-pond. She was attended, as usual, by two of her maidens.

So then the mistress and the young steward met each other on the red-sanded path, and their encounter went off something like this:

Joseph, perceiving the group, gave a little " Oh! " of startled respect; raising his hands he began to move backwards, bowing as he went. Mut on her side, smiling a little, in vague surprise, shaped a casual and questioning " Ah? " with her sinuous lips, above which her eyes looked sternly, even forbiddingly at him. She walked forward as he retreated a few ceremonial steps, then signed to him by a little downward motion with one hand to await her. She stood still at the same time, and behind her her dark-skinned maidens did the same, casting delighted glances with their paint-lengthened eyes as did all the servants when they saw Joseph. In their ears, peeping from among black woolly fringes, they wore great enamelled disks.

It was not a meeting to afford one of the two any of the disillusion of which I spoke. The light fell slanting across the garden, bathing the scene in colour and beauty;

it gilded the summerhouse and the duck-pond with rich
tints, turned the sand of the path to a fiery red, gave
lustre to the flowers, lighted the waving foliage of the
trees, and made little mirrors of men's eyes, like the mirror of the pond, whereon the ducks, both domestic and
exotic, looked less like real ducks than painted and lac-
quered toys. And the human beings, too, looked painted
and celestial in this light, as though freed from all taint
of inadequacy or care; not only in their gleaming eyes
but with their whole figures, they looked like gods and
tomb images, painted and beautified by the flattering
brightness, so that each must have had joy at sight of
the other, as they looked out of their mirror-eyes into each
other's illumined faces.

Mut was enraptured to see in all his perfection him
whom she knew she loved. For the loving woman is ever
on the look-out for justification of her love; palpitatingly
sensitive to every flaw in the image of the beloved, tri-
umphantly grateful for every favourable illusion. And
if its splendour, which for the sake of her honour she
cherishes, is a source of pain, because it belongs to everybody, is apparent to everybody, and must disquiet her
with fear of rivals on every hand — yet even the pain
is sweet beyond words, so that she presses the sword to
her heart, heedless of everything if only its sharpness be
not blunted by any clouding or detraction from the image.
And then Eni might joyfully conclude from Joseph's
beauty that she too was beautified, and hope that he found
her lovely in his turn, even though broad daylight might
perhaps betray that she was no longer in her first youthful bloom. She knew that the long open white woollen
mantle that she wore, closed at the throat over her

necklace with an agraffe, for it was near the winter season, gave majesty to her figure; and that her breasts stood out firm and youthful under the batiste of her garment, which fitted her closely and was embroidered with red beads round the hem. Look at it, Osarsiph! It had clasps and ribbons at the shoulders, and how well she knew that it left free her smooth and chiselled arms and revealed the splendid high haunches of her wonderful limbs! Was that not reason enough for her love to hold its head high? It did so. She pridefully behaved as though she could scarcely raise her eyelids and so must throw her head back to look out underneath them. Her face was framed this time in a golden-brown headcloth, held in place by a broad, loosely fitting band set with precious stones — a face, she trembled to think, no longer the youngest, and very unusual and irregular with its shadowed cheeks, its saddle-nose and deep-cornered mouth. Only the thought of how its ivory paleness must set off her painted jewel-like eyes gave her courage to hope that it would not disadvantage the effect of her arms, legs, and breasts.

Conscious, with mingled pride and misgiving, of her own beauty, she looked at his; at the beauty of Rachel's son in its Egyptian guise. Highly civilized it was, though the costume had an out-of-doors negligence about it. His head, indeed, was very carefully dressed, with a headcloth of ribbed black silk which suggested a wig and finished in curls at the bottom; beneath it, with artful effectiveness, peeped out a corner of the clean white linen cap. But save this peruke, and the enamelled collar, armbands, and flat chain of reed and gold with a scarab, he wore only the knee-length double skirt round his narrow hips; very elegantly cut indeed, and of a sheer white which set off charmingly the warm tone of his flesh, turned into bronze by the slanting light and decked with its jewelled adornments. That youthful body, so exactly right in its build, strong and delicate at once, irradiated by the sunset light and freshened by the cool air, seemed not to belong to the world of the flesh, but to the purer world of Ptah's thoughts made visible. Especially the shrewd-looking head seemed to accentuate and embody — for himself as for everyone who looked at him — a gratifying union of beauty and wisdom.

Very conscious of herself, in pride and misgiving, the wife of Potiphar looked at him, at his dark-skinned features, large by comparison with her own, and into the friendly night of Rachel's eyes, whose expressiveness, in the face of the son, was heightened by the masculine power of understanding. She took in at once his shoulders' golden-bronze gleam; the slender arm whose muscles rounded pleasantly but not unduly to hold the walking-staff. And such a wave of maternal admiration and tenderness swept over her that she gasped; her bosom was so shaken by her desperate ecstasy that it quaked visibly beneath its thin white sheath and she could only hope that her proud bearing would give it the lie in his sight.

Thus, then, and so shaken she must speak to him. And she did so, with a self-conquest in itself alarming because it cost her such a heroic effort.

" I see," said she, coolly, " that we walk here very untimely, we idle women, and disturb the offices of him who is set over the house."

" Set over the house, my mistress, is yourself alone;

for you stand above it as the morning and evening star, which in the land of my mother they call Ishtar. She too is idle, because divine, and we toiling ones look up for refreshment to her tranquil shining."

She acknowledged his words with a gesture and a smile of understanding. She was both enchanted and pained by the spoilt way in which he wove into the compliment an allusion to his unknown mother; and seized by a gnawing jealousy of that mother, who had borne him and nourished him, guided his steps, stroked his hair out of his eyes, and kissed him by the right of her love.

"We will go away," said she, "I and my handmaids, who accompany me today as always, that we may not hinder the steward, who doubtless would make sure before twilight falls that all is well in Petepre's garden, perhaps even up in the little house on the mound."

"Garden and temple," replied Joseph, "concern me but little when I stand before my mistress."

"But I think they should at all times concern you, and reward you for your concern more than all the rest," she answered — and already how frightfully, how wildly sweet it was, simply that they addressed each other and said "I" and "you," sending out across the two paces of distance between their bodies the breath which created the bond and union of speech — "for I have heard that they are the beginning and fount of your good fortune. I am told that it was in the little house you first did service as dumb servant; and in the orchard Petepre's eye first fell upon you when you were setting blossoms to ride."

"Thus it was," he laughed. And his laugh cut through her, like a sacrilege. "Just as you say, my lady! I was doing the service of the wind in Petepre's palm trees, at the bidding of the gardener, whom they call — but I know not why, nor may I repeat his name before you, for it is a gross and common name, unsuited to your gracious ear." She looked at his laughing face but did not smile herself. He obviously did not know how little she was minded to jest, nor why; that was well, was inevitable, yet it hurt her. He might interpret her seriousness and lack of smiling response as a remnant of her earlier hostility; but he should perceive it. — " Yes," he said, " I did the wind's work by the gardener's direction, when the friend of Pharaoh came and summoned me to speech, and as I found favour before him, much took its issue from this hour."

" Men lived and died," she said, " that you might prosper."

" The Hidden One does all," he replied, using an inoffensive designation for the Highest. " His name be praised! But truly I often question myself whether He has not advanced me beyond my deserts; and I am anxious for my youth, that such an office is laid upon me and I have become at not much more than twenty the eldest servant of this house. Great lady, I speak openly to you, though you hear me not alone and are not come alone into the garden, but accompanied by maids of honour as befits your rank. They hear me too, and for good or ill hearken while the steward deplores his youth and expresses doubts of his capacity for such high service. But let them hear. For I must put up with their presence, which may not constrain me in my frankness to you, who are the sovereign of my head and my heart, my hands and my feet."

There are after all certain advantages in falling in love

beneath one's station. For the station of the beloved makes natural turns of phrase which give us pleasure, though he may think little or nothing about them.

"Of course," she said, with even more majestic poise, "I do not walk alone. I could never do that. But speak without thought of injury to yourself, for the ears of Hedjes and Me'et are as my ears. What would you say?"

"Only this, my lady: my responsibilities are more numerous than my years and it could not have surprised your servant had not alone good will but some ill will and contrariety accompanied my swift rise to the steward's office. I had a father who brought me up in the goodness of his heart, the Osiris Mont-kaw; would that the Hidden One had let him still live, for much better was my youth, and I might still speak of good fortune, when I was his mouthpiece and his right hand. But he has entered the mysterious gates to the splendid places of the lords of eternity and I am alone with more cares and sorrows than the tale of my years and have no one in the world with whom to take counsel in my unripeness or to share the burden which bows me to the earth. Petepre, my great master — may he live long in good health! — is well known to take naught upon himself save that he eats and drinks and boldly confronts the horse of the Nile. When I come before him with the accounts and books he will say: 'Good, Osarsiph, my friend. All that you have written seems to me right, so far as I can see, and I take it that you have no intent to cheat me, for you know the nature of sin and have understanding for the special offence to me which would lie therein. And therefore I need not trouble myself.' Thus the master, in his greatness, may blessing be upon his head! " He searched her face for a corresponding smile. It was a slight, a very slight treachery which he here committed: an attempt, though in all love and respect, to set up an understanding with the mistress over Petepre's head. He thought he might go so far without offence to the bond. He still thought, for some time yet, that he might without danger go so and so far. But there was no smile of understanding. And he was glad to see that, though faintly ashamed. He went on:

"So am I alone in my youth and unripeness, with my many problems of trade and production, of increase and maintenance. As you saw me approach, my head was full of the cares of the sowing. For the river ebbs and the beautiful feast of mourning approaches, when we dig the earth and bury the god in the darkness and plough for the barley and wheat. Then here is the problem which goes round and round in my head, for it is question of a change: whether we should not do well to sow much more durra corn on Potiphar's fields which are the island in the river, instead of the barley as heretofore; it is the Moorish millet, the negro corn, the white kind, for we have already planted plenty of brown durra for fodder and it satisfies the horses and is good for the cattle. But the question is, would it not be an improvement to change over to the white to even greater extent; that is, planting over much ground to feed the servants, that they may be nourished by good bread instead of with lentils and barley and grow stronger in their service? For the kernel of the white corn is full of meal and has taken up the richness of the earth so that a worker needs less than of the lentils or barley, and we feed them quicker and better. So all that goes round in my head, I cannot tell how, and when I saw you, my lady, approaching through the sunset garden, with your handmaids, then I thought in my soul and spoke to myself as to another: Lo, you are alone in your unripeness with the cares of this house and have no one with whom to share them, for the master takes upon himself none of these things. But now comes the mistress in her beauty, followed by two maids, as is fitting to her rank. Confide, then, in her upon the matter of the new plan and the durra corn; try her opinion, and her good counsel will sustain your unripe youth! "

Eni blushed, partly for joy, partly for embarrassment, for she knew nothing at all about negro corn and was ignorant of the advantage of planting it. She said in some confusion:

" The matter is worthy of discussion, that is clear. I will consider it. Is the soil of the island favourable to this innovation? "

" The mistress," remarked Joseph, " displays her judgment and experience, in that she seizes at once upon the heart of the matter in all things. The soil is fertile enough, yet one must be prepared for failure at first. For the field workers do not yet know how to sow the white corn for food, but only the brown for fodder. What does my mistress think that it may cost till they are instructed in the fine cultivation of the ground with the hoe, as the durra requires, or till they understand that it cannot tolerate weeds like the brown? For if no heed be paid to the roots and shoots, then there is fodder but no nourishment."

" You may well have your difficulties with your workpeople in their lack of understanding," said she, and went red and pale with embarrassment, for she knew nothing of these things and had no sensible answer ready, though she had wished that he might speak with her about them. Her conscience smote her with shame before her servant, she felt humiliated; for he spoke of honest practical matters like food for human beings, whereas she knew and desired nothing but that she loved him and longed for him.

" It must be very difficult," she repeated, and controlled her trembling. " But they say that you know well how to deal with the labourers and keep them to their work. So that you will surely succeed in teaching them this new thing as well."

His gaze betrayed that he had not heard what she said, and she was glad, though this was at the same time an offence. He stood there plunged in his practical considerations.

"The straw from the corn is very strong and pliant. It makes good brushes and brooms, so that it is not all loss should the crop fail."

She was silent, painfully conscious that his mind was not on her but on the brooms, which were certainly a more honourable topic than her love. But at least he noticed her silence, for he started and said with that conquering smile:

" Forgive me, my mistress, that our converse is upon such lowly themes as can but bore you. But it is on account of my single-handed unripeness in these cares and because I was so tempted to take counsel with you."

"There is naught to forgive," she answered. " The matter is important and the possibility of making brooms lessens the loss. I thought so at once when you spoke of your new plan and I will also consider the matter further."

She could not stand still, her feet urged her away from him and his too dear nearness. All lovers know this conflict: the strife between seeking and flight. And old as the hills is the practice of speaking honesty with the tongue while the eyes belie it with their seeking, shifting glance, and the mouth wries what it utters. Fear lest he know that her talk about corn and brooms concealed only one desire: that she might put her hand on his forehead and kiss him with possessive maternity; the frightful wish that he might know it and not despise her for it but rather share her wish; these, and her great uncertainty in all pertaining to food and fodder, which was the subject of their talk, for her but a lying pretext — though how can one lie when one has no knowledge of the pretended subject and is condemned to stumble blindly through it? — all these unnerved and shamed her so that she went hot and cold and could think only of panic flight.

Her feet twitched to be off, her heart held her still on the spot — in the immemorial struggle of the love-possessed. She drew her mantle closer about her and spoke in a strangled voice:

"We must continue, steward, another time and in another place. Evening is falling, I shall soon be shivering with cold." She was in fact taken with an unmistakable shivering which she thought to explain on this ground. "You have my promise that I will take counsel of myself as to your new plan; likewise I permit you to come before me again when you feel yourself too solitary in your youth." She should not have tried to utter this last word, it stuck in her throat. For with it he and only he became the subject of their talk; it was a stronger synonym for the " you " she had used in their lying converse, the only true thing in it. It was the word of the magic he practised, the word of her maternal longing, laden with tenderness and pain. It overcame her quite, it died away in a whisper. " Farewell," she breathed, and fled, her maidens ahead of her, past Joseph, as he stood bowing in respectful salutation.

One cannot too much wonder at the weakness of love, nor too long pause upon its strangeness. For it is not as a stale, everyday affair that we would consider it, but as the unique, novel, and isolated occasion which it really was, and is to this very day. A great lady, elegant, superior, proud, worldly, hitherto self-contained within her personal and religious arrogance — and now all at once fallen victim to a you, and a you — from her own point of view — entirely unworthy and unsuitable. Fallen victim to such weakness, with such abandonment of her rank, that she was hardly capable of sustaining even the rôle of mistress and challenger, but knew herself to be already a slave, as with shaking knees she fled, half-blind, her thoughts flickering in her head, murmuring broken words, heedless of the maids whom she had pridefully taken with her to the rendezvous.

" Lost, lost, betrayed, betrayed — I am lost, I betrayed myself to him, he saw it all, the lie in my eyes, my restless feet, my trembling; he saw it all, he despised me, it is over, I must die. We must plant more durra, we must destroy the weeds, the stalks are good for brooms. What did I answer? I betrayed myself with my stammering, he was laughing at me, it was frightful, I will kill myself. But was I beautiful, at least? For if I was, in that light, then it was only half bad and I need not kill myself. The golden bronze of his shoulders — oh, Amun in thy chapel! 'Sovereign of my head and heart, my hands and my feet'! O Osarsiph, speak not thus to me with your mouth, laughing the while in your heart at my stammering and the weakness of my knees! I hope — I hope — though all may be lost and I must die after this mischance, yet I must hope and not despair; for I am not utterly unhappy, there was much happiness in that I am your mistress, boy, and you were obliged to speak to me with such sweetness, saying: 'Sovereign of my head and heart,' though it was only lip-service and empty homage. But words are strong; one cannot speak them without consequences, they leave traces on the mind; spoken without feeling, they yet speak to the feeling of the speaker; if they are lying words, yet the magic of them changes one a little in the direction of their sense, so that they are no longer quite lies. That is very happy and hopeful; for the soil of your nature, boy, must be turned by your words, making it a good soil for the sowing of my beauty, if I have the good fortune to appear before you in a favouring light. For the subservience of your words, together with my beauty, will bring me healing and bliss; from it will grow a worshipful feeling only needing encouragement to become desire — for so it is, little boy, worship encouraged becomes desire. Ah, what a depraved woman am I, with my wily thoughts! Shame upon my head and heart! Forgive me, Osarsiph, forgive me, my master and deliverer, O morning and evening star of my life! Why had it today to go all wrong, so that all seemed lost, because of my restless feet? Yet I will not kill myself, not yet send for an asp to lay upon my bosom, for there is still much hope of happiness left. There is to-morrow, and all the other days. He will remain here, Peteprê refused to send him away, to sell him, I must see him every day, every sun rises with hope and good prospects. 'We must continue, steward, another time. I will take counsel of myself and permit another meeting.' That was good, it was providing for the next time. Oh, yes, that was sensible, Eni, that in all your madness you had thought for continuance. He must come again; and if he delay out of shyness, I will send to him Dudu the dwarf to remind him. How shall I make good all that to-day went wry? I will meet him calmly, and my feet will stand still, and only betray a little, a very little, encouragement to his homage, as it pleases me. Perhaps he will seem less beautiful to me, this very next time, so that my heart shall cool and I can smile and jest with a free mind and inflame him while I suffer not at all? No, ah, no, Osarsiph, it shall not be, those are wily thoughts, and gladly will I suffer for you, my lord and my salvation, for your glory is like that of a new-born bull. . . ."

This rhapsody, of which the maids Hedjes and Me'et caught some words, to their vast amazement, was but one of many, of a hundred such which escaped the mistress that year, while she sought to conceal her love from Joseph. The dialogue about the Moorish corn, which preceded it, likewise represents many of the same kind, carried on at various times of day in various places: in the garden, in the fountain court of the house of women, even up in the little summerhouse, whither, however, Eni never came unattended and where Joseph was likewise accompanied by two scribes carrying paper rolls, accounts to be submitted, and other documents. For they always talked of domestic affairs: ploughing, sowing, and reaping, trade and crafts; and the young steward gave accounting to the mistress, instructed her, or sought her advice. Such was the lying content of their talk; and we must realize — if with a somewhat doubtful smile — that Joseph laid stress on it and tried to make something real out of the pretence to give the mistress a serious account of these practical matters and gain her interest in them, even if only on the ground of her interest in himself.

It was a sort of cure. Young Joseph fancied himself in the rôle of pedagogue. His plan was — he thought, at least — to lead the thoughts of his mistress from the personal to the objective; from his eyes to his occupations, thus assuaging, cooling, and neutralizing them. Thus he should profit by the honour, advantage, and great pleasure of her favour and her company, without risking the pit with which the anxious little vizier threatened him. One cannot but see a certain overweeningness in the young steward's pedagogic design, with which he thought to keep in leading-strings the soul of a woman like his mistress, Mut-em-enet. If he wanted to avoid the danger of the pit, he might much better have avoided her, instead of holding educational conferences. That the son of Jacob preferred the latter may well rouse the suspicion that the cure was a hocus-pocus, and his idea of taking their pretended conversations as genuine, itself a pretence and a pretext for thoughts which no longer served pure mind but tended to proneness.

In any case, such was the suspicion, or rather the shrewd little dwarfish conclusion, of Joseph's gnomelike friend. And he made no concealment of his view, almost daily wringing his hands and begging him not to condescend to evasions and beating the air, but to be as wise as he was good and beautiful and flee from the devastating breath of the fiery bull. In vain. For his young friend, the steward, the full-sized man, knew better. And when a man is used, with good reason, to depend upon his own judgment, he is in the greater danger when that reason is clouded.

Dudu, meanwhile, the solid-substantial dwarf, acted his traditional rôle: that of go-between and crafty pander playing on the weakness of both sides; running back and forth between two who would sin, winking and blinking, hinting and pointing, setting himself to one or other, with his mouth on one side, his lips closed, and retailing all sorts of insidious and provocative gossip out of the corner. He played his part without knowledge of his predecessors and successors in it, as though he were its first and only actor — for each of us must consider himself that in every part he plays, as though he had made it all up himself, yet with a sureness and dignity which comes to him, when he plays it, so to speak, in daylight for the first time, not from his supposed invention of the rôle, but on the contrary from the well-grounded consciousness that he is once more presenting something legitimate and traditional, and must perform it, however repellent, to the best of his ability according to the pattern.

But for the present he did not take all the steps which belong to the rôle. I mean, he did not yet tread a path which always branches off from the one running between the two parties concerned and leads to a third — in other

words, to Potiphar. To infect that sensitive gentleman
with doubt, to trickle suspicion in his ear, on the subject
of certain meetings — that would come, but as yet the
time seemed not to be ripe. It did not please Dudu that
despite all his industry in making the occasions, all the
half-invented messages he gave out of the corner of his
mouth, at both ends of the road, his mistress and the
young steward as good as never met alone, but conversed
almost always in the presence of attendants. And he did
not like what they talked about, either; Joseph's pedagogic enterprise was not to his taste, it annoyed him,
although he saw through it and recognized its rationalized proneness to " all fours " quite as well as did his
pure-minded little brother dwarf. All this exchange of
practical information seemed to him to delay a desirable
development of his project; he was concerned lest the
plan meet with success and the thoughts of the mistress be
elevated and purified and no longer to the point. Even to
her good guardian of the wardrobe she would now talk
about such matters as production and trade, the price of
oil and wax, supplies and provisioning. It did not escape
his sun-perception that she was simply using it all to
speak of Joseph, who had taught it to her. But it vexed
him; he bent all his energies, directed all the insinuations
at both ends of his route, to a single goal. The young
steward, he would say, was often sad. He was privileged,
indeed, to be with the mistress when his toil was done, or
sometimes even in between, to bathe his soul in her
beauty, and might speak with her, but only of dull domestic concerns, instead of more intimate and animating
affairs. And at the other end: the mistress had ordered
Dudu to express to the young steward her regret, her

bitterness, that he was so little aware of the favour he received in his audiences with her, and would always talk of household matters instead of coming round to himself and gratifying her curiosity about his person and former life, his wretched home, his mother, his virgin birth, his descent to the pit, his resurrection, and so on. Such things were of course more interesting for a lady like Mut-em-enet than lectures on paper-making and installing looms. If the steward wished to make progress with Mut, progress toward a goal higher and splendider than any he had yet reached in the house, he must embolden himself to deal with themes not quite so heavy.

"Let that be my affair, the goal equally with the means," Joseph answered crossly. "And you might speak straight out, instead of out of the corner of your mouth; I do not like it; also I could wish, husband of Djeset, that you yourself kept more to the point. Forget not that the understanding between us is a worldly one, not an affair of the heart. Continue to report to me what you hear in house and courtyard. I have not encouraged you to offer friendly advice."

"By the heads of my children! " Dudu swore. "According to my bond I have but told you what I gathered from the mistress's bitter sighs because your discourse is so dry. Not Dudu but herself it is that counsels you to be a little more entertaining."

That was more than half a lie. Actually, he had said to her that if she wanted to spy out the source of the young steward's magic and bring him to a fall she must get closer to his person instead of letting him hide behind his office and his business. To which she had replied:

" It does me good, and somewhat quietens my mind, to hear of his doings when I do not see him."

A revealing answer, even a touching one. For it betrays the envy of the loving woman for the fuller life of the man; the jealousy of the nature wholly occupied with feeling, against the content which plays so large a part in the life of the beloved and makes her aware of the painful idleness of her own. The effort made by the woman to share in the man's life springs from this jealousy, even when his interests are not of a practical but of an intellectual kind.

It did the mistress good to let Joseph introduce her into the practical side of life, on the ground that he yearned to have his youth instructed by her wisdom. And how little it matters, indeed, what the talk is about when it is his voice that embodies it, his lips which shape it, his gaze which accompanies it, and his nearness which can inform the driest and coldest matter, as sun and water warm and moisten the earth! Every speech becomes a love-speech — but it could actually not be carried on as such, consisting as it would have to of the words " I " and " thou," and with nothing else at all would come to an end out of sheer monotony. So that other things must inevitably come in. Yet it is clear from Eni's simple reply that she treasured even the subject-matter of their talk; that it nourished her soul through the vacant, hopeless, enervating days when Joseph was away on business up or down the river, and there could be no moment-meeting of the eyes at table nor could or might she feverishly await his visit in the house of women or elsewhere. Then she fed on the things he had told her, exalted them

in her heart, and got much good from her knowledge of
his errand, in this or that city and its villages, at this market or that fair; for thus at least her woman's misery of
utter feeling might be lightened by knowing the content
of his masculine days. She could not help boasting her
knowledge, before the chattering women in her house,
before her maids, and before Dudu when he waited on
her.

" The young steward," she would say, " has gone down
the river to Nekheb, to the feast of the goddess Nekhbet;
with two barges full of doum and balanite fruit, figs
and onions, garlic, melons, cucumbers from Aggur, and
castor-oil seeds. He will trade them, under the pinions of
the goddess, for wood and leather for sandals, which
Petepre needs in the workshops. The steward by consultation with me chose a moment for the shipment when
vegetables fetch a high price and wood and leather are
relatively cheap."

Her voice rang and vibrated as she spoke; Dudu put
his hand to his ear to hearken and bethought himself
whether the moment would not soon come when he should
take his hidden way to Petepre to rouse his suspicions.

How much else we might tell of this year when out of
pride and shame Mut was still hiding her love from Joseph, and even from the outer world was still thinking
that she hid it? Her own struggle against her feelings,
the struggle with herself, carried on for a while with such
violence, was over, and for better or worse the feelings
had won. Now she only fought to conceal her state before men and before the beloved himself; for in her soul
she gave herself more utterly to this new marvel, with the
more rapture, one might say with the more simplicity,

in that she had been before so ignorant of it, had remained so long the elegant saint and cool worldly moon-
nun before she had awakened to feeling. With the deeper
revulsion she now looked back upon those times unblest
by passion; she could not find herself again in their
aridity, she shrank from a return to them with all the
strength of her awakened femininity. The intoxicating
enchancement which fullness of love can bring to a life
like hers is well known — though indescribable. But
gratitude for that blessing of desire and torture seeks an
object, and finds it only in him from whom it all proceeds
or seems to proceed. Is it any wonder, then, that fulfilment in him, increased by gratitude, becomes adoration?
We have seen that there were brief, uncertain moments
in which Joseph seemed half and half, or even more than
half and half a god. But were those momentary prompt-
ings to be called idolatry? For so much positive rapture,
so much finality lies in the word, as the logic of love
understands it! That is a logic strange and audacious
enough. He who has done this, so it runs, to my life, he
who has given to the once dead this burning and freezing,
this jubilation and these tears — he must be a god, nothing else is possible. Actually he has done nothing, and
everything proceeds from the possessed one herself. But
she will not believe it; with prayers of gratitude she
creates out of her own rapture the other's godhead. " O
paradise of feeling! Thou hast made rich my life — it
burgeons! " That was a prayer, a fragment of one of
Mut-em-enet's prayers of gratitude addressed to Joseph,
as she knelt at the end of her couch, when no one saw her,
stammering and weeping. But why, with her life so rich
and burgeoning, why was she more than once on the point

of sending her Nubian slave for the asp that she might put it to her bosom? Yes, why had she once even given the order and had the viper already at hand, in a little reed basket, and had only at the last moment desisted from her purpose? Well, because she was convinced that she had at their last meeting spoiled everything and not only looked ugly but had by her look and her trembling betrayed to her lover her love — the love of an ugly old woman — after which there was nothing left but to die, so punishing herself and him, and by her death revealing to him the secret for whose betrayal she had sentenced herself.

Oh, muddled, fantastic logic of love! So familiar, it is hardly worth telling; so old, that it was already old in the time of Potiphar's wife, and seems new only to those who, like her, are in the throes of what they believe to be a unique experience. She whispered: " Oh, hearken, music! . . . A ghost of sound breathes blissful on my ear! " That is familiar too: it is the aural delusion of the ecstatic, which visits the love-intoxicated as well as the god-intoxicated and indicates that the two states are re-lated and mingled, the one having much of the divine, the other of the human. Familiar too, so that we need not go into detail, are those fevered nights, taken up with a sequence of brief dreams in which the other is always present and turns coldly and suspiciously away: a succes-sion of meetings with his image, wretched, crushing, yet tirelessly resumed by the slumbrous soul, between con-stant abrupt wakings; the sufferer starts up, wrestles for breath, makes light: "O God, O God, how can it be? How can such torments exist? " But does she fly from him, the author of such nights? By no means. When morning releases her from agony she sits exhausted on the edge of her bed and sends a whisper thence to where he is: "I thank thee, my joy, my star, my salvation! "

The well-wishing friend can but shake his head at such a reaction to such frightful anguish. He feels confused, even made a fool of, by his pity for her. But when the author and giver of the anguish is thought of as not human but divine, then the reaction is possible and natural; the authorship is shared between the I and the you, so that though it seem bound up with the one, yet at the same time it is localized in the other; consisting in the enlacement and union of an inward and an outward, an image and a soul — a marriage, that is, such as has before now had gods as issue, and can thus, without absurdity, be spoken of as divine in its manifestations. A being whom we bless for the tortures he inflicts must be a god, not a man, else we should curse him. A certain logicality cannot be denied. A being upon whom depends all the joy and sorrow of our days — for that is love — belongs in the ranks of the divine; nothing could be clearer; for this dependence is the very essence of an awareness of God. But has anybody ever yet cursed his god? It has been tried, perhaps. But then the curse turned into something else — what it sounded like we have heard.

All this for the consolation of the well-wishing friend, if not perhaps altogether to his satisfaction. But had our Eni not a peculiar justification for making a god out of her beloved? Surely; for thus she got rid of the humiliation otherwise inseparable from her weakness for a foreign slave, with which she had struggled so long. A god from above, taking on a slave's shape, only apparent

by his undisguisable beauty and his shoulders' golden
bronze: she evoked this idea out of her thought-world,
and most happily, for it was the explanation and excuse
for her state. But the hope that her dream might be fulfilled, that dream of healing when he had opened her
eyes and stanched her blood — that hope was nourished
by another and more remote vision which likewise she
discovered in her own mind. It was the vision of a mortal
overshadowed by a god. It may well be that in her groping back to so fantastic a conception lay some of the anguish she felt when her husband made his revelations
about Joseph's consecrated state, and the meaning of the
garland that he wore.

THE SECOND YEAR

WITH the coming of the second year something gave way
in Mut-em-enet's soul, so that she began to let Joseph see
her love. She could no longer help it; she loved him too
much. At the same time, and in consequence, she began
to confide her state to certain persons in her entourage —
not quite to Dudu, for indeed she well knew that his sun-
brightened wits had found it out long before; besides,
despite the change in her, it would have gone against her
pride to admit it to him. They abode by their old understanding, that she was seeking to discover the source of
the magic practised by the foreign slave, in order to
" bring him to a fall." This was the established phrase,
becoming less equivocal from day to day. But there were
two women whom she suddenly made her confidantes, she
who had never had confidantes before, so that they were
no little exalted by the honour. She confided in each

separately: the concubine Mekh-en-Weseht, a lively little
person, arrayed in transparent garments, with flowing
hair; and an old rubber-eater, Tabubu by name, slave
of the toilette-table and the rouge-pots — grey of hair,
black of skin, with sagging breasts like leather wineskins.
To these two Eni opened her heart in whispers, after her
behaviour had been such that they began to wheedle her
for its cause. She so sighed, that is, and smiled, and
sat plunged in such obvious day-dreaming that the two
women, one beside the basin in the court, the other at
the toilette-table, implored her to tell them the reason.
For a while she still twisted and turned; but then as
though overtaken by a seizure she confessed her state to
them, murmuring in their ears with drunken tongue,
while they shuddered too.

Though they may have guessed before, by putting this
and that together, they now held up their hands, or covered their faces, kissed her hands and feet, and cooed
over her solemnly and tenderly — almost as though she
had told them she was with child. In such wise did these
women receive the great news, so important to their sex,
that Mut, the mistress, found herself in love. They became very busy with consolation and congratulations,
stroking the afflicted one as though her body had become
the vessel of some precious and perilous thing; displaying in all sorts of ways their fearful delight with the turn
of affairs, the great transformation, the opening of a time
of feminine mysteries and joys, sweet deceptions, and
the enhancement of the daily round by intrigue. Black
Tabubu, who knew all sorts of Negro magic and how to
conjure up forbidden gods, was all for practising her
arts to subject the youth and bring him to her mistress's

feet a blissful prey. But the daughter of Mi-Sakhme, the prince of the nome, rejected the idea with disgust — for the present; displaying a higher stage of civilization than the woman from Kush, and also the decency of her own feelings, however suspect they really were. On the other hand, Mekh, the concubine, thought not of magic, considering such practices beside the mark. Surely the matter, aside from the danger of it, was simple enough.

"Blissful one," said she, "why sigh? Is not the handsome youth the bought slave of this house, although set over it, and your property from the very first? If you would have him, what have you else to do but beckon? He cannot but consider it the greatest honour to put his head and feet to yours for your rejoicing! "

"For the sake of the Hidden One! " whispered Mut, hiding her face. " Speak not so openly, for you know not what you say, and it rives my heart! "

She could not chide the simple soul, for she knew, with a certain envy, that the concubine was pure and free from love and love's guilty desires and so might speak with good conscience of putting heads and feet together, however it anguished her mistress to hear her. Mut went on:

" One can see you were never in such a state, my child. Never have you been hurried and harried, but might spend your time munching and prattling with your sisters in Petepre's house of women. Else you could not say that I have but to lift my eyebrow; you would know that in my love the state of mistress and slave is cancelled out, even if not reversed. Rather I hang upon his gloriously pencilled brows, to see if they are smooth and pleasant, and not bent with amazement and reproof upon my quaking form. Lo, you are no better than the base Tabubu, who would have me practise black magic with her, that the youth might fall victim in the flesh, and in all innocence. For shame, you ignorant ones, who with your advice thrust a sword into my heart and turn it round! For you speak as though he were but body, and not soul and spirit to boot. And over these my beckoning would have no power, no more than magic; for both can only command the body and bring me only that — a living corpse. Were he ever mine, obedient to the beckoning of my brow, then by my love he hath his freedom, his full freedom, foolish Mekh, and I give up my sovereignty with joy and wear his yoke, enslaved in bliss and torment to his living soul. This is the truth; and I suffer endlessly that it is not daylight truth, but that he must by day be ever the slave and under my orders. For when he calls me sovereign of his head and heart, his hands and feet, I cannot tell whether he speaks in the phrases of a slave or perhaps as a living soul. I hope the latter but am ever fearful. Heed what I say! If his mouth were all, then might I listen in my need to what you say of beckonings and magic, for the mouth is of the body. But there is the lovely night of his eyes, speaking freedom and the soul — ah, how I specially fear that freedom, for that it may be freedom from the longing which thralls me, the lost one, in its sullen bondage; perhaps he laughs at me, perhaps not just at me but at my longing, so that I am shamed and ruined, for my admiration of his freedom but heightens my longing and weaves my bonds the tighter. Can you understand that, my Mekh? And more: I must fear the anger of his eyes, and his rejection of me, because my feeling for him is a betrayal of Petepre the courtier, his master and mine, to whom he is loyal, in whom he labours to keep self-esteem erect. While I would tempt him to shame the master, upon my heart! All this I read in his threatening eyes; from which you can see that it has to do with more than his mouth and that he is more than body. For a man who was only body would not be involved in entanglements which condition him as well as our relation to him and make it difficult by weighing it down with all sorts of considerations and consequences, turning it into a question of rules and honour and moral precepts and cutting the wings of our desire so that it limps along the ground! How much, Mekh, by night and day, have I pondered on these things! For a body is free and single, has no reference, and for love's purpose we need be only bodies, swinging free in space and embracing each other without care or consequence, mouth on mouth, with closed eyes. That would be bliss — and yet bliss which I reject. For can I wish that the beloved should be a detached body, a corpse, not a person? That I cannot; for I love not alone his mouth, I love his eyes, them most of all, and thus your counsels are repellent to me, yours and Tabubu's, and I reject them with impatience."

"I cannot understand," said Mekh, the concubine, " your tangled imaginings. I thought, since you love him, the only matter was to put your heads and feet together for your enjoyment."

As though simply this were not after all the final goal of her longings — the longings of Mut-em-enet, the lovely Mutemone! The thought that her feet, so restless in Joseph's presence, might rest nestled close to his — the thought enraptured her and shook her to her very depths. When Mekh-en-Weseht gave it words, without having spent a tithe of thought upon it, compared to Mut, she encouraged the inward yielding, of which her disclosures to her women had been a sign, and she began to betray to the young steward her fallen state, in word and deed.

The deeds were significant, if also childlike in kind and even touching: small attentions from the mistress to the servant, who found it not easy to put the right face upon their true meaning. For instance, one day — and often afterwards — she received him in Asiatic dress, a rich garment, the stuff for which she had bought in the city of the living, at the shop of a bearded Syrian; her slave the dressmaker Heti had made it up. It had much more colour than Egyptian wear; in fashion like two pieces of embroidered woollen stuff, one blue and one red, wound together and bordered with coloured braid. It was extravagant and exotic. The shoulders were covered by the lappets proper to the style, and on top of the embroidered and gaily coloured head-band, called *sanip* in its native land, Eni had thrown the indispensable head-cloth, reaching below her hips. Thus clad, she looked at Joseph, her eyes widened both by the application of galena and by an expectation half-mischievous, half-concerned.

" How strange, yet how splendid you look, my lady! " said he, betraying his understanding by an embarrassed smile.

" Strange? " she asked, smiling too — but her smile, though tender, was forced and confused. "Familiar, I should rather think. Do I not appear as a daughter of your own land in this garb, which for a change I put on today? If indeed it be my garb you have in mind? "

"Familiar," he said, his eyes cast down, "is the garment indeed and the fashion of it; yet a little strange on you."

"Do you not find that it suits me so that I wear it to advantage?" she tremulously challenged him.

He answered guardedly: "The stuff is not woven nor the garment fashioned, were it even of sackcloth, that would not serve your beauty, my sovereign."

"Then it is all the same to you what I wear," she retorted, "and the trouble is lost that I have taken with this costume! For I arrayed myself in it in honour of your visit and as a response to your own custom. For you, a youth from the Retenu, wear Egyptian garb with us, doing honour to our customs. I thought not to be behind you on mine own part, but to meet you in the dress that your mother wore. Thus as in the feast have we exchanged garments; in such an exchange there has been ever something festal, when the men wear the garb of the women and the women the men's and distinctions fall away."

"To which," he responded, "I am bound to add that there is naught familiar to me in such a custom. For it savours rather of light-headedness and a falling away from godly sobriety, and my father would not be glad to see it."

"Then have I erred indeed," said she. "Have you aught to tell me of the house?"

She was profoundly hurt, that he seemed not to understand (though understanding but too well) that she had offered up to him her feelings, in that she, the child of Amun, bride of the mighty one and partisan of his power, honoured the stranger in her dress, because the stranger was her beloved. The offering had been sweet to her, it was bliss to divest herself of her opinions for his sake; so now she was most unhappy, because he had accepted it so lifelessly. Another time she succeeded better — though the symbolic gesture she made was even more self-abnegatory.

In the retreat she liked best, her apartments in the house of women, was a small hall facing the desert. One might give it that name, for the wide-open door with its wooden jambs had its view cut by two columns with simple square capitals under the eaves, standing flat on the threshold, without bases. The room gave on a court with low flat-roofed white buildings on its right. Here were the quarters of the concubines, and adjoining them a higher building, like a pylon, with columns. A clay wall, shoulder-high, ran diagonally behind it, so that one could see nothing beyond save the sky. The little salon was simple and elegant, the ceiling not very high. The shadows of the columns lay black on the floor, the walls and ceiling were a plain lemon-colour with a simple band of decoration in pale tints. There was little in the room save a graceful couch in the background, with cushions on it and skins on the floor in front. Here Mut-em-enet often awaited Joseph.

He would appear in the court, raising the palms of his hands toward the room and the woman on the couch; tucked under his arm were his rolls and accounts. She would sign to him to enter and speak before her. But one day he saw at once that there was a change in the room; saw it by her air of mingled pleasure and embarrassment, as when she had worn the Syrian dress. But he behaved as though he noticed nothing, greeted her with

suitable salutations, and began at once to speak of household matters. Then she said:

"Look round you, Osarsiph! What do you see that
is new?"

She might well call it new. It was almost incredible.
At the back of the room, on a little altar with an embroidered cloth, stood an open shrine with a gilt statuette
of Atum-Re!

The Lord of the Horizon was unmistakable; he looked
like his written symbol, sitting with his knees drawn up
on a little square pedestal, the falcon's head on his shoulders, even the oval sun-disk on top, with the inflated head
and the ringed tail of the uræus at front and back. On a
tripod beside the altar were incense-pans on standards,
with gear for making fire and little pellets of incense in
a dish.

Astonishing, almost impossible it was — likewise very
touching, a childishly direct expression of the longing of
her heart for utterance. The lady Mut, of the house of
women of him rich in bulls; sweet singer and sacred
dancer before the ram-browed god of the kingdom, friend
of his statesmanly chief shiny-head; partisan of his con-
servative sun-sense — she had erected in her own inner
sanctum a shrine to the lord of the wide horizon, on whom
Pharaoh's thinkers tried their thoughts, complaisant and
friendly brother to foreign and Asiatic sun-lords — to
Re-Horakhte-Aton from On in the apex of the Delta.
Thus she gave expression to her love, in this language she
took refuge, the speech of space and time, which was
common to them both, the Egyptian woman and the
Hebrew servant. How could he have failed to understand

her? He had long since understood, and one must honour his emotions at this moment: what he felt was joy, mingled with alarm and concern. His head drooped.

"I see your devotion, mistress," he said very low. "It somewhat alarms me. For what if Beknechons, the great priest, were to visit you and see what I see?"

"I fear not Beknechons," she answered, her voice thrilling with triumph. "Pharaoh is greater."

"May he live long and prosper!" he murmured mechanically. "But you," he added, still lower, "you belong to the lord of Ipet-Isowet."

"Pharaoh is the son of his body," she responded so quickly that it was plain she was prepared. "I too may serve the god whom he loves, whom he has commanded his wise men to study. Where could there be an older, a greater in all the lands? He is like Amun, and Amun is like him. Amun has named himself with his name, and said: 'Who serves me, serves Re.' So then I too serve Amun when I serve him."

"As you say," he answered softly.

"We will burn incense to him," she said, "before we take up the household affairs."

And she took him by the hand and led him before the image, to the tripod with the implements of the offering.

"Put in frankincense," she commanded (she said "*senter neter*," which is Egyptian for "divine odour"), "and light it, if you will be so kind!" But he hesitated.

"It is not good, my lady," he said, "that I should burn incense before an image. It is forbidden among my people."

She looked at him, silently, with such unconcealed

pain that he shrank afresh. Her look said: "You will not with me burn incense to him who permits that I love you?"

He thought of On in the Delta, the mild doctrine of its teachers, and the head priest, whose smile had said that whoso sacrificed to Horakhte did so at the same time to his own god in the meaning of the triangle. And he answered to her look:

"Gladly will I be your ministrant, lay the fire and light it and assist your sacrifice."

And he put some of the pellets of terebinth in the pan, struck fire and kindled it, and gave her the stick that she might incense. And while she caused the smoke of the fragrance to rise before Atum's nose, he lifted his hands and served the tolerant god — with reserve, and trusting that what he did might be overlooked. But Eni's breast swelled at the symbolic act, throughout the whole of the dry conversation that followed.

In such ways did she confess her longing. But the poor soul could not much longer refrain from words. For her craving to tell the beloved that which she had struggled so long for her life to conceal grew finally overpowering. And being constantly encouraged by Dudu and incited to lead the conversation away from the impersonal toward more intimate matters, that she might slip up upon his secret and "bring him to a fall," she tore with hot hands at the pretended fabric of their converse — his fig-leaf, as it were — to uncover the naked truth of the thou and I. She could not know what frightful associations were bound up in Joseph's mind with the idea of uncovering: Canaanitish associations warning against the forbidden thing, against every kind of drunken shamelessness, going back to the beginning and the place where nakedness and knowledge had sharply confronted each other, with the resulting distinction between good and evil. Such a distinction was foreign to Mut's traditions; with all her sense of honour and her sense of shame she was quite without understanding of sin, there was no word for it in her vocabulary. Least of all could she connect any such idea with nakedness; or know the shuddering Baal-horror, impersonal to him and transmitted in his blood, which nakedness of speech inspired in the youth. As often as he would draw the garment of objectivity over their talk, so often would she draw it away and make him speak not of household economy but of himself, of his life and earlier life; she asked him about his mother, whom he had already mentioned; learned of her proverbial loveliness; whence it was but a step to his own inheritance of charm and good favour; and she no longer refrained from speaking of it, at first with smiling words, but going on to praise it with more and more passion and fervour.

"Seldom," said she — she was leaning back in her great armchair, which stood at the tail end of a lion's skin, while the beast's maw yawned at Joseph's feet, and her own lay under stern control, crossed on a footstool — "Seldom," she said, in answer to a remark of his, " does one hear of a person, and have her described, while at the same time her very image stands before one. It is strange, very strange, to see directed upon me while you tell me of them the very eyes of that lovely mother-sheep, and the friendly night of them, whose tears of impatience were kissed away by that man of the west, your father. For not idly did you say how like you were to the departed, so that she lived in you after her death and your father loved you both together, mother and son. You look at me with her eyes, Osarsiph, and describe them as passing lovely. But for long I knew not whence you had them, those eyes which win the hearts of men for you as you go up and down the river and the land. They were, up to now, if I may so express myself, an isolated phenomenon. But it is welcome and agreeable, not to say consoling, to become familiar with the origin and history of a manifestation which speaks to our souls."

We must not be surprised at the painful nature of such talk. Being in love is a sickness; though a healthy one, so to speak, like pregnancy and childbirth — yet like them not without danger. The woman's senses were benumbed; true, she expressed herself like an Egyptian woman of culture, even with literary skill, and in her way reasonably; but her power to distinguish between what is possible and what not was greatly lessened and befogged. What made things worse — or, in a sense, excused them — was that as the mistress she was unused to self-restraint and in the habit of expressing herself as she chose, confident that it was not natural to her to offend against aristocratic good taste. And in the days before her sickness she was right in her self-confidence. But now she neglected to allow for the change in her circumstances, and spoke with her usual freedom, with the result that she said many things most awkward to listen to. There is no doubt that Joseph found them awkward and offensive; not only on her account, but even on his own. He saw his careful pedagogic plan, symbolized by the rolls and accounts under his arm, suffering shipwreck; but even that was less annoying than the lofty lack of

self-control in which she persisted in their changed relations — saying, for instance, things to him about his
eyes which are only said by a lover to his mistress. The
feminine form of the word " master " retains the masculine element even in its changed application: a mistress,
physically speaking, is a master in female form; but
figuratively it is a woman with the character of a man,
thus the conception of a mistress can never lack a certain
ambivalence, though the male element predominates.
On the other hand, beauty is a passive, feminine quality,
in that it awakens longing and calls out active masculine
motives of admiration, desire, and courtship in the breast
of him who sees her, so that she too is able to respond
and show that double nature, though presided over by
the female element. Now Joseph, of course, was very
much at home in this double realm. He understood it,
in the sense that a maiden and a youth united in the person of Ishtar, and that in him who exchanged the veil
with her, Tammuz, the shepherd lad, the brother, son,
and husband, the same manifestation repeated itself, so
that actually all together there were four of them. These
memories to be sure were very distant and strange, but
Joseph received the same instruction from his own
sphere. Israel, the spiritual name of his father, in its extended meaning signified also a virgin, betrothed to the
Lord his God, as bride and as bridegroom, a man and a
woman. And He Himself, the solitary, the jealous One?
Was He not at once Father and Mother of the world, with
two faces, one a man's, turned toward the daylight, and
the other a woman's, looking into the darkness? Yes, was
not this two-sidedness of the nature of God the first fac-
tor, by which the double nature of Israel's relation to

Him, and especially that of Joseph's personal relation, so strongly bridelike and feminine, were first defined?

All that was very right and true. But it will not have escaped the attentive reader that certain changes had taken place in Joseph's consciousness which made it unpleasant to him to be the object of desire and courtship on the part of a mistress who paid him compliments as a man does a maiden. It did not suit him; and the growing masculinity which was the consequence not only of his twenty-five years but also of his official position and his success in bringing under his control and supervision a considerable area of the economic life of Egypt, sufficiently explains why he found it unpleasant. But though the explanation is easy, it is perhaps not quite sufficient; and there were other grounds for his discomfort. This increasing manliness of the boy Joseph was represented in his own mind by a certain image: the awakening of the dead Osiris by the female vulture which hovered over him and received from him the god Horus. Do we need to point out the correspondence between this picture and the actual circumstances — the fact, for instance, that Mut, when she danced before Amun as his bride, wore the vulture head-dress? There can be no doubt: she herself, the smitten one, was the cause of Joseph's increased masculinity, which began to claim the rights of desire and courtship for itself and found it unfitting to be the recipient of masterful compliments.

So now Joseph only looked at her in silence with his belauded eyes and then turned to the roll in his hands, making bold to ask if they might not now, after the personal digression, get back to business. Mut, however, encouraged in her wilfulness by Dudu's hints, affected not to hear, but continued to yield to her craving to make her love known. I am speaking here not of the single scene but of many, very like it, occurring during the second year. Without self-restraint, acting like one possessed, she gave vent to raptures not only about his eyes but about his stature, his voice, his hair; always taking his mother as the point of departure and marvelling at the law of inheritance which permitted advantages that in one generation took on feminine shape, to descend to the next in masculine shape and quality. What should he do? Let us remember that he was kindly and very sweet to her, that he spoke with affection; we can even find him deliberately taking refuge in the defects of that which she admired, hoping to cool her ardour.

" Let be, my lady," he would say. " Pray speak not so. These appearances, to which you have vouchsafed your regard — what of them? They are vanity and vexation of spirit, as one does well to remind oneself — and anyone who tends to smile upon them. For we know but in our weakness would forget of what poor stuff it is, if indeed it may be said to be at all, so pathetically perishable is it! Remember that in a little this hair must fall out, and these teeth too, that now are white. The eyes are but a jelly of water and blood, they will dissolve, as indeed the whole outward show must shrivel and melt away to vileness and nothing. Lo, now, it seems to me proper not to keep these reasonable considerations to myself, but to put them at your service in case you might find them useful."

But she did not believe in them; her condition made them quite unavailable as educational propaganda. Not that she could have been angry with him for his penitential exhortation; she was far too glad that they were not talking about Moorish corn or suchlike painful proprieties, but moved in a region where she felt her feminine competence and her feet need not be seized with a desire to flee.

" How wonderfully you speak, Osarsiph! " she replied, her lips caressing his name. " Yet your words are false and cruel — false because cruel; for even if true and indisputable to the reason, they are not in the least so for the heart and spirit, to which they are naught but sounding brass. For that substance is perishable is no ground for us to feel less admiration for form, but rather more; since we mingle in our feelings an element of pathos quite lacking to those which we have for the durable beauty of bronze or stone. Our regard for living loveliness is far more lively than it is for the images from Ptah's workshop, however beautiful and lasting they may be. And how shall you teach the heart that the stuff of life is of baser quality than its enduring copies? The heart refuses the knowledge, could never learn it. For permanence is dead and only dead things endure. Ptah's busy workmen may set sparks in the eyes of their images, they may seem to look at one; but they see not, you only see them, they cannot respond, as does a you who is likewise an I and of the same nature with yourself. But we are moved by the beauty of our kind. Who could possibly be tempted to lay his hand upon the brow of an image, or to kiss its mouth? See then how much more living is our feeling for the living form, no matter how perishable! Perishable! Why speak to me of the perishable, Osarsiph, warning me in its name? Do we then carry the mummy round the banqueting-hall to put an end to the feast because all must perish? Nay, on the contrary; for on its brow is written: ' Celebrate the joyful day! ' "

A good, even a capital answer — in its way; the way, that is, of that madness which makes to serve its ends the wisdom of its saner days. Joseph only sighed and said no more. He had done what he could, and dwelt no further upon the abominations of which all flesh, under the surface, consisted. For he realized that it was of the nature of the madness to ignore all that; the " heart and spirit " would simply not hear of it. He had other tasks than convincing this woman that life was either illusion as images were, or the beauty of the perishable children of men; and that truth, wherein life and beauty are a solid and imperishable unity, belongs to a different order of things, upon which one would do well to direct one's thoughts. For instance, he had great trouble in warding off the presents which Eni nowadays wanted to shower upon him. She did so out of a primitive impulse, always present in those who love; rooted in a sense of dependence upon the being whom they have made a god, and the need of bringing him offerings, of adorning, glorifying, and bribing him. But still more: for the gift serves also the purpose of attaching and pre-empting the recipient, of staking him out, as it were, and marking him with a prior claim. If you wear my gift, you are mine. The most preferred gift is the ring; who gives it knows very well what he wants, and who receives it must be aware of its meaning, for every ring is the visible link of an invisible chain. Thus Eni, ostensibly in gratitude for his services in initiating her into the household affairs, gave him — with a self-conscious air — a very costly

ring, with a carved scarab; likewise, in the course of
time, other valuable ornaments, such as gold bracelets
and collars set with precious stones. She even gave him
feast-day garments of great elegance. Or, rather, she
wanted to give him all these things and kept pressing
them upon him, in artless words. But after he had
respectfully received one or two, he refused the rest,
at first gently and pleadingly, then more and more
brusquely. And it was these gifts which showed him his
situation, so that he recognized it for what it was.

For instance one day, when he rejected the present of
a feast-day garment, saying curtly: " My garment and
my shirt content me," he had clearly recognized what
was involved, and unconsciously replied in the words
of Gilgamesh when Ishtar made assault on his beauty
and said: " Come then, Gilgamesh, thou shalt mate with
me and give me thy fruit! " and promised many splendid
presents in return for his compliance. Such a recognition can have its soothing as well as its disturbing side.
A man says to himself: " Here we have it again! " —
with a sense of the solid ground, the shelter afforded by
the myth, the reality, or even better, the truth, of what
is happening — all of which reassures him. But at the
same time he is startled to find himself playing a part
in the feast and representing such and such a myth as is
then being made present — he feels as though he were
in a dream. " Yes, yes," thought Joseph, as he looked at
poor Mut. " Verily thou art the abandoned daughter of
Anu, though thou knowest it not. I might chide thee for
it, reproaching thee with thy many lovers, whom thou
smotest with thy love and turned them into a bat, a
brightly coloured bird, a savage dog, so that his own

shepherds hunted him, the chief shepherd of the flocks, and the dogs tore his skin. ' To me also would it happen ' — as my part makes me say. Why did Gilgamesh say that, insulting thee, so thou didst run to Anu in thy rage and made him send the fire-breathing bull of heaven to chastise the disobedient? I know why now, for in him I see myself, as through myself I understand him. He spoke in displeasure of thy masterful homage, and turned maid before thee, girding himself with chastity against thy wooing and thy presents, O Ishtar in the beard! "

OF JOSEPH'S CHASTITY

THUS Joseph, the reader of tablets, assimilated his thoughts to those of him who went before him in the pattern. And in that he did so he gives me the cue for an explanation which is at the same time a summing up, and which I am convinced is here due to the fine spirit of scientific inquiry. The cue is " chastity." The theme has for thousands of years been associated with the figure of Joseph, it supplies the classical epithet inseparable from his name. " The chaste Joseph," we say; or even, giving it a general and symbolic application, we say " a chaste Joseph." That is the pretty, prudish phrase in which his memory lives in an age separated from his own by so many abysses of time; and I shall not feel that I have made a true and reliable reconstruction of his story unless, at the appropriate time, I gather together the scattered threads, the tangled and varicoloured strands of that much-talked-of chastity and make them as comprehensible as possible to the reader who out of natural sympathy for Mut-em-enet's anguish may incline to be angry at Joseph's resistance.

It goes without saying that there can be no chastity where there is no capacity — honorary captains and mutilated sun-chamberlains, for instance, are not chaste. We set out with the premise that Joseph was a whole and virile man. Indeed, we know that in later years he married, under the protection of royalty, and had as issue two sons, Ephraim and Manasseh, who will come into the story later on. So that his chastity was not permanent throughout his life, but only for the term of his youth, with which the conception was apparently bound up. It is plain that he kept his virginity (the word may perhaps be applied to young men as well as to maidens) only so long as he associated with its surrender the idea of prohibition, temptation, and fall. Later, when, so to speak, it was of no importance, he gave it up without a thought. So the classical epithet fits him only for a certain period of his life.

We must not make the mistake of thinking that his youthful chastity was that of some simple country bumpkin, whose awkwardness is at fault though his temper may be as ardent as you like. Jacob's darling was no blunderer in affairs of the heart — such an idea is inconsistent with the picture we first saw of him, saw, indeed, with the father's anxious eyes: the seventeen-year-old youth by the well, coquetting with the moon and matching her beauty with his own. His famous chastity was so far from being due to inexperience that it was closer to the opposite: resting rather upon a feeling that the mutual relations between him and all the world were permeated with the spirit of love; he was in love with everything, with a love deserving of the adjective universal, because it did not stop at the earthly but was present as a pervasive atmosphere, as an inference, a subtle significance and unconscious background to every relation in life, even the holiest and most awe-inspiring. From this feeling his chastity proceeded.

Earlier in my narrative I have discussed the phenomenon of the lively jealousy of God, as displayed in the unequivocally violent persecutions with which the one-time demon of the desert, even in a much further advanced stage of his relation with the spirit of man, visited the objects of idolatry or unbridled excess of feeling. It was this which poor Rachel had experienced. And I said then that Joseph, her son, would better understand this attitude of God and be more pliable in coming to terms with it than Jacob, his over-emotional begetter. Joseph's chastity, then, was above all an expression of this understanding and compliant spirit. He knew, of course, that his sufferings and death — with whatever large designs they might be connected — were a punishment for Jacob's pride, which had imitated, in a way not to be borne, the deity's majestic exercise of the power of selection. They were a manifestation of jealousy, directed against the poor old man. In this sense Joseph's misfortunes had to do only with the father, and were the continuation of Rachel's, since Jacob, in simply transferring his affection to her son, had never ceased to love her too much. But jealousy can have a twofold reference. One may be jealous of an object because another person, whose whole love one claims, loves it too; or one may strive for the object out of love for itself which cannot brook a rival. There is a third possibility: the combination of both these other two to make up the complete conception. Joseph was not fundamentally wrong when he assumed the third case. In his view, he had been ravished and snatched away, not only and not even chiefly for the chastisement of Jacob — or rather for this chastisement, indeed, but on the ground that he himself was the object of an over-whelming exercise of the power of selection, of a majestic covetousness and jealous pre-emption. Jacob's own set-tled paternalism had not yet arrived at the height of such complicated craftiness; he could not understand, though his anxiety might make him sometimes suspect it. I know that our modern sense too may be confused and offended by ideas like these, by such an emphasis on the relations between creator and creature, as foreign to us as would be Jacob's settled paternalism. Yet they have their place in time and evolution; there is no doubt, psychologically speaking, that more than one pregnant dialogue, handed down by tradition, taking place in a cloud between the Unseeable (whatever name He bore) and His disciple and favourite, was characterized by an abnormal capri-ciousness. Thus Joseph's view of things is at bottom justi-fiable; its probability rests upon his own personal worth, which I would not wish to dispute.

"Yea, I keep myself clean." Little Benjamin had once heard the words from the lips of his admired brother, in the grove of Adonis. He was speaking of keeping his face clean of a beard and thus enhancing the peculiar beauty of his seventeen years; but also of his relation to the outer world, which had been, and still remained, abstemious, though as remote as possible from awkward inexperience. His restraint was nothing less than cau-tion, an inspired shrewdness, a religious circumspection;

and the experience of frightful violation, the tearing of wreath and robe, must have strengthened it mightily. We must suppose that it was associated with a certain haughtiness of spirit which did away with the bleakness of renunciation. There can be no talk here of painful mortification of the flesh, in whose haggard image our modern world almost inevitably clothes the idea of chastity. Yet even the modern world might have to concede the possible existence of another kind: a blithe, even supercilious chastity. Joseph decided for this, first by virtue of his clear and bold mentality; but his choice was made easier, where for others it would have entailed cruel hardship, because of the pleasure he took in the pious conceit of his brideship with God. Mut the mistress, in talk with the concubine Mekh-en-Weseht, had let fall a complaint about the mockery she read in the young steward's eyes. It was, she thought, a jeering at the cruel bondage of desire, so shameful to him who feels it. The observation was a shrewd one; for certainly of the three animals which according to Joseph kept guard in the orchard of the little fowler — shame, guilt, and mocking laughter — the last was the most his familiar. Yet not in the sense that he suffered from it, in the meaning of the legend. It was he himself who indulged in the mocking laughter, and nothing else could be seen in his eyes when the wanton women peered after him from the house-tops. Such an attitude toward the sphere of sexual infatuation does doubtless exist; it is produced by the consciousness of a higher bond, to which one is chosen. Some may see in it an arrogant contempt of human claims and find that it is culpable to look at passion in a comic light. To these let me say that we are approaching a time in our tale

when Joseph laughed no more; and the second catastrophe in his life, his second descent to the grave, was
brought on him by just that power to which in his youthful pride he had thought to deny tribute.

Here, then, was the first reason why Joseph denied
himself to the desire of Potiphar's wife: he was betrothed
to God, he practised a shrewd foresight, he took account
of the peculiar pain which faithlessness inflicts on the solitary. And his second reason was closely allied to his
first, being its mirror, being actually its earthly and social form: it was loyalty to the letter of the pact made
with the departed Mont-kaw: loyalty to his difficult master, the highest in his sphere.

This juggling with ideas of the absolutely Highest
compared with him only relatively and locally so, as it
went on in the head of the descendant of Abraham, must
strike a modern sense as absurd and even glaring. For
all that, we must realize and accept it if we wish to understand how it looked inside that mind, so early and yet
so modern, which thought its thoughts with as much inevitability, composure, and reasonableness as we do ours.
Joseph's fantasy actually did no less than see, in the
obese aristocratic person of Mut's honorary husband
the courtier of the sun, and in his melancholy egotism, the
earthly counterpart and fleshly reproduction of the wife-
less and childless, lonely and jealous God of his fathers,
with whom he was bent on keeping loving human faith.
He made a fantasy-parallel, which yet was not without
some trace of speculation on the practical side. Add to
that the solemn vow he had made to Mont-kaw on his
death-bed, to sustain the master's sensitive dignity to the
best of his powers and protect it from harm — and we

shall better understand that the now scarcely concealed desires of poor Mut must have seemed to him like a devouring temptation to experience the knowledge of good and evil and to repeat the folly of Adam. That was the second reason.

For the third, it is enough to say that his aroused masculinity objected to being degraded into the feminine and passive by the wooing of a mistress who behaved like a man; he would be the arrow, not the goal of desire. That is understandable. — And the fourth follows quite naturally, for it also had to do with pride, but spiritual pride.

Joseph shuddered when he thought of that which Mut, the Egyptian woman, embodied to him. A proud tradition of racial purity warned him not to mingle his blood with hers. She was the ancientness of this land into which he had been sold; the enduringness, the unchanging, unpromising desolation which stared out into a future savage and dead and void of expectation, yet seemed as though it would raise its paw to snatch to its bosom the reasoning child of the promise as he stood before it, that he might name it his name, of whatever sex it was. For the hopelessly old was at the same time lewd, lustful of young blood — young not alone in years but, and especially, also in its promise for the future. This election of his Joseph had in his heart never forgotten, since he came a slave, a nobody and nothing, into this land. With all his native worldly adaptability, by means of which he had ingratiated himself among the children of the land of mud and thought to go far amongst them, he had kept detached, he had clung to his inward reserve, well knowing that in the last analysis he might not make himself common, for they were taboo; distinctly feeling in his heart of whose spirit he was child and of what father son.

His father! There was the fifth reason — if indeed it was not the first and strongest. He knew not, the poor, beaten old man, who had painfully grown used to thinking of his child as safe in death, he knew not where it lived and moved, arrayed already in a new and strange bodily garment. Were he to learn, he would fall down and collapse with grief. When Joseph, in his mind, dwelt on the third of his three imaginings: the snatching away, the elevation, the following after, he never concealed from himself that much resistance would need to be overcome in Jacob, knowing the stately old man's pathetic prejudice against Mizraim, his paternal-childish horror of Hagar's land, the monkey-land of Egypt. The good soul's etymology was wrong; he derived the name of Kemt, which signified the black earth, from Ham, the shameless one and shamer of his father; and cherished immoderate ideas about the abominable folly of the children of the land in matters of morality and discipline; Joseph had always suspected them of one-sidedness, and learned to smile at them as mythical since his coming to the land. For the luxury here was not worse than the luxury of other lands; and whence would the panting, tax-paying, drudging little peasants and systematically flogged water-carriers whom Joseph had known now for nine years have got the lustiness to behave like sodomites? In short, the old man had all sorts of quaint notions about the conduct of the people of Egypt — as though they lived in a way that must have infected all the children of God with wantonness.

But Joseph was the last person to have concealed from

himself the grain of truth in Jacob's moral condemnation of the land where the inhabitants worshipped animals and the dead. Some good downright epithets echoed in his brain at this time, which the anxious old man had uttered about people who set up their beds with the neighbours' whenever they pleased and exchanged their wives; of women who would go to market and see a youth who took their fancy, when they would lie down with him without more ado, without a notion of sin. Joseph knew the sphere whence the father drew these ideas: it was the sphere of Canaan and the abominable fluctuations of its worship, against all reason; the sphere of the Moloch-madness, of singing and dancing, abandonment and aulasaukaula, when they went whoring after the images of fertility in an abandonment of ritual copulation. Joseph, son of Jacob, would not go whoring after the gods of Baal; this was the fifth of the seven reasons why he practised reserve. And the sixth reason lies to hand; though in passing, our sympathy with poor Mut should make us cast an eye on the perversity of her fate, in that precisely he upon whom her late-roused fancies dwelt saw her in the light of his father's mythical misunderstandings and heard in the cry of her heart's longing so much shameless temptation — which was as good as not there at all. Eni's yearning for Joseph had little to do with the follies of Baal and aulasaukaula; it was a deeper and more honourable wound from his youth and beauty, a fervid desire, as decent and as indecent as any other and no more lewd than it is the nature of love to be. If later it degenerated, and destroyed her reason, the fault lay with her anguish over the sevenfold armour of resistance which it encountered. A cruel fate would have it that her love was weighed not by what she was but by what she meant for Joseph: in other words, and sixthly, the " bond with Sheol."

Here again we must take care to be clear in our minds. This was a situation in which Joseph desired to act with good sense and consideration, to lose nothing himself nor do anyone harm. And in it his mentality must lead him to associate his Canaanitish hostility to the stammering and staggering folly of Baal with another conception, fundamentally Egyptian, which was the greatest difficulty of all. I mean the reverence for death and the dead, which was nothing else than the Egyptian form of whoring after Baal. It was Mut's misfortune that it was just this she represented to Joseph. We cannot envisage too clearly the importance of the ancient warning, the primeval No in Joseph's blood, which spoke out against any bond with the lower world or its inhabitants, against that combined idea of death and dissoluteness. To sin against its command, to err in this inscrutably fundamental matter, was for him literally to lose all. His thoughts, and the serious obstacles they created for him, may easily seem fantastic to our modern reason; but it is for precisely them that I seek to win understanding from initiate and allied minds, however separated by time from his sphere. And yet it was reason itself, speaking with his father's voice, that set itself against the temptations of shameless unreason. Not in the least that Joseph would have been without understanding for unreason; the anxious old man at home had known that. But must one not understand sin in order to be able to sin? It takes understanding to sin; yes, at bottom, all spirit is nothing else than understanding of sin.

The God of Joseph's fathers was a God of the spirit —
at least that was the goal of His evolution, for the sake
of which He had made a bond with men. Never since He
united with theirs His will to salvation had He anything
to do with death and the nether world or with any madness rooted in the dark bottom of fruitfulness. In man
He had become aware that such things were an abomination unto Him; and in his turn man too had become aware
of it in Him. Joseph, when he said his good-nights to
the dying Mont-kaw, had of course dealt soothingly with
his death-anguish and told him how it would be with him
in the hereafter, saying consolingly that they would be
together for ever and always because they belonged together in their sagas. But that was a friendly concession
to human distress, a benevolent open-mindedness which
for the moment looked aside from what he knew to be
fixed: from the strict and stern renunciation of any view
of the hereafter, which had been the way the fathers —
and their self-sanctifying God — took to make by such
a ruling a clear divorce between themselves and the
corpse-gods of their neighbours in their temple graves
and their death-rigidity. For only by comparison does
man distinguish and learn what he is in order to become
what he should be. Thus the famous chastity of Joseph,
a future husband and father, was no theoretic and self-
flagellating denial of the sphere of love and procreation,
which would have been inconsistent with the promise to
Abraham that his seed should be numerous as the desert
sand; rather it was the inherited dictate of his blood to
uphold the godly claims of reason in this field and to
avoid all horned folly and aulasaukaula, which in his
mind formed an inseparable logical and metaphysical

unity with the service of the dead. It was Mut's misfortune that he saw in her wooing a temptation from this complex of death and unchastity, the temptation of Sheol, to yield to which would have meant laying himself bare to annihilation.

Here we have the seventh and last reason — the last also in the sense that it comprehended all the others. For all together what they came to was just this fear: the fear of laying himself bare. That was what he heard when Mut had tried to divest their conversation of the fig-leaf of objectivity; but we must consider it here in the sober light of its manifold sense-reference and the vast scope of its consequences.

How strangely it can fare with the meaning of a word when it breaks up into its elements in the mind, as a ray of light from a cloud is broken up into the colours of the rainbow! Let even one of these refractions make unhappy contact with an evil association and become a curse, and it loses its good repute in all, it becomes an abomination in every one of its senses, so that it can be and is condemned to be used solely to characterize abominations. If red, let us say, is a bad colour, the colour of the desert, the colour of the polar star, then it is all over with the blithe innocence of the whole white ray of heaven. The idea of barenness and baring did not originally lack innocence and blitheness; it had no red about it and no curse. But since the accursed affair of Noah in his tent, with Ham and Kenaan, his wicked son, it got, so to speak, a permanent split, became red and evil in this refraction, and blushed through and through. There was nothing else to do after that but to use it to describe abominations. It even happened that every abomination, or almost all, cried out for this name and recognized itself in it. In the attitude of the anxious Jacob by the well — almost nine years before — when he sternly rebuked his son for the nakedness with which he responded to the loveliness of the moon, in that attitude lay a regrettable blackening of an idea in itself as bright as the sight of a naked boy by a well. Baring, in the simple and literal physical sense, was in the beginning quite unsuspect, it was as neutral as the light of heaven. It only began to blush when it acquired a transferred significance, as Baal folly and the shameful blood-sin of looking upon the nakedness of a father. But now the redness had reflected back upon the innocent original meaning and cast such a glow upon it that it became a name for every sort of deadly sin, those actually committed and those only realized in look and wish. So that finally everything forbidden, thought of as accursed, in the realm of sensual lust and fleshly intercourse — and especially, by association with the shame of Noah, the invasion of the son into the rights of the father — was thought of as " baring." And even that was not all; for a new and peculiar association and comparison grew up, and the error of Reuben, the offence done by the son to the father's bed, began to stand for the whole conception — until every meeting of glances, every wish, every act, became almost equivalent, in quality and even name, to a shaming of the father.

These, then, whether we like it or not, were the pictures in Joseph's mind. To do that to which the sphinx of this dead land incited him seemed to him a shaming of his father — and was it not, in truth, when we remember what wickedness the land of mud meant to the old man at

home, and with what outraged alarm he would have
learned that his child, instead of being safely garnered
up in death, was living in such sore temptation? In those
anxious brown eyes with the soft tear-glands beneath —
Joseph could feel them resting upon him — he would be
committing that sinful " baring " of himself; forgetting
himself as grossly as Reuben had done, what time he had
shown himself unstable as water and been deprived of
the blessing. Since then the blessing had hovered over
Joseph's head; should he, too, be unstable and fling it
away by sporting with this dubious cat-goddess as Reuben
once had sported with Bilhah? Who can wonder that
his inward answer to the question was: " Not for the
world! " Who, I repeat, can be surprised, considering all
the associations and identifications bound up in Joseph's
mind with the idea of his father, and the thought of offending him? Can even the liveliest mind, or the person most
receptive to the tender passion, find anything strange in a
chastity which consisted in a resolution counselled by the
purest religious prudence; namely, that he would avoid
the grossest error he could commit and the one most in-
jurious to his future prospects?

These, then, were the seven reasons why Joseph desired
not to respond to the call of his mistress's blood — not for
anything in the world. I have set them down in the order
of their number and weight, and regard them with a certain sense of reassurance — which, however, considering
the hour at which we have arrived, is by no means in
place, since Joseph is still enduring temptation, and as
the story tells itself, there was as yet no certainty whether
he would come out of it a whole man or not. He did come
well out of it; that is, he escaped with a black eye, as we

know. But why did he venture so far? Why did he disregard the whispered warning of his pure-hearted little friend, who already saw the pit yawning, and make friends instead with the phallic-minded manikin who played Lothario and mumbled out of the corner of his mouth? In a word, why did he not avoid the mistress instead of letting things reach the pass they did for him and for her? Yes, that was coquetting with the world, it was sympathy with the forbidden thing; it was also a falling away from the death-name he had chosen and from the state of salvation in which he had stood. And it had a savour of arrogant self-assurance, of a notion that he could venture into danger and retreat whenever he liked. To look at it on its good side, it was a willingness to take a dare, an ambition to face the worst and run the risk, to push matters to the uttermost in order to carry off a greater triumph — to be a virtuoso of virtue and thus more precious to the father than a more restricted and an easier trial would have shown him. Perhaps, even, it was a secret knowledge of his own course and the line it took, the suspicion that its next lesser round was to complete itself and bring him to the pit, which was inevitable if all that was to be fulfilled which was written in the plan.

7

THE PIT

BILLETS-DOUX

WE see and we have said that Potiphar's wife, in the third year of her passion, the tenth of Joseph's sojourn in the chamberlain's house, began to tender her love to Joseph, and with growing vehemence. At bottom there is no great difference between the revealing of the second year and the tendering of the third; the one was comprised in the other and the line between them was fluid. But there was a line none the less; and to pass from attentions and longing looks, even though desire was implicit in them, to actual invitation cost the woman a self-conquest almost equal to the effort required to conquer her weakness and renounce her desire for her servant — almost, but probably not quite, since obviously she must have preferred this to the other.

She did not do it; rather than overcome her love she overcame her pride and her shame — hard enough, but yet somewhat easier, a little, because she was not alone in this struggle as she would have been in the other, for Dudu, the begetting dwarf, helped her; going to and fro between her and the son of Jacob, playing with great dignity and in his own mind for the first time the rôle of

attached patron, counsellor, and messenger, and fanning
the flame on both sides with all the strength of his lungs.
For Dudu at length understood that there were two fires,
not only one; that Joseph's pedagogic plan of salvation,
by means of which he need not avoid the mistress but
might stand before her nearly every day, was just an absurd and asinine pretext, since he — consciously or not
— already found himself in the state of the god when
his wrappings were rent. Dudu understood all this quite
as well as did the quaking little mock-vizier; for in this
sphere his perceptions were not only equal but superior
to those of his small colleague.

" Steward," said he, at Joseph's end of the route, " you
have so far known how to make your fortune — even
envy, of which I am incapable, would concede that. You
have trodden down those above you, despite your doubtless respectable but modest origins. You sleep in the
private room of trust, and the perquisites in which the
Osiris Mont-kaw once rejoiced, the corn, beer, bread,
geese, linen, and leather — you are now the one whom
they rejoice. You take them to market, since it is impossible you should consume them; you increase your
wealth and seem to be a made man. But what is made
can be unmade and what is won can run away, as happens often in the world when a man knows not how to
hold his good fortune nor how to secure it by unshakable
foundations that it may endure for ever like a temple of
the dead. Indeed, it must happen again and again that
only some one thing is lacking to crown such a man's
fortune and make his unshakable success; and he would
need but to put forth his hand to grasp it. But from shy-

ness or obstinacy, slackness or even conceit, the fool re-
frains, folds his hand in his garment, and wilfully does
not put it out to grasp this final success, but neglects it,
despises it, and whistles it down the wind. And the consequence? The sad consequence is that all his luck and
his gains ebb away, his good fortune is level with the
ground, and his place knows him no more, all because of
that one refusal. For he lost credit with powers which
had thought to accompany his success with their last and
highest favour that it might last for ever, but being thus
despised and insulted, rage like the sea, their eyes shoot
fire, and their hearts rouse up a sand-storm like the mountains of the East, so that they not only turn their faces
away from the man's fortune, but set themselves against
it in their wrath so that they entirely destroy it, which
costs them no effort at all. I doubt not that you see my
concern as an honest man for your welfare — indeed,
not for yours alone but also and equally for that of the
person to whom my words, I hope unmistakably, refer.
Yet they are the same: her good fortune is yours and
yours hers; this conjunction is long since a happy truth,
and it only remains to give it blissful reality. For when
I think and ruminate in my soul what voluptuous delight
this union must prepare for you, I, the strong man, reel
and am giddy. I speak not of fleshly bliss — in the first
place out of modesty, and in the second because it goes
without saying that it will be very great, considering the
silken skin of the person in question and the wonder of
her build. I refer to the delight of the soul, through which
the fleshly must be heightened beyond any measure; and
will consist in the thought that you, of certainly respect-

able but yet quite modest origins and a foreigner, are holding in your arms the loveliest and most noble lady in the two lands, and that you have evoked her profoundest sighs, as it were in token that you, a youth of the desert and of misery, have subdued Egypt, which sighs beneath your weight. And wherewith do you repay this mutual bliss, of which one ever spurs the other up to fresh heights? You pay it not, but are paid for it; paid by the unshatterable perpetuation of your fortune, in that you will have risen to be the true lord and master over this house. For who possesses the mistress," said Dudu, " is in truth the master." He raised his stumps of arms as though before Potiphar, and symbolically kissed the ground before Joseph's feet.

The latter had listened, though with disgust, to the pander's very common and offensive words. But he had listened; so that the arrogance with which he replied was not wholly becoming:

" I should, dwarf, be better pleased if you spoke not so much of your own motion nor developed so many of your marvellous ideas, for they are little to the purpose; but instead would confine yourself to your office as messenger and informer. If you have something to tell me from a higher source, then do so. If not, then begone! "

" I should," answered Dudu, " put myself in error to be gone before I discharged my office. For I have something to deliver and hand over. It will perhaps be permitted to the messenger and announcer from so high a source that he somewhat adorns and enlarges upon the message."

"What is it? " asked Joseph.

And the gnome handed something up to him, a note on papyrus, a long, narrow slip, on which Mut, the mistress, had written some words.

For at the other end of the route the mischief-monger had said:

" Let your loyal servant, my lady (by which I mean myself), speak to your very soul in saying that the pace of time in which things move forward is a vexation to me, for it is sluggish and stagnant. And that pinches my inwards with anger and grief for your sake, for that your beauty might suffer under it. Not that I have seen it suffer — thanks to the gods, it flourishes in plenteous bloom and has such abundance that it might lose much and still radiantly excel the common human measure. Thus far all is well. But your honour suffers if your beauty does not, and therewith mine too, under the state of things and in your relation with the youth who is set over the house, who calls himself Osarsiph, but whom I would call Nefernefru, for certainly he is the most beautiful of the beautiful — does the name please you? I have contrived it for your use — or not actually contrived, rather overheard and picked up to put at your service, for so is he often named in the house as upon the land and the water-ways and in the city, yes, the women on the house-tops choose to call him so, against whose behaviour unfortunately one could not take any serious measures. But let me go on with my considered words. For it gnaws your devoted servant in his very liver, for the sake of your honour, that you approach so slowly your goal in the matter of this Nefernefru — your known purpose being that you may come upon the sources of his power and bring him to a fall as he names to you his name. I have indeed contrived and brought about that mistress and man no longer approach each other with scribes and attendants, but converse without restraint or burdensome formality, just four eyes and two mouths, and in some appointed place. That improves the prospect that in some most sweet and secret hour he will at last name you his name and you will swoon with the bliss of your triumph over him, the wicked one, and all those whom his mouth and eyes have beguiled. For you will seal his mouth in such wise that his beguiling speech will fail him and his all-enchanting eye grow dim in the bliss of surrender. But the trouble is that the youth defends himself against trying a fall with you, which in my eyes is rank sedition and a sort of shameless shamefacedness, as Dudu does not hesitate to call it. For what is it? You would assault him and bring him to his fall; you, child of Amun, the flower of the southern house of women; and he, the Shabirite Amu, the foreign slave and son of the depths, he forsooth resists, he will not what you will, he hides himself behind accounts and affairs of the household. That is not to be borne, it is rebellion and presumption on the part of the gods of Asia, who owe tribute to Amun, the Lord in his Chapel. Thus the affront to the house, which earlier consisted in the growth and advancement of this slave, has now become the open insurrection of the gods of Asia, who will not pay their due tribute to Amun, which is the downfall of this youth to your power, who are a child of Amun. To this must it come. I have given timely warning. But neither, great lady, can a just mind quite absolve you or wash you white of guilt in this abomination, that the affair does not go forward. For you do not press it; in maiden

delicacy you allow the youth to play his game with
Amun, the king of the gods, by feints and shifts putting him off from moon to moon. That is frightful.
But it is your maidenliness that is responsible, by
lacking in boldness and in ripe experience; you will
pardon your true servant his words, for else whence shall
you acquire that which you lack? For now it must be
that without scruple or ceremony you must summon the
slippery one and challenge him to his fall, so that he cannot escape. If your modesty forbids you to achieve this
by word of mouth, then there is the written way and the
billet-doux, which he must understand when he reads,
whether he will or no, for it should run in some such
wise as: 'Will you overcome me today at a game? Shall
we try conclusions alone together?' For so can ripeness
and audacity clothe itself in a maidenly garment of
speech, yet make itself understood. Let me prepare the
writing instruments and write as I dictate, that I may
bring him to it and make a conclusion of the business to
the honour of Amun! "

Thus Dudu at this end, the sun-potent dwarf. And Eni,
dazed and femininely submissive to his authority and
knowledge of the field, did write to his direction that
which Joseph now read. He could not conceal the redness of Atum that flew to his cheeks; though it angered
him so that he ungently drove away the messenger without any ado. Yet despite anxious whisperings from another quarter, bidding him not obey the artful challenge,
he did obey it, playing a game with the mistress in the
columned hall beneath the image of Re-Horakhte. Once
he " drove her into the water " and once let her drive
him, so that defeat and victory were even and the result

of the meeting was nothing at all — to the great disappointment of Dudu, at this new hitch in affairs.

So then he took the next and last step; and presently he could say to Joseph, out of the corner of his mouth:

"I have something to deliver, from a certain source."

"What is it? " Joseph asked.

Then the dwarf handed up to him a narrow slip, of which one may say that it did indeed give a desperate push to the plot; for it contained, quite baldly and unmistakably, the word which I called a word of mistaking — on the ground that it was not the word of a strumpet but of a woman overwhelmed. True, it was couched in the roundabout way which the written word permits and in especial the Egyptian, in which it was of course set down. The delicate conciseness of the picture-writing, which with the vowels left to the imagination, with the everywhere interspersed symbols suggesting the category of the consonantally crisply invoked sounds, always has something of the magic rebus, of flowery half-concealment and witty anagram, so that in fact it seems made for the confection of billets-doux, and the simplest statement receives an allusive and ingenious cast. The decisive part of Mut-em-enet's communication, what we should call the point of it, consisted of three word-symbols, with others equally pretty preceding them, and following them the quickly sketched symbol of a lion-headed couch with a mummy lying on it. The rebus looked like this:

and it meant " lying " or " sleeping." For the two words are the same in the language of Kemt; and the whole line on the papyrus slip, signed with the symbol of a vulture, said quite plainly and unmistakably: " Come, let us sleep together for an hour."

What a document! Precious as gold, highly moving and self-respecting if also most evil, distressing, and dangerous in its nature. We have here, in its original form, in the original version and the phrasing of the Egyptian language, the words in which the wife of Potiphar according to tradition couched her imploring offer to Joseph — for first in this written form she addressed it to him, empowered by Dudu, the begetting dwarf, who prompted her out of the corner of his mouth. But if the sight of it moves even us, then how must Joseph have felt when he had deciphered it! Pale and startled, he crumpled the paper in his hand and chased Dudu away with the handle of his fly-brush. But he had now received the message, the sweet suggestion, the longing and promising call of his loving mistress; and if he could not in honour be greatly surprised at it, yet it shook him mightily and made such havoc in his blood that we might fear for the strength of the seven reasons, if we did not, while still involved in the present feast-hour of our story, already know how it came out. But Joseph, to whom it happened when it played itself for the first time, actually lived in that hour, was unable to see beyond it, and could by no means be certain of the outcome. It was all in suspense, at the point whither we are arrived; and at the moment when it was actually decided, it was to be touch and go whether the seven reasons would hold or would be dissipated into air and Joseph yield to sin. It might just as well have gone wrong as to have gone, as it did, right by the thickness of a hair. Certainly Joseph knew himself

resolved not to commit the great error, not to wreck
his good faith with God. But the wise little dwarf had
been right when he had seen in Joseph's pleasure in
his freedom of choice between good and evil something very like pleasure in evil itself, not only in the
freedom to choose it. Certainly an unconfessed inclination to evil, interpreted only as a pleasure in the glorious freedom of choice, includes the other inclination:
namely, to pull the wool over one's own eyes and
cloud one's understanding to the point of seeing the
good in it. God had such wonderful intentions with regard to Joseph — did He really mean to grudge him
the proud and honeyed satisfaction which offered itself,
which perhaps He Himself was offering? Might not this
satisfaction be the destined means of the elevation in the
hope of which the " snatched-away " one lived and which
had so far prospered in the house that now the mistress
had cast her eyes upon him to covet him, naming to him
her sweet name, longing to name the name of all Egypt,
and thereby to make him, so to speak, the lord of all the
world? What youth to whom the beloved yields herself
would not liken this to his elevation to the lordship of
the world? And was it not just this, to make him lord
of the world, that God designed for Joseph?

We see the temptations to which his clouded reason
was exposed. Good and evil were in a fair way to be
thoroughly confused in his mind. There were moments
when he was tempted to interpret evil as good. The symbol coming after " lie " on the slip of paper was calculated — thanks to the mummy on it — to open his eyes to
the kingdom whence the temptation came, and to show
him that to yield to it would be an unpardonable affront

toward Him who was no mummy-god promising endur-
ance and nothing else, but rather a God of the future;
yet even so Joseph had every ground to mistrust the
strength of his seven reasons and the course which future
feast-hours would take, and to lend an ear to the whisperings of a certain little friend who implored him to go no
more to the mistress, to receive no more billets-doux from
the malicious go-between, and to fear the bull which even
now was beginning to turn the smiling meadow into a
field of ashes with his fiery breath. True, for Joseph to
avoid the mistress was more easily said than done; after
all, she was the mistress and when she called he had to
go. But how prone is man to keep open the door to evil
choice, rejoicing in freedom and playing with fire —
whether out of self-confidence that thinks it can take the
bull by the horns, or out of light-headedness and secret
desire, who can tell?

THE PAINFUL TONGUE
(PLAY AND EPILOGUE)

THERE came that night in the third year, when Mut-em-
inet, Potiphar's wife, bit her tongue, because it so over-
poweringly craved to say to her husband's young steward
that which she had already written to him in a rebus;
while at the same time her pride and shame would have
prevented her tongue from speaking and from offering
to the slave her blood that he might stanch its flow. The
conflict lay in her rôle as mistress. On the one hand it
was frightful to her so to speak and to offer him her flesh
and blood in exchange for his own; while on the other
it was her fitting part to behave as the male and, so to

speak, as the bearded active principle in love. Thus it was she bit her tongue by night, above and below, so that it was nearly bitten through, and next day she lisped from the wound, like a little child.

For some days after the sending of the letter she would not see Joseph, but denied him her countenance because she could not look into his, after challenging him in writing to try a fall. But just this renunciation of his presence it was that made her ripe to utter with her own lips what she had said in magic writing. The longing for his presence took the form of the longing to utter the words which it was forbidden to him, the slave of love, to speak. For if she were ever to learn whether he spoke from his soul, there was nothing left but for her, the mistress, to speak and to offer him her flesh and blood in the fervent hope that she responded to his own desire and took the words from his lips. Her rôle as mistress condemned her to shamelessness, for which she had already punished herself at night, by biting her tongue; so that now she might take leave to say what she must say, as well as she could after the punishment, lisping like a child — which was also a refuge, since it gave an air of helplessness and innocence to the shamelessness and turned into pathos what would else have been gross.

She had summoned Joseph through Dudu to a business session and a game afterwards, and she received him in the hall with the image of Atum, about an hour after the meal, when Joseph would have finished reading to Potiphar. She came to him from her bedchamber; and as she approached he made the observation, for the first time, or for the first time consciously, that she was greatly changed. I also have until this hour refrained from no-

tice of the change which had taken place since the beginning of her passion — and also as a result of it.

It was a peculiar change, in characterizing and describ-
ing which I run the risk of being either offensive or mis-
understood. To Joseph, when he at last perceived it, it
afforded much food for wonderment and profound reflection. For life lies deep, not only in the spirit but in
the flesh. It was not that Mut had aged in this time; her
love would have prevented that. Had she grown more
beautiful? Yes, and no — but on the whole no. Even
decidedly no, if by beauty we mean the utterly admirable
and satisfyingly complete, a splendid image, something
glorious to enfold in one's arms, yet afterwards claiming
no place in our thoughts because it appeals to our most
clarified sense, the eye, and not the mouth or the hand —
in so far as it appeals to anything at all. For however
richly sensuous, beauty has about it something abstract
and spiritual; it asserts its independence and the priority
of the idea before the manifestation; it is not the product
and tool of sex, but rather sex is its stuff and instrument.
Feminine beauty — that may be beauty embodied in the
feminine, the feminine as beauty's means of expression.
But if the relation between spirit and matter is reversed,
so that one speaks of beautiful femininity rather than of
feminine beauty, because the feminine has become the
premise and primary idea, and the beauty its attribute
instead of the reverse — what then? What if sex, I would
ask, deals with beauty as its material, embodying itself
in it, so that beauty serves and is functional as a means of
expressing the feminine? It is clear that the result is a
quite different kind of beauty from that which I spoke of
above — a suspect, an uncanny kind, which may even

approach the ugly and wield for evil the power over the
emotions which it is the gift of beauty to wield; by virtue,
that is, of sex, which has usurped beauty's place and takes
its name. Then it is no longer a spiritual beauty revealed
in the feminine, but a beauty in which the feminine re-
veals itself, an eruption of sex, the beauty of a witch.

The word I have used, startling as it is, is indispensable
to a description of the change which had taken place during the year in Mut's physical being. It was a change
pathetic and disturbing at once, evil and apparent, a
witchlike metamorphosis. We must not imagine a hag,
we must reject such an idea — though perhaps a faint
suggestion of something like it might enter in. A witch
is certainly not of necessity haglike. And yet in the most
charming witch one might descry a trace — it does belong to the picture in our minds. Mut's new body was that
of a witch, informed by love and sex, and thus remotely
haglike, though the only manifestation was a combined
development of leanness and voluptuosity. A proper
example of a hag was for instance black Tabubu, who
presided over the mysteries of the make-up and had
breasts like wineskins. Mut's own breasts, once so tender
and maidenly, had, thanks to her suffering, developed in
voluptuous splendour; standing out like great fruits of
love and suggesting the haglike only by comparison with
the thinness, the emaciation of the fragile shoulder-
blades. The shoulders themselves looked too narrow,
fragile, even childishly touching, and the arms had lost
much of their roundness, they were wellnigh thin. On the
other hand the thighs had developed, one might almost
say, illicitly, by comparison with the upper extremities;
they were large and vigorous, and gave the impression

that they gripped a broomstick between them, over which the creature bent, with shrunken back and swelling breasts, and rode to the mountains. The fancy not only lay to hand, it fairly urged itself upon the observer. And the face helped it out, with its frame of black curls — that saddle-nosed, shadow-cheeked face, so long the theatre of a conflict to which only now the right name can be given, since only now did it arrive at its climax: the quite witchlike contradiction between the stern, the threatening and sinister expression of the eyes and the sinuous audacity of the deep-cornered mouth. This distressing contrast, now at its height, lent the face a morbid, masklike tension, intensified, probably, by the burning smart of the bitten tongue. But among the reasons why she had bitten it was probably this: that she knew she would be obliged to lisp like an innocent child and that the childlikeness of her lisping would perhaps disguise and palliate the witch-aspect of her new body, of which she was but too well aware.

We may guess the distress which the cause of all these changes felt at the sight of them. Now for the first time he began to realize how lightly he had behaved in paying no heed to the prayers of his pure-minded little friend and, instead of avoiding the mistress, let it come to this, that his swan maiden was transformed witch. The folly of his pedagogic scheme struck him; for the first time he had a glimmer of the fact that his behaviour in the affair of his second life was not less culpable than his conduct toward the brethren. This insight, which was to ripen from a misgiving to a conviction, explains much that happened later.

At first his bad conscience and his distressful unease

over the transformation of his mistress into a hag for love
hid itself behind the special reverence, yes, veneration,
of his tone and manner. Wisely or unwisely he proceeded
as on all other occasions with his idiotic plan of pedagogic
treatment; showed his rolls of accounts and spoke of the
supplies and consumption of various commodities for
the house of women, the dismissing of certain servants,
and the appointing of others. Thus he did not at once
notice the injury to her tongue; for she only listened to
him nervously and said almost nothing. But when they
sat down to play their game, at the beautifully carven
board, she on her couch of ebony and ivory, he on an
ox-legged tabouret; sorted the pieces shaped like cou-
chant lions, and agreed upon the play, he could no longer
fail, with mounting anxiety, to note that she lisped. When
he had listened a few times and confirmed his perception
he ventured to ask:

"What do I hear, my lady? It seems you have some
difficulty in your speech?"

And he was forced to hear that the lady had "painth"
in her tongue; she had hurt herthelf in the night and bitten her tongue, the thteward mutht pay no heed.

So she spoke — I reproduce the childish accents in our
tongue instead of hers, but with no great difference in the
effect. Joseph, profoundly shocked, lifted his hands from
the board and wished not to play until she had tended her
wound and taken balsam in her mouth, which Khun-
Anpu, the barber-surgeon, must straightway be summoned to prepare. But she would not hear of it; she
lightly reproached him that he wished to avoid the game,
which at the beginning stood unfavourably for him and
it looked as though he would be pushed into the water.

Therefore he would save himself by breaking up the game and seeking for the apothecary. In short, she held him to his seat, lisping and babbling like a child, for involuntarily she suited her words to the helplessness of her tongue and spoke like a small girl, seeking to give her strained and suffering face an expression of infantine charm. I will not try to imitate her as she went on talking about puthing hith piethes into the water; for I would not seem to mock at her, who had death at her heart and was in act to throw away every vestige of pride and spiritual honour, in the overpowering urge to appease the honour of her flesh and see fulfilled the dream of healing which she had dreamed.

He too, who had awaked this urge in her, he too felt death at his heart — and only too justly. He did not dare to look up from the board, and he bit his lip, for his conscience spoke against him. Yet he played carefully; it would be hard to say whether reason controlled him or he his reason. She too took her pieces, lifted and moved them, but so absently that she was soon in a corner with no way out, was hopelessly beaten without seeing it at all, but went on playing until she was recalled by the fact that he no longer moved, when she looked down with a nervous smile upon the confusion of her hopes. He in his delusion thought that by speaking sensibly and courteously he could mend the disordered situation and set it to rights, so he said discreetly: " We must try again, now or some other time, for the game went wrong, very likely because I made an awkward opening, and you see that we can get no further, you have checkmated me and I you, so that nobody has won or lost, for we have both done both."

He hesitated and his voice was toneless, he spoke on only because he had begun, for he could no longer hope to save the situation by speaking of it. Even as he spoke, the worst had happened: she had broken down, laying her head and face on his arm that rested on the edge of the board. Her hair, with its gold and silver powder, upset the couching lions, and her hot breath brushed his arm as she feverishly lisped and stammered. Out of respect for her pain I refrain from reproducing the childish, sickly sounds, but their sense and nonsense ran somewhat like this:

" Yes, yes, we can go no further, the play is played out, there is only a downfall for us both, Osarsiph, my beautiful god from afar, my swan and bull, my highly and hotly and eternally beloved; so we may die together and go down into the darkness of blissful despair! Tell me, speak to me, and freely, since you cannot see my face, because it lies upon your arm, at last upon your arm and my lost lips touch your flesh and blood as I implore you: tell me, not seeing my eyes, if you have had my letter that I wrote before I bit my tongue to prevent myself from saying what I wrote and what I even so must say, because I am the mistress and it lies with me to speak the word you may not speak and may not embolden yourself to utter though the reason has long since become no reason. But I know not whether you would gladly say it, which is the sum of my anguish; for if I knew that you would burn to say it if you could, then I would take the words from your lips and blissfully utter them as your mistress, even though lisping and stammering, with my face hidden on your arm. Say if you had my letter from the dwarf, as I wrote, and did you read it? Were you glad to see my hand, so that all your blood rose in a wave to beat on your soul's shore? Do you love me, Osarsiph, my god in a slave's form, my sublime falcon, as I have loved you, for so long, so long, in bliss and torment, and does your blood burn for mine as mine for yours, so that I had to write the letter, after long struggle; ensnared by the golden bronze of your shoulders and the love all bear you, but above all by the godlike glance, beneath which my body has changed and my breasts become like fruits of love? *Sleep — with me!* Give me, give me your youth and splendour and I will give you bliss undreamed of, for I know what I speak! Let us put our heads and our feet together for our delight, that we may together die of our mutual bliss, for no longer can I bear it that we live together as two! "

Thus the woman spoke, in her abandonment. I have not imitated the actual sound of her plea and the lisping of her cloven tongue, for every syllable cut her like a knife, yet she lisped it all in one breath against his arm — for women can bear great pain. But so much must be clearly envisaged and settled: that the word of mistaking, the incisive phrase which has been handed down, did not issue from the sound lips of a grown person, but was thrust through and through by pain and spoken as a child speaks: " Thleep — with me! " she said. For this was the purpose of the mangling of her tongue.

And Joseph? He sat and ran over his seven reasons in his mind, conning them forwards and back. I would not assert that his blood did not rise in a wave to beat on the shore of his soul. But it met the wall of his seven reasons and they held firm. To his credit be it said, that he did not turn harshly against her or treat the witch with

contempt because she tempted him to destroy himself
with God; but was mild and gentle and sought in all
honour to console her, despite the danger to himself
which, as anyone can see, lay in such a course. For
where, once begun, would the consolations end? He did
not even pull away his arm, regardless of the humid heat
of her breath as she lisped and the touch of her lips, but
left it where it was while she lisped herself out, and even
a little longer, while he replied:

"What do you, my mistress, with your face hidden on
my arm, and what are you saying in the fever of your
wound? Come to yourself, I implore you; for you forget yourself and me! For consider: your room is open,
and we might be seen, by a dwarf or by some ordinary
man, who would spy where you have your head — forgive me, for if you permit I must now take my arm away
and see if outside — "

He did as he said. She, too, lifted herself, but with
violence, from the place where his arm no longer was,
and stood stiffly erect, with flashing eyes and suddenly
ringing voice, crying out words which should have taught
him with whom he had to deal and what he might expect
from her who but now had been crushed and imploring,
and now seemed to lift her claws like a lioness. For the
moment she did not even lisp; for when she bore the
pain she could force her tongue, and she cried out with
great distinctness:

"Leave the hall open that the whole world may look in
upon me and you, whom I love! Are you afeared? I fear
neither gods nor dwarfs nor men that they see me with
you and spy upon our meeting. Let them come, let them
come in hosts to see us! I will fling to them like trash my

modesty and shame, for they are naught to me but thrash and trumpery compared with what is between us and the world-forgotten need of my soul! Am I afeared? I alone am frightful in my love. Isis am I, and upon him who sees us would I cast a look from my eyes so frightful that he would pale in death upon the spot."

Thus Mut the lioness, unmindful of her wound and the stabbing pain in every word. But he drew the curtains across between the pillars and said:

" Let me then be careful for you, since it is given me to foresee what might happen were we spied upon. For that must be sacred to me which you would fling at the world's feet, which is not worthy of it, not even worthy to die of the scorn of your look."

But when after drawing the curtain he came back to her in the shadow of the room she was no longer a lioness but a lisping child, yet with the wiliness of the serpent too, for she turned round upon him his words and stammered sweetly:

" Have you shut us in, wicked one, enfolding us in shadow against the world, that it may no more protect me against your harshness? Ah, Osarsiph, how cruel you are, that you have so namelessly bewitched me and changed my body and soul, that I know myself no more! What would your mother say if she knew how you bewitch human beings and make them so that they know themselves no more? Were son of mine so lovely and so evil, and I might see him in you, my lovely, evil son, my sun-youth, whom I bore and who at midday puts head and feet together with his mother to beget himself upon her anew! Osarsiph, do you love me upon earth as in heaven? Have I painted your soul when I painted the letter I sent you, and did your inwards quake as you read, as I too shuddered to my innermost soul with unquenchable shame and desire as I wrote? When you dupe me with your mouth, calling me the sovereign of your head and your heart — what does that mean? Do you say it because it is fitting, or in fervent sincerity? Confess to me here in the shadow! After so many nights of torturing doubt, when I lay alone, lay without you, and my blood cried out helplessly, you must heal me, my saviour, and redeem me, confessing that you spoke the lying language of beauty but to tell me the truth of your love!"

Joseph: "Not so, great lady. . . . But yes, as you say — yet spare yourself, if I must believe you look on me with favour; spare yourself and me, I implore, for it pierces my heart to hear you force your injured tongue to shape your words, instead of cooling it with balsam. To shape cruel words! How could I not love you, you, my mistress? Upon my bended knees I love you; upon my bended knees I beg you not to pry into the nature of that love, its humbleness and fervour, its reverence and sweetness, but graciously let it rest in its component parts which make up a delicate and precious whole, underserving of untwisting and unravelling in pitiless curiosity. No, bear with me still and let me tell you. . . . Gladly you hearkened when I spoke before you in many matters — hear me then in this. For a good servant loves his master, if he be noble, for so is it ordained. But when the master becomes mistress and a lovely woman, then there comes a great sweetness and adoring fervour into the love and permeates it — it is humility and sweetness, which are adoring tenderness, ardour, and inward imprecation against the cruel one who would approach it too closely with prying touch and angry glance — for that cannot come to good. When I call you sovereign of my head and heart, surely it is for the form's sake and fitting. But how sweet that it is fitting so to speak — there lies a mystery which must be veiled in delicate silence. Is it then gracious or wise to break the silence and ask my meaning, leaving me in my answer a choice between a lie and a sin? That is a false and cruel choice, I can none of it. And I beg you on my knees that you will show kindness and mercy to the life of the heart! "

The woman: " O Osarsiph, you are frightful in your speaking beauty, which makes you appear godlike before men so that they serve you, yet the art of your speaking drives me to despair. That is a terrible deity, your art, child of intelligence and beauty; a mortal spell for the unhappily loving heart. You chide me for speaking, yet you speak in eloquent chiding, and say that beauty must be silent and not speak; that there must be silence about beauty as about the holy grave at Abdu, for love shall be silent like death, yes, in silence they are like each other and speaking wounds them. You demand that I show kindness and mercy to the life of the heart, and would seem to be on its side against my unravelling curiosity. But that is to turn the world upside down; for it is I who in my sore need fight for the life of the heart when I am driven to examine it. What else shall I do, beloved, and how help myself? I am mistress to you, my lord and saviour, for whom I yearn, and I cannot spare your heart nor let your love rest in peace for pity of it. I must be cuel, I must lay siege to it as the bearded man

lays siege to the tender maiden who does not know herself, and must wrest fervour from her humility and desire from her meekness, that she may be bold and able to
grasp the thought that you sleep close beside me, for
therein lies all the salvation of the world that you do so
with me; it is a question of bliss or the torment of hell.
It has become for me the torment of hell that our limbs
are separate, yours there and mine here; and if you only
speak of your knees I am seized with unspeakable jealousy of them, that they are yours and not also mine, and
they must be near to me, that you sleep with me or I perish and am destroyed! "

Joseph: "Dear child, that cannot be, let your servant
implore you to consider and not cling fixedly to this idea,
for it is born of evil. You put an exaggerated, a morbid
value upon the idea that dust must lie close to dust; it
would be lovely for a moment, but that it would outweigh
the evil consequences and all the remorse coming after
could be true only in your fevered dream. Lo, it is not
good and could never come to good that you should lay
siege to me as the bearded man and woo me as your
mistress for the satisfaction of my love. There is an
abomination in it, it is unfitting to our days. For I am
not slave enough for that, and I can myself conceive the
idea — only too well, I assure you; yet may we not bring
it to pass, for more than one reason, many more than one,
a great number of them, like the constellation in the image of the bull. I beg you to understand that I may not
set my teeth in the lovely apple which you offer me, that
we should eat transgression and lose all. Therefore I
speak and am not silent, take it kindly of me, my child,

for since I may not be silent with you I must speak and choose consoling words, for your consolation, dearest mistress, lies close to my heart."

The woman: " Too late, Osarsiph; too late for you and for us both. You cannot retreat, nor I, for we are mingled. Have you not drawn the curtains and shut us in together in shadow apart from the world, so that we are paired together? Do you not already say ' we ' and ' us ' — ' we might be seen,' drawing yourself and me together in sweet union in this precious word, the figure of all the bliss I offer you, which is already comprehended in it so that the act has no new element after we have said ' we,' for we have a secret together against all the world and are two together with it apart from the world, and naught remains but to — "

Joseph: " No, but hear me, my child, that is not true, and you do violence to truth, so that I must resist! It was your self-forgetfulness forced me to draw the curtain, for your honour's sake, that it might not be seen from the court where your head was lying. And now you will so turn it that naught is any matter and the act already done because we have a secret and must shut ourselves in with it! That is not true, for I have no secret, I would but protect yours; and only in this sense can there be talk of we and us, and nothing has happened nor can, for a whole constellation of reasons."

The woman: " Osarsiph, sweet liar! You will deny our union and our secret, when you have but now confessed that you could but too well understand my wooing, since it lay all too near to your heart? Is that, wicked one, to have no secret together from the world? Do you then not think of me as I think of you? But how would you think of me and of lying with me if you could once imagine the pleasure that awaits you, my golden sun-boy, in the arms of your heavenly goddess! Let me tell you and promise you in your ear, shut away from all the world, in shadowy depths, what awaits you! For I have never loved, never received a man into my body, have never given even the smallest part of the treasure of my love; it is all treasured up for you, and you shall be so extravagantly rich with it as you could never dream! Hearken to what I whisper: for you, Osarsiph, my body has changed and been transformed to a vessel of love from tip to toe; when you come to me and yield me the glory of your youth, you will not believe that you lie next a human woman, but will satisfy the lust of a god with mother, wife, and sister, for lo, I am she! I am the oil that craves your salt that the lamp may burn bright in the feast of night! I am the meadow that thirsts after you and the flood of your manhood's water, bull of your mother, that you swell above her and over her in espous-ing me, before you leave me, beautiful god, and forget your lotus wreath beside me in the moist earth! Hear, hear now what I whisper. For with every word I draw you deeper into the mystery which we share, and you can no longer withdraw, for we are in the thick of it together, so that there can be no reason in withholding what I ask."

Joseph: " Yes, dearest child — forgive me that I call you so, since we are so far, certainly, in a secret together that I had to draw the curtain because of your distraction; but it has its good sense, and sevenfold, that I must refuse your honeyed suggestion; for it is marshy ground upon which you would lure me, where nothing grows but wild grass, no corn; and would make of me an adulterous ass,

of yourself a roving bitch. Then how shall I not protect
you against yourself, and myself against the vile transformation? Consider how it would be with us if we were
seized of our crime and it fell upon our heads? Shall I
let it come to this, that they strangle you and throw your
body to the dogs, or cut off your nose? One cannot think
of it. But the ass's share would be uncounted beatings, a
thousand blows for his senseless lechery, if he were not
thrown to the crocodiles. These corrections threaten us
if our deed take possession of our souls."

The woman: "O cowardly boy, if you but let yourself
dream of the bliss that awaits you by my side, you would
think no further, but laugh at punishment, for whoever
meted it out it could not measure to the height of our
joy!"

"Yet behold," he said, "dear friend, how madness
reduces you for a time below the level of the human! For
its advantage and special property it is to think beyond
the moment and consider what comes after. Nor would
I fear at all—"

They were standing close together in the darkened
room, speaking softly but urgently like people who de-
bate something of great moment, with lifted brows, faces
flushed with excitement.

"Nor would I fear at all," he was saying, "the punishment for you and me, that were the least of it. But I
fear Petepre, our master, himself, not his punishments,
as one fears God, not on account of the evil He can visit
on one, but Himself, in the fear of God. From him have
I all my light, and what I am here in house and land I
owe to him. How should I then dare to tread before him
and look into his mild eyes, though I had no punishment

to fear, after I had lain with you? Hearken, Eni, and in God's name recall your understanding for that which I would say, for my words will stand, and when our story comes into the mouths of the people, so will it sound. For all that happens can become history and literature, and it may easily be that we are the stuff of history. Therefore have a care for yourself and take pity upon your story, that you do not become a warning in it and the mother of sin. Much could I say, and give words to many involved matters, to resist your desire and mine own; but for the people's mouth, should it come to be put into it, will I say the simplest and most pertinent thing, which every child can understand, thus: *My master hath committed all that he hath to my hand; there is none greater in this house than I; neither hath he kept back anything from me but thee, because thou art his wife. How then can I do this great wickedness, and sin against God?* These are the words which I say to you for all the future, against the desire which we have for each other. For we are not alone in the world, to enjoy the flesh the one of the other, for there is also Petepre, our great master, in his loneliness, against whom we may not act, instead of doing loyal service to his soul, nor affront him with such an act, which could bring to shame his sensitive dignity and break the bond of loyalty. He stands in the way of our bliss, and that is an end."

"Osarsiph," she whispered close behind him, and girded herself up to make a proposal. "Osarsiph, my beloved, who are long since joined with me in a mystery, hearken and understand your Eni aright. I could — I could . . ."

This was the moment which revealed why and to what

end Mut-em-enet had bitten her tongue; and what were
the long-since-ready words for which she had prepared it
that it might utter them in the most beguiling, helpless,
and pathetic guise. Not only the words of the offer —
that came first but not last; for the final and actual ones,
for which she had taught her tongue to lisp like a child,
were meant for the proposal she now made, laying on his
shoulder the lovely masterpiece that was her hand, blue-
veined and decked with precious stones, and nestling her
cheek to it as she said, sweetly, with pouting lips:

" But I might kill him."

He started back. The prettiness of it was too much
for him, he would never have thought of it nor expected
it of her, even after he had seen her lift her lioness paws
and heard her hoarse breath: " Frightful am I alone! "

She nestled to him as he shrank away. " We could kill
him and put him out of the way, what ith there to that,
my falcon? It ith nothing. Tabubu could brew me in a
twinkling a clear decoction or crystalline deposit of mysterious powers; I would give it you in your hand to shake
into the wine he drinks to warm his flesh, but when he
drinks he would grow cold by degrees and no one perceive anything, thanks to the skill of the Negro lands in
brewing such potions; and he embarks for the West and
is out of the world and can no longer stand in the way of
our bliss. Let me only do this, beloved, and revolt not
against so simple a measure. For is not his flesh dead
already while he lives, is it of any use but to flourish
and increase to no end? How I hate his lazy flesh, since
my love for you has lacerated my heart and made my
own flesh to a vessel of love — I cannot say, I can only
shriek it. So, sweet Osarsiph, let us make him cold, for

it is a little thing. Or is it something to you, to knock down a fungus with a stick, some foul tindery mushroom or puff-ball? That is nothing to do, to do away with such. But when he is in his grave and the house empty of him, then are we free and alone, blissful vessels of love, unbound to consequences, and may embrace each other, fearless, mouth on mouth. For you are right, my divine boy, to say that he stands in the way of our joy and we may do naught to him — you are right in your misgiving. But just therefore must you see that we must make him cold and send him out of the world, that the misgiving may be satisfied and we do him no more harm in our embracing. Do you understand, my little one? Picture to yourself our raptures and how it will be when the mushroom is struck down and put out of the way and we are alone in the house, and you, in all your youth, are its master. You the master, because I am the mistress, for he who sleeps with the mistress is the master. And we shall drink of bliss by night, and in the day rest beside each other on purple cushions and breathe incense of nard, while garlanded girls and youths posture before us and play on their lutes, while we lie and dream of the night that was and the night that will be. For I will hand you the cup, where we shall drink from one and the same place, with our lips on its golden rim, and as we drink, our eyes will meet in the thought of the delight which we had the past night and that which we plan for this night, and we put our feet together — "

" Hearken now, Mut in the valley of desolation," said he. " For I must conjure you — that is an expression, but I mean it literally, I must conjure you in all truth, or rather the demon that speaks out of you and by whom you

are clearly possessed, for so it must be. Little pity have
you for your legend, I must say; for you give yourself the
name of mother of sin, for all future times. But remember that we are perhaps, yes, very likely, in a saga; then
pull yourself together! For I too, as you can see, must do
the same against your urging of delights, though it is
easier for me because of my horror at your mad proposal
to murder Petepre, my master and your husband. That is
a frightful thing. It lacks only that you tell me that we
are together also in this secret because you have im-
parted to me your thought, and that it is now mine. But
it is my case and concern that it shall remain but a thought
and that we shall make no such history as that! Dear
Mut! I have no liking to your proposal that we live here
together thus in your house after we have done away with
its master. When I think how I should live, in the house
of murder with you, as the slave to your love, and derive
my mastership from that, I feel self-contempt! Shall I
not wear a woman's garment from Byssus and you command me every night for your lust, a master seduced to
murder his father that he might sleep with his mother?
For just so would it be with me: Potiphar, my lord, is to
me like a father; were I to live with you in the house of
murder it would be as though I lived with my mother.
Therefore, dear, good child, I conjure you, in all friendliness, console yourself and incite me not to such an evil
deed!"

" Fool! Fool and child! " she answered in her ringing
tones. " How like a foolish boy you answer in your fear,
which as your mistress in love I must break down! With
his mother each man sleeps — the woman is the mother
of the world, her son is her husband, and every man be-

gets upon his mother — do you not know, must I teach you these simple things? Isis am I, the Great Mother, and wear the vulture hood, and you shall name me your name, sweet son, in the sacred sweetness of the begetting night — "

"No, no, not so!" he cried. " It is not as you say, I must correct you. The Father of the world is no mother's son, nor is he the Lord by a lady's grace. To Him I belong, before Him I walk, the son of my father, and once for all I tell you I will not so sin against God the Lord, to whom I belong, to shame my father and murder him and pair with my mother like a shameless hippopotamus. — Now, my child, I must go. Dear mistress, I beg your leave. I will not forsake you in your distraction, surely not. I will console you with words and speak to you kindly as I can, for that I owe you. But now must I take my leave and go to look after my master's house."

He left her. She cried after him:

"Do you think to escape me? Do you think we shall escape each other? I know, I know already of your zealot god to whom you are sealed and whose wreath you wear. But I fear no stranger god and I will tear your wreath, of whatever it is made, and give you to wear a wreath of ivy and vine for the mother-feast of our love! Stay, beloved! Stay, loveliest of the lovely! Stay, Osarsiph, stay!"

And she fell down and wept.

He parted the curtains with his hands and went quickly out. But in their folds as he thrust them to right and left, on each side was a dwarf; one named Dudu, the other little Shepses-Bes, for they had found themselves together, stealing up from either side to listen; they stood there, each with one hand on his knee, the other to his ear, eagerly listening, the first out of malice, the second trembling with fright. And each ever and anon shook his fist at the other and gnashed his teeth, beckoning him to go away. Neither had stirred, though each had been no little hindrance to the other in hearing; yet neither had left the field.

And behind Joseph, emerging from the folds, they flew at each other with hisses, fists raised to their temples, choking with fury, deadly in their enmity because they were like in kind yet so different in nature.

" What business have you got here? " panted Dudu, spouse of Djeset, " you hunch-back, you mite, you empty little barley-corn! You must crawl hither to this crack, where I alone have a right and claim to be, and will not budge however much I sign to you to make yourself scarce! You miller's thumb, you cod's head, you shotten herring! I will thrash you till you cannot stir a leg, you worm, you misbegotten, crawling vermin! You must come sneaking and spying hither, you empty bladder, and stand guard for your master and crony, the pretty-phiz, the bastard from the swamps, the scum he brought into the house to shame it, taking the upper hand till it is a disgrace to the two lands, and on top of all making a thing of the mistress — "

" Oh, oh, you villain, you bully, you vile mischief-making devil! " piped the other, his little face flawed into a thousand wrinkles with rage, his ointment-cone askew on his head. " Who is it here lurking and listening to the devilry which he himself has brewed with his billets-doux and his playing with fire, feasting his eyes at a crack on the torture and agony of the big folk, that they may be snared in destruction according to his shameless scheming — who but you, you pouch-mouth, you moocher, you scullion, — oh, you scarecrow, you jumping-jack, you busnacker, with nothing about you of dwarf or giant but just one thing, you walking dardsman, you much-married knave — "

"Wait! " the other gave back shrilly. " Wait, you less than nothing, you atomy, you loss-and-lack, you worthless nocky! Away from this spot where Dudu guards the honor of the house, or I will disgrace you with my manly weapon, wretch, and give you something to remember! What shame awaits you now, if I go to Petepre and tell him what goes on here in the dark, and what sort of words the steward whispers to the mistress in the curtained room — that you shall soon learn! You brought him into the house, the good-for-nothing, not resting from your little tittle-tattle before the departed Mont-kaw; boasting of your keen eye for goods and men and goods in men, till he bought the knave from the other knaves against my advice and set him here in the house to dishonour the mistress and make a cuckold of Pharaoh's eunuch. You are to blame for the mess, you above all, and in the very beginning. You are due to the crocodile, and shall be served up to him as a tidbit and sweetmeat after they feed him your bosom friend when they have bound and beaten him."

" Oh, oh, you foul-mouth! " railed the little one, trembling and writhing with rage. " You backbiter, whose words come not out of his understanding but rise out of unknown depths and are slavering obscenity! I dare you to touch me, or make any attempt to disgrace me, else, though I am only a poor dwarf, you shall feel my nails in your face and the hollows of your eyes, for

they are sharp, and to the pure weapons are given against
the vicious. I, a little dwarf, guilty of the agony and
affliction there within? Guilty is the evil thing, the all-
devouring pestilence wherein you boast yourself a master; and have used it to the devilish ends of your hatred
and envy, to dig a pit for Osarsiph, my friend. But see
you not, you goat-dwarf, that you have failed, for no
lack showed itself in my beautiful one? Since you listened, you must have heard that he was constant as a
novice before the mysteries, and heroically defended
his saga? What else have you heard at your crack, and
what misheard, since your dwarf-ear has lost all its
cunning and sharpness and become thick and stupid with
playing the cock? I should like to know what you would
or could tell the master of Osarsiph, when your dull ears
could have caught nothing important at your eavesdropping."

"Oho!" Dudu cried out. "The husband of Djeset
can vie with you, weak wight, in sharpness of ear and
hearing, when the matter is one he is at home in, while
you, you chirruping lack-brain, have no understanding
of it at all! Have you not heard the billing and cooing
there within, and how the fine little pair were calling and
prancing like birds when they mate? My ear is good for
all that; it heard him call her ' dear child,' and ' little
treasure,' the slave the mistress, but she said ' falcon '
and ' bull ' in the most honeyed tones. I heard them con-
niving how they would enjoy each other's flesh and blood.
Do you not see that Dudu is not wanting as a witness?
But the best thing I heard as I listened is that they made
up, in their heat, to bring about Petepre's death, to lay
him low with a club — "

"You lie, you lie! For it is plain you have heard but the crassest nonsense at your post and will tell Petepre the sheerest lies about them both. For my youth called the mistress child and friend out of simple goodness and kindness to soothe her in her distraction, and honourably dissuaded her from her plan of felling even a puff-ball with a stick. Marvellously did he bear himself for his years, and as yet not the smallest blemish comes into his legend despite all those sweet blandishments."

"And so you think, crab-louse, that I could not accuse him just the same and ruin him with the master? There is precisely the trick of it, and my trump card in this game, of which a puppet like you understands nothing at all. For it matters not a scrap how the fool behaves, more properly or more lustfully; the point is that the mistress is head over ears in love with him and has no room for thought save how to bill and coo — and therein lies his ruin, from which nothing can save him. A slave about whom the mistress is crazy — he simply goes to the crocodiles, nothing else for him, and that is just the game. If he yields and makes love to her, I have him. But if he refuses, then he but pricks her madness and it is even worse, he is for the crocodile either way, or at best for the knife, which will ruin his bill for cooing and cure the mistress of her fit."

"Oh, you monster, you blasphemer!" shrieked Shepses-Bes. "You are the best case in the world of what abomination can come and straddle about on this earth when one of the race of dwarfs loses his rightful goodness and fineness and tries to take on full-grown dignity. For such a one is a rascal like you, you runagate, you coney-hunter, you — "

To which Dudu retorted that when the knife had been wielded, then Osarsiph would be a better match for his emasculate friend. Thus the two pigmies expended themselves in mutual reviling, until the courtyard folk ran together. Then they parted; the one to report Joseph to the master, the other to seek his friend and warn him, that he might still try by some means to escape from the pit.

DUDU'S COMPLAINT

POTIPHAR, as everybody knew, could not abide Dudu — on the ground of the pompousness he saw in the stout little man. The Osiris Mont-kaw had always been irritated by the dwarf, and for the same reason. I have said already that the courtier held at a distance the keeper of his jewel-chests; did not see him if he could help it, and interposed other servants between them — people of the regulation size, who for that reason were better able to dress and undress that towering form and adorn it, whereas Dudu would have had to use a pair of steps. But aside from that, being of the same size as other people, they laid less stress on certain natural gifts and sunpowers and assumed less dignity on account of them than Dudu did, to whom they amounted to a lifelong marvel and proud distinction.

Thus it was by no means easy for the pygmy to arrive at speech with the master, now that he had at last decided to take the bypath which branched off from the road so assiduously trodden between mistress and steward. He did not succeed all at once, after that quarrel with the mock-vizier before the curtained room; not days but weeks had he to wait, to announce himself, before he got audience. He, the scribe of the jewels, had to bribe the slaves, or else threaten them that he would withhold this or that dress or ornament, would simply not unlock his wardrobes, so that they would get into trouble with the master, if they did not force it upon his notice that Dudu would and must speak to him on a very weighty domestic concern. A whole quarter of a moon he had to work, beg, cajole, and storm before he achieved the favour of an audience, which he the more ardently desired because he thought that, once exploited, there would be an end to his troubles; such a service as he meant to render the master must ensure him the latter's abiding favour.

The indomitable creature had plied two of the slaves of the bath with presents, to the end that with every jug of water which they poured over their puffing master's shoulders and chest they should repeat: " Master, remember Dudu! " They said it again when the dripping tower of flesh stepped out of the sunken basin on to the tiled floor to be dried with perfumed towels; one after the other: " Master, remember Dudu! " until in exasperation he said: " Let him come and speak before me! " They signed to the slaves who were waiting in the bedchamber to anoint and massage; these had likewise been bribed, and summoned the dwarf out of the western hall, where he was like to die with impatience, into the room with the bed standing in a niche. He raised his little palms aloft, toward the kneading-bench, where Pharaoh's friend stretched himself out and gave his flesh to the ministrations of the slaves. Dudu's dwarf-head drooped meekly to one side between his lifted arms, as he awaited a syllable from Petepre's mouth or a glance from his eye.

But neither came; the master only grunted softly as the slaves attacked his flesh, working his shoulders, hips, and thighs, the fat feminine arms and fleshy bosom with oil of nard, even turning the small fine head the other way as it lay on the leather cushion, so that it did not look at Dudu. That was vexatious; but his affair was so hopeful that he would not desist or be cast down.

" May your destiny endure a thousand years," he said, " first of mankind, warrior of the highest! Four jars for your entrails, and for your abiding image a coffin of alabaster! "

"Thanks," Petepre answered him. He said it in Babylonian, as we might say " *Merci*," and added: " Will the man take long with what he has to say? "

" The man " was bitter. But Dudu's hopes were too high, he would not be abashed.

" Not long, my sun and master," he gave answer. " Rather, briefly and to the point."

And at a sign from Petepre's little hand he put one foot before him, laid his stumpy arms on his back, and began, his nether lip drawn in, the other sticking out over it like a thatch. He knew that he could not say all that he had to say before the slaves, but felt sure that Petepre would soon dismiss them to listen in private.

His beginning might be called skilful — except that it lacked in fine feeling. He began with praise of Min, god of the harvest, who in some localities was honoured as a form of the sun-power, but had had to name his name to Amun-Re and became, as Amun-Min or Min-Amun-Re, one person with him, so that Pharaoh as readily spoke of " my father Min " as of " My father Amun," especially at the harvest festival or the feast of the crowning, when

the Min aspect of Amun was predominant and he became
the fruitful god, protector of desert wanderers, towering
in feathers and mighty in procreative power, the ithy-
phallic sun. Him then Dudu evoked in all his dignity,
appealing to him as he implored the countenance of his
master, in that he, as upper servant of the house and
scribe of the master's wardrobe, did not confine his zeal
for his office to the narrower round of his duties but, husband and father as he was, author of the being of two
well-proportioned children, called so-and-so, to whom,
unless all signs failed and there was nothing in the coy
confession which Djeset his wife whispered to him, a
third would soon be added — as he was saying, then, he,
who had himself given increase to the house and was
bound by especial reverence to the majesty of Min (and
thus to Amun in his Min aspect), gave an eye to the welfare of the house in general and in particular from the
point of view of human fruitfulness and propagation. He
had taken under his special protection and supervision
everything that came to pass in the household in this field:
all such happy events as marriages and consummations,
bringing home the bride, fertility of the womb, childbed
and so on; encouraging all the household folk in such
activities, spurring them on and in his own person setting
them an example of diligence and established order. For
much depended upon a good example from those in authority — not quite the highest authority, of course, for
naturally, where nothing could be taken upon oneself,
this could not either. So much the more important and
necessary was it that precautions be taken to avoid disturbing the sacred tranquillity of that apex of their household structure which stood above the need of setting an

example. But those just beneath him were, in his, Dudu's, opinion, bound to lead an exemplary life, not only orderly but also diligent in the activities before-mentioned. He hoped that thus far the speaker had the approval of his lord and sun.

Petepre shrugged his shoulders and rolled over on his belly, to give the rubbers a chance to work on his massive back. But he lifted his small, well-shaped head to ask what Dudu meant by his words about disturbing the master's tranquillity, and the remarks about dignity and the reverse.

"Your upper servant will come to that at once," replied the dwarf. And spoke of the departed Mont-kaw, whose course of life had been so upright, and who had married early the child of a state official and would have become a father had not fate dealt hardly by him and shattered his prospects, so that well-meaning as he was, he had ended his days as a downcast widower. So much for Mont-kaw. But now he would speak of the brightness of the present, bright in so far that the deceased had found a successor of equal standing, or, if not quite equal, being a foreigner, yet not inferior to him in gifts, and they had welcomed to the headship over the house a youth of very considerable parts. His name, to be sure, had a somewhat decadent sound; but his face was ingratiating, he talked well and seemed astute — in short, an individual of very evident advantages.

"Ass!" muttered Petepre into his folded arms. For nothing sounds sillier to us than praise of an object whose true worth we think ourselves better able to gauge than anyone else.

Dudu pretended not to hear. The master may have

called him an ass, but it was better to take no notice, in
order to keep up his courage.

He could not, he said, give enough praise to the fasci-
nating, yes, really dazzling and for some people distract-
ing qualities of the youth in question. For it was just
these which gave weight to the anxiety he, Dudu, felt for
the stability and well-being of the household, to the headship of which these qualities had raised the young man.

"What is he jabbering about?" Petepre said, lifting
his head a little and turning it in the direction of the rub-
ber. "The steward's qualities threaten the stability of
the household?"

Jabbering was pretty bitter too. But the dwarf was not
to be put off.

They need not, in the least, under other circumstances,
be anything but a blessing to the house; that is, if they
were legally circumscribed and ameliorated — or, still
better, had been so circumscribed beforehand. For such
qualities — such an attractive face, such astuteness and
eloquence — could otherwise become the source of much
unrest, ferment, and derangement in their vicinity. And
Dudu expressed regret that the youthful steward, whose
religious affiliations were quite obscure, had refrained
from paying due tribute to the majesty of Min, had remained unmarried in his high office and not taken to himself a bedfellow suitable to his birth — for instance the
Babylonian slave Ishtarummi of the house of women —
and added his offspring to the children in the courtyard.
That was regrettable, it was bad, it was serious — it was
even dangerous. For not alone did the household suffer
diminution to its state, but a bad example was set in the
point of stability and fruitfulness. And even that was not

the worst. For, thirdly, there was, so to speak, no check upon the beguiling charms which undeniably the young steward possessed, and of which they stood in such need and had for a long time needed, to guard against their inflammable, head-turning, sense-destroying effect upon the household; to prevent them, in short, from sowing the wind not only upon their own social level but also in spheres far above it.

There was a pause. Petepre lent himself to be massaged and did not answer. It was either — or, Dudu declared. Such a young man must either submit to the marriage yoke, so that his gifts might not strew destruction like wildfire throughout the house, but be brought into the peaceful haven of wedlock; or else it would be better to wield the knife as a preventive measure and effect the sanative neutralization which would secure exalted persons from the disturbance of their rest and preserve their honour and dignity unscathed.

Another silence. Petepre suddenly turned on his back, so that the masseurs working upon him were interrupted and stood with their hands in the air. He lifted his head toward the dwarf, measuring him from head to foot and back again — a short distance for Petepre's eyes — and then glanced over to the armchair where lay his clothes, his sandals, his fan, and other insignia. Then he rolled round again, his head in his arms.

He was filled with a cold, shuddering anger, a sort of outraged alarm at the threat to his peace of mind from this disgusting hop-o'-my-thumb. Obviously the misbegotten fool knew something and wanted to tell it to him. And if it was true, certainly he, Petepre, had to know it; though he felt that to be told it was the grossest unkindness. "Is all well in the house? Naught untoward has happened? Is the mistress happy?" Yes, that was it; he was going to be given the wrong answer to the question. He hated the man — this man, most of all, not being prepared to hate anybody else, and aside from any question of the truth of what the dwarf would say. He would have to send away the masseurs and be alone with this valiant little guardian of his honour, to let him rouse it up, whether with truth or with calumny. Honour: what was that, in the present connection? It was sexual honour, the honour of the cock, which consists in the faithfulness of the hen, as a sign that he is a complete specimen of cockishness, from whom she will get such satisfaction that it will never occur to her to take up with anyone else nor would she be tempted by the advances of any other cock, no matter how well equipped. But if this happens, and she has to do with another, everything is altered: there is sexual dishonour, the cock becomes a cuckold, which is as good as saying he becomes a capon. He is made ridiculous with horns which she sets on his head, and if anything is still to be saved he must save it by running a sword through the rival whom she hoped to enjoy, and perhaps better yet by killing her too, in order by that striking and sanguinary deed to re-establish his self-respect in his own eyes and those of the world.

Honour. Petepre had no honour whatever. He lacked it in his very flesh, he had no comprehension of what this cockish attribute might be; and it seemed frightful to him when others, for instance this pompous little scribe, wanted to make much of it. But he had a heart, one capable of doing justice; that is, he had a sense of the rights of others. It was a sensitive heart, dependent upon the love and loyalty of others. He hoped for their love and, being betrayed, was so constituted as to suffer bitterly. During this pause, while the masseurs set to work again on his tremendous back and he kept his face buried in his fat feminine arms, all sorts of thoughts coursed through his mind. They had to do with two persons on whose love and loyalty he so fervently built that one might say he loved them: Mut, his chief wife, whom he hated a little too, because of the reproach which of course she could not utter and yet did by her very existence utter none the less; to whom he would dearly have liked to show himself strong and loving; and Joseph, who did him so much good, who knew how to make him feel better than wine, and for whose sake, to his own great regret, he had had to refuse to show himself strong and loving to his wife in that twilight hour in the western hall. Petepre was not without an intuition of what he had then refused her. To tell the truth, even during that conjugal conversation he had been vaguely aware that the reasons she gave for her request were only a pretext, the real ground being fear of herself and for his honour. But since he lacked that kind of honour, her fear had seemed less important to him than the retaining of the youth who did him good. He had preferred him to her; and by abandoning his wife to her fear he had challenged them both to prefer each other and betray him.

He saw all that. And it wounded him, for he had a heart. Yet he saw it, for that heart was inclined to fairness, if perhaps only out of indolence, and because fairness can counteract anger and thirst for revenge. Probably he felt, too, that it is also the safest refuge of dignity. Evidently this hateful guardian of his honour was try-

ing to tell him that his dignity was being betrayed by
treachery. As though, he thought, dignity ceased to be
dignity when it had to hide its head and suffer from
treachery! As though the betrayed were not more dignified than the betrayer! But if he is not, because he has
himself incurred guilt and invited treachery, yet justice,
fair-mindedness, is always there, so that dignity may
find in it its own guilt and the rights of others and there
establish itself anew.

So then Petepre, the eunuch, strove after justice —
at once and before everything else, whatever might be
brought up against him from the side of honour. Justice
is a spiritual quality, by contrast with the fleshliness of
honour; and as he lacked the latter he was perforce, he
knew, thrown back upon justice. It was on the spiritual
he had relied, with both of these who now, as this informer and intriguant seemed to want to tell him, had
broken their faith. So far as he knew, both were secured
by powerful spiritual considerations against the flesh,
for they were both set apart and in the spirit belonged together: the woman, with all her compensations, Amun's
wife and bride of his temple, who danced before him
in the narrow garment of the goddess; and the devoted
youth with the wreath of consecration in his hair, the
boy " touch-me-not." Had the flesh mastered them? He
grew cold with terror at the thought, for the flesh was
his enemy, despite his superfluity of it; and always, when
he came home and asked: " Is all well? Naught untoward has happened? " his subconscious anxiety had
been lest the flesh have somehow gained the mastery over
the forbearing, careful, yet not trustworthy bond of the
spirit and brought about some frightful disruption. But

his cold shivers did not exclude some anger too; for did
he have to know, could they not have left him in peace
anyhow? If those two dedicated persons had been overpowered by the flesh behind his back and had secrets
from him, yet in that very secrecy and betrayal lay a forbearing love for which he was very ready to be grateful.
But for that creature there, the pompous little guardian
of honour, who was trying to give him unasked-for en-
lightenment and make a vulgar attack upon his peace of
mind — for him he felt nothing but inexpressible dislike.

"Are you nearly done?" he asked. He was thinking
of the masseurs, whom he would have to send away, and
did not want to be compelled by that spy and sneak to do
so against his will. But there was nothing for it. They
were perfect blockheads, you might say that they had
made themselves clods because it suited their calling
to be so. But though certainly they had not understood
a word up to now, nor were any more likely to understand the rest, yet Petepre could scarcely ignore the
silent intimation of his tormentor that he would speak
with him alone. It made him dislike him still more ve-
hemently.

"Go not before you have finished," he said, "and
there is no special need of haste. But if you are done,
give me my sheet and then go when you like."

They would never have understood that they were to
go, whether finished or no; but since they really were,
they smoothed the linen sheet up to their master's chin,
over his ponderous bulk, flung themselves on their faces,
touching their narrow foreheads to the ground, and went
off with arms akimbo, in a sort of waddling trot, which

was evidence enough of their self-satisfied stupidity, were more needed.

"Come closer, my friend," said the chamberlain. "Come as close as you will and find proper for what you have to tell me, for it seems to be something better not shouted to the house-tops, but rather something that brings us to close grips, which I take to be an advantage, whatever else may be said of it. You are a valuable servant, small indeed, far below the average, and in this respect a figure of fun; but you have poise and dignity and qualities which justify you in assuming responsibility beyond the duties of your office, having an eye over the house and especially over its fertility. Not that I remember installing you in this charge, for I do not. But I do so now, for I cannot avoid recognizing your calling to it. If I understood aright, your love and duty urge you to impart to me certain disturbing information in your special field of oversight and accounting, of events which might kindle disorder in the house? "

"That is so," Joseph's enemy replied with emphasis to this address, whose offensive insinuations he swallowed down for the sake of its otherwise encouraging nature. "Loyal and anxious concern bring me before your countenance, to warn you, my lord and my sun, of a danger so pressing that it merited my admission earlier to your presence; for too easily, yes, at any moment it may be too late."

"You alarm me."

"I am sorry. And yet it is my purpose to alarm you, for the danger is imminent, and with all the keen perception of which I am master I cannot, I your servant,

be sure that it is not already too late and your disgrace
already accomplished fact. In that case it would still in
one respect not be too late, for you are still alive."

" So I am threatened with death? "

" With both shame and death."

" I should consider the one welcome could I not avoid
the other," said Petepre grandly. " And whence do these
things threaten me? "

" I have already," responded Dudu, " gone so far in
indicating the source of the danger that it is unmistakable,
unless for an ear too fearful to hear it."

" Your impertinence makes plain to me in what an evil
case I am," retorted Petepre. " Obviously it corresponds
to my situation, and I am reduced to praising the zeal
which is its source. I admit that my fear is insuperable.
Help me, my friend, and tell me the truth so straightfor-
wardly that even my fear has no place to hide from it."

" Very good, then," answered the dwarf, changing his
legs and putting one hand on his hip. " This is your
situation: the unsatisfied and contagious qualities of the
young steward Osarsiph have kindled a fire in the breast
of your wife Mut-em-enet and the flames already with
crackling and smoke lick at the supports of your honour, which are near to collapsing and burying your life
beneath them."

Petepre drew up the linen sheet over his chin and
mouth, as far as his nose.

" You would say," he asked from under the sheet,
" that the mistress and the young steward have not only
cast eyes on each other but that they also threaten my
life? "

" Quite," replied the dwarf. He changed fists with a

bounce. "That is the situation of a man who but late was so great."

"And what evidence," asked the captain in a subdued voice, the sheet going up and down on his mouth, " have you for so frightful a charge? "

"My watchfulness," Dudu gave answer, " my eyes and ears, the penetration which was given me by my zeal for the welfare of the house may be witness, my poor master, for the lamentable and regrettable truth of my revelations. Who can say which of the two — for so must we now speak of these persons who in virtue of their rank are so widely separated — the two, we must say; which of them first cast his eyes upon the other? Yet their eyes met; they lost themselves criminally in each other's depths — and there you have it. We must consider, my master, that Mut-em-enet, in the valley of desolation, is a woman of a lonely bed; as for the steward, he is inflammable and inflaming. What servant would be beckoned in vain by such a mistress? That would presume a love and loyalty to the lady's husband which obviously does not exist in the person of the highest steward but only in the next-lower ranks. Guilt? To what end inquire who first lifted eyes to the other or in whose senses the evil first took root? The young steward's guilt consists not only in his acts but in that he is here at all. His presence in the house kindles and inflames with a fire neither unallayed by lawful wedlock nor made innocuous by the knife. If the mistress is on fire for the slave, it is his existence is at fault, the sin lies at his door, his guilt is the same as though he had made indecent assault upon the innocent, and accordingly should he be served. But this now is the state of things: they have most forward understanding, billets-doux pass between them which I have myself seen, and can vouch for their ardour. Under pretext of consultation on affairs of the house they meet, now here, now there; in the hall of the women, where the mistress has set up an image of Horakhte to please the slave; in the garden and in the garden-house on the mound, yes, even in the mistress's own room in this house — in all these places the pair come together secretly, and long since their talk has ceased to be of open matters, it is vanity and idle billing and cooing. How far they have gone, and if they have yet enjoyed each other's flesh so that it is too late to prevent it and only revenge remains, I cannot say with full and complete certainty. But what I can take upon mine own head, before all the gods and before you, you humiliated man, is certain truth, because with my own ear I heard it as I listened at the crack: that they in their blissful madness appoint and arrange to kill you, striking you with a club on the head; and when you are gone they will live here in the house as master and mistress and indulge their lust on a garlanded bed."

At these words Petepre drew the sheet over his whole head and became invisible. So he stayed for some time, so that Dudu began to feel how long it was, though at first he had enjoyed the sight of the master lying there a formless mass, covered and hidden by his shame. But suddenly he thrust back the sheet to his middle and half sat up, facing the dwarf with his little head propped on his hand.

" I must express my hearty thanks, guardian of my chests," said he, " for these revelations " (he used a Babylonian word, as we might use a French one) " about the saving of my honour, or alternatively about the fact that it is already lost and perhaps nothing but my bare life is left. And I must save it, not for itself, but for the sake of revenge, to which it must be devoted from now on. I am in danger of dwelling on this and losing sight of my due gratitude and recognition of the debt I owe you for your information. For my astonishment at the evidence of your loyalty and love equals the anger and horror which I feel. Yes, I confess my surprise — I know that I ought to moderate it; for how often do not the best things come to us from an unlikely quarter, one perhaps where we have bestowed no great signs of confidence and respect! Still, I cannot get over my surprise. You are after all a misbegotten changeling, a sort of dwarf jester, and hold your office more as a joke than anything else; a type half repulsive and half absurd, and accentuated both ways by your pomposity. Does it not border on the incredible, or even overstep the border, that you should succeed in penetrating into the private affairs of persons who are after me the highest in the house — for instance to read their love-letters which according to your account pass between the mistress and the young steward? Must I — or may I — not doubt the existence of these letters, when it is already unbelievable to me that you should have seen their contents? To do that, my friend, you must have wormed yourself into the confidence of the person who carried them — and how, considering your undeniable repulsiveness, can that seem in the least likely? "

" Your dread," responded Dudu, " of having to believe in your shame and humiliation, my poor master, makes you seek grounds for mistrust of me. But believe me, the grounds are ill-chosen. Though so great is your fear and trembling before the truth, which shows you so mocking and miserable a face, that it is really no wonder. Hear, then, how unfounded are your doubts! I needed not to slip into the confidence of the confidential messenger who carried the wanton letters, for that selected person was myself."

" Simply immense! " said Petepre. " You grotesque little man, so you carried them yourself? My respect grows, even to hear you say it; but it would have to grow still more before I actually believed it. What, you are so far in the mistress's confidence, and on so familiar a footing, that she thus entrusted to your keeping her happiness and her guilt? "

" Certainly," said Dudu, changing legs and fists again with another bounce. " Not only did she give me the letters to carry, but I dictated them to her. For she knows nothing about billets-doux and needed to be instructed in the sweet art."

" Who would have thought it? " murmured the chamberlain, as in surprise. " I see more and more how I have underestimated you, and my respect is growing by leaps and bounds. I assume that you have so acted to have matters come to a head and to see how far the mistress's folly would carry her."

" Of course," Dudu agreed. " Out of love and loyalty to you, my humbled lord. Should I else be standing here to incite you to revenge? "

" But how did you, contemptible and hideous as you appear at first sight, win the friendship and confidence of the mistress and make yourself master of her secret? " Petepre wanted to know.

"They happened at the same time," answered the dwarf. "Both together. For I, as all good people would, felt anger and affliction for Amun, that this foreigner had craftily advanced himself so far in the house; I mistrusted him, and the guile of his nature — not without justice, as you will admit, since he has now betrayed you and shamed your marriage bed, and after you had heaped benefits upon his head, has made you the laughing-stock of the capital and probably of the two lands. In my anger and suspicion I complained to Mut, your wife, about the affront and injustice and pointed out and called attention to the person of the wretch. At first she did not know whom I meant. But soon she hearkened so eagerly to my complaints, and in so contrary a way, speaking so wantonly and amorously under cover of a just concern, that I was not long in knowing that she lusted in her bowels after the youth and was smitten like a very kitchen-maid, having completely surrendered all her pride — for the which his presence is to blame. And if a man like me had not taken hold of the affair and associated himself with it, in order to explode the whole plot at the right moment, it would have been all up with your honour. So seeing your wife's thoughts take such devious ways, I slipped after them like a thief in the night, whom one will catch in the act. I inspired her with the idea of the billets-doux, to tempt her and to try how things were with her and how far she would go; and I found all my expectation exceeded, for by dint of the confidence she reposed in me, because she thought me a man of the world and ready to serve her lust, I learned to my horror that the young steward had inflamed our noble lady so far that she would stop at nothing, and that not only your honour but your life is in immediate danger."

" Ah! " said Petepre. " So you called him to her attention and inspired her acts. Well, so much for the mistress. But even now I simply cannot believe that a man with your drawbacks could have won the steward's trust — that I consider simply impossible."

" Your scepticism, my dear dishonoured lord, must give way before the facts. I consider your dread responsible, but likewise your particular and sacred constitution, which, one must admit, is responsible for all the harm, and which makes it impossible for you to understand people and realize how greatly a man's view of others, and his liking for them, no matter whether they are short or tall, depend on their readiness to serve his pleasure and desires. I needed only to display this readiness and to offer him my services, as a man of the world, as a go-between, between our lady and his lust, to have the fool in the snare. My standing with him was such that he soon kept nothing from me and I was able not only to know all the treacherous dealings of the couple but to lead them on and blow up the fire, that I might see how high it would blaze, to what extreme of guilt they would be led, in which I might trap them. For such a course is prescribed for the guardians of the established order, of which I am a model representative. And by this assiduous conduct I was able to come at their mutual views and the purpose they cherish: namely, that he who sleeps with the mistress of the house is master of it. That, my poor gentleman, is the luxurious and murderous plot which they daily discuss; and from it, from their own lips indeed, they deduce their higher right to fall upon you with a club and do you out of the way, that they may celebrate their feast of roses as mistress and as master of the mistress's love. But when things were so far advanced that I heard this from their own lips, the boil seemed ripe for lancing, so I have come to you, in your abasement and misery, to tell you all, that we may trap them."

"That shall we," said Petepre. "We shall come upon them and overwhelm them with fear — you, my dear dwarf, and I, and their sin shall find them out. What think you we should do with them, what punishment do you find at once painful and pitiable enough to be visited upon them?"

"My judgment is mild," answered Dudu, "at least in respect of our Mut, the lovely sinner; for that she has no bedfellow excuses much; also even though you suffer from their sin, it is not fitting, just between ourselves, for you to make great outcry. Besides, it is as I said: if the mistress loses her head over a slave, the slave is to blame, for it is due to his very presence that the misfortune occurs and he should be the one to pay. Yet even toward him I have some mercy; I would not demand that he be bound and thrown to the crocodiles, though he has richly deserved it by his good and his ill luck. For Dudu thinks not so much of revenge as of repentance and prevention, to make an end of the danger; we should but bind him and let the knife do its work, thus rooting out the cause of the sin, that he become unavailable to Mut-em-enet and his charm have no more meaning in the woman's eyes. I am myself ready to do the deed, if he is properly bound beforehand."

"I find it very dutiful," said Petepre, "that you are

willing to do this too, after all you have done for me. Do you not think that thus justice would in more than one respect be re-established in the world, in that you, by this change, would be advanced in proportion as he is diminished, and put in a position of advantage which must afford you a compensation for his advancement, highly satisfying, considering your peculiar build? "

" There is something in that," Dudu replied, " I will not deny that it might be a consideration, though secondary." And he folded his arms, thrust one shoulder forward, and began to sway to and fro with his front leg going up and down. He seesawed there, nodding his head and looking pertly about as his spirits rose higher and higher.

" But again," went on Petepre, " he could hardly remain at the head of the house after you had revenged yourself thus upon him? "

"No, of course not," laughed Dudu, continuing to posture. "To be at the head of the house and give orders to the household is no office for a chastened criminal. It is the service of a capable and unmutilated man, competent to represent the master in every affair which he cannot and will not take upon himself."

" Then," concluded the captain, "I should know at once the suitable reward for your great service, that I may thank and pay you for your service as spy, and for striving to save me from shame and death."

" I should hope! " cried Dudu, abandoned to arrogance. " I may hope that you will understand my merits and be clear as to their reward and the succession. For it is not too much to say that I have saved you from shame and death, and our lovely sinner as well. She should know that I begged for mercy for her on the ground of her loneliness in bed, giving her her life, so that she has breath only through my favour! For if I choose, and she prove ungrateful, I can publish abroad her shame in city and land, and you would be forced to strangle her after all and lay her delicate body in ashes, or at least to send her back to her family minus her nose and ears. Let her be advised, poor light-of-love; let her turn her jewelled eyes away from unfruitful beauty to bend them upon Dudu, who knows how to console; master of the mistress, stout little steward over all the house! "

And he cast ever blither glances on this side and that into space, wreathed and writhed with shoulders and hips, pranced on his little feet — and, in short, behaved just like a cock at courting time, blind and deaf to his peril, utterly absorbed in his performance. And it befell him too as it befalls the cock. For with one bound Petepre the master was out from under the sheet; quite naked, a tower of flesh with the little head atop. Another bound took him to the chair where his clothes lay, and he swung his cudgel. We have seen this ornamental emblem of office in his hand — or one like it: the thick stick covered with gilded leather, with a pine-cone on top and a gilt wreath round it. It was probably a symbol of power, also probably a fetish and cult-object in female ritual. The master swung it suddenly and let it fall on Dudu's shoulders and back; he beat him until the dwarf was deaf and blind — though on quite other grounds than before — and squealed like a stuck pig.

" Oh, oh! Ow, ow! " he yelled, and writhed at his hips. " Oh, it hurts, it is killing me, my bones are broken, I bleed! Mercy, mercy! Have pity on your faithful servant!" But Petepre had none: "There, that's for you, you shameless spy, you sneak — you snake-in-the-grass, who have confessed to me all your treachery!" And drove him under a rain of blows round and round the bedroom until the faithful servant found the door, took to his legs, and ran.

THE THREAT

AND it came to pass, the story tells us, that Potiphar's wife spake to Joseph day by day and entreated him that he should lie with her. So he gave her occasion, then? Even after the episode of the injured tongue he did not avoid her presence but still came together with her in various places and at various times? He did. He probably had to; for she was the mistress, a female master, and could command his presence when she liked. But also he had promised not to forsake her in her distress, but to console her with words as he alone could, because he owed her that much. He saw this. He was bound to her by the consciousness of his guilt; admitting in his heart that he had light-headedly let things come to this pass, and that his pedagogic plan of salvation had been a very culpable pretence, whose consequences he must now endure and as far as possible amend, however dangerous, difficult, and unlikely any amendment seemed. Shall we then count it to his credit that he did not withdraw his countenance from the smitten one, but " day by day " — or, shall we say, nearly every day — exposed himself to the breath of the fiery bull; that he still dared, and went on daring, to face one of the strongest temptations which have probably ever assailed any youth in the history of the world? Yes, probably; conditionally and in part. Some of his motives were excellent, we may grant him that. His sense of guilt and obligation was praiseworthy; so was his stout-hearted reliance on God and his seven reasons in the hour of need. Perhaps we may respect even the defiance which had begun to guide his conduct, and which demanded of him that he measure the strength of his reason against the madness of this woman. For she had threatened him; she had sworn to tear off the garland he wore for the sake of his God and crown him with her own. He found that shameless, and I must say here that another element came in which in time made him think of the matter as something between his God and the gods of Egypt; just as to her, also, her zeal for Amun gradually became — or was made by others — a ground for her desire. We may understand, we may even approve, his feeling that it was not permitted him to shirk; that he must see the matter through to the bitter end and make it redound to the honour of his God.

All very well. Yet not quite wholly so. For there was an admixture of another motive for his obeying her, going to her and meeting her — and this, he very well knew, was not quite so creditable. Shall I call it curiosity, irresponsibility? The unwillingness to give up the free choice of the bad course, the desire to preserve his freedom for a while yet, though without any intention of deciding on the wrong side? However serious, even dangerous the situation, did he take pleasure in being alone with the mistress, on a certain footing, in calling her " my child " and feeling justified on the ground of her passion and despair? A commonplace assumption, yet justifiable, along with another, more godly or more profound: that product of his fantasy, the highly alluring, deeply thrilling thought, that is, of his death and deification as Osarsiph, and the state of sacred readiness that belonged with it, above which, none the less, there hung the ass's curse.

Enough, then, he went to the mistress. He stuck by her. He suffered her to speak to him day by day and to entreat him: "Lie with me!" He suffered it, I say, for it was no joke and no small matter, to persevere with this woman possessed by desire, to speak kindly to her and yet on his own side to sustain the seven reasons in full force and fend off her demands, despite the sympathy which in some measure flowed toward them from his own dead and deified state. Truly, one is inclined to overlook the less praiseworthy among the motives of the son of Jacob, when one considers the trouble he must have had with the unhappy woman, for she daily so besieged him that he had moments when he understood Gilgamesh, who in furious impatience one day tore out the phallus of the sacred bull and flung it in Ishtar's face.

For she degenerated daily and grew less and less delicate in the importunities with which she besought him that they might put their heads and feet together. She never, at least, came back to that idea of hers to murder the master and do away with him that they might reign as mistress and lord of love in soft garments amid flowers and lead a life of bliss. She saw that the idea was entirely repugnant to him and must have feared to estrange him by repeating it. Her drunken and clouded state did not prevent her from seeing the perfect justice of his decided refusal even to consider the wild project, and that he did not need to conceal his indignant rejection of a proposal which even she would find it hard to bring up again with a whole tongue and without the excuse of a childish lisp. But she did not abandon the plea that there was no sense in refusing her, since they already shared the secret and might just as well, so to speak, get the good of it; she went back to it again and again, holding out the promise of unspeakable bliss which he would find in her loving arms, in her body, which had stored all its treasures up for him. And when to that sweet wooing he only answered: " My child, we may not," she proceeded to try to spur him on with doubts about his masculinity.

Not that she took these seriously herself — it is hardly possible. But on the face of it she was somewhat justified by his response to her mockery. Joseph could not come out with his seven reasons — most of them she could not even have understood — and what he offered instead was certainly feeble, stupid, and badly invented. What, for instance, could she, in her passion and extremity, make of the moral thesis which he would once and for all have made his answer, that it might be on the lips of the peoples in case this story of theirs became history: namely, that his master had put all that he had into his hands save only herself because she was his wife, and how then could he do this great wickedness and sin with her? That was threadbare rubbish, it could not serve her need and passion. And even if she found herself in a history, Mutem-enet was convinced that everybody and at all times would find it justifiable that such a pair as she and Joseph were should put their heads and feet together regardless of the captain of the guard and her titular husband; she was sure that anybody would take much more pleasure in it than in a moral thesis.

What else did he say? Something like this:

"You want me to come by night and sleep with you? But it has been just by night that our God, whom you do not know, has mostly revealed Himself to men. If then He would reveal Himself to me in the night and found me thus — what would become of me? "

That was childish. Or he would say:

" I fear because of Adam, who was driven out of the garden on account of so small a sin. How then would I be punished? "

She found that as pitiable as the one which followed:

" You cannot know all these things. But my brother Reuben lost his first-born right because he was unstable, and the father gave it to me. He would take it away again, if he knew that you had made an ass of me."

That must have seemed to her the sheerest pusillanimity. He could not be surprised, when he had dragged in some such lame excuses by the hair, that she answered them, weeping tears of rage the while, by saying that there was nothing left but for her to believe that the garland which he wore was nothing else than the straw wreath of impotence. She could hardly have meant what she said. Rather it was a desperate challenge to the honour of his flesh, and the look with which he answered her shamed and inflamed her equally, for it spoke with more eloquence and emotion even than his words:

" Do you think so? " he said bitterly. " Then be quiet. For if it were with me as you pretend to think, then were it easy, and my temptation were not like a dragon and a roaring lion. Believe me, woman, I have

had the thought of putting an end to your agony and
mine by making of myself what you impute to me, like
the youth in one of your legends, who took a sharp leaf
of the sword plant and cut himself and threw the offending member into the river for fish to devour, to witness
his innocence. But I may not; the sin were as great as
though I yielded, and I should be no use to God any
more. For He will that I remain whole and sound."

"Horrible!" she cried. "Osarsiph, whither did your
thoughts tend? Do it not, my beloved, my glorious one,
it would be such a dreadful pity! Never could I mean
what I said! You love me, you love me, your angry look
betrays your love and your blasphemous purpose. Sweet
one, oh, come and save me, stanch my streaming blood,
for pity of its flowing!"

But he answered: "It may not be."

Then she grew wrathful and began to threaten him
with martyrdom and death. So far had she come; it was
this that haunted me when I said that she grew less and
less fastidious in her choice of means. He learned now
with whom he had to do and what she had meant by her
ringing cry: "Frightful am I alone in my love!" The
giant cat lifted her paw, threateningly she put out her
claws from their velvet sheath, to tear his flesh. If he
would not do her will, not yield her his sacred wreath
to receive in exchange the garland of bliss, then she must
and would destroy him. Urgently she implored him to
take her words seriously and not for empty sound, for
he could see that she was ready for any- and everything.
She would accuse him to Petepre of that which he denied
her, and tax him with assault upon her virtue. She would
say that he had done violence to her and the accusation

would be a joy, and she would know how to act the ruined
and maculate so that no one would doubt what she said.
Her word and oath, he might be sure, would count before
his in this house, and no denial would help him. Besides
she was convinced that he would not deny, but in silence
take the guilt upon himself; for that it had come to this despair and fury with her was his fault, the fault of his
eyes, his mouth, his golden shoulders, and his denial of
her love; he would see that it was all one in what accusa-
tions one clothed his guilt, for every accusation became
true by virtue of the truth of his guilt and he must be
prepared to suffer death. But it would be a death which
would make him rue his silence and even perhaps his
cruel denial of her love. For men like Petepre were in-
ventive in revenge and for the libertine who debauched
the mistress there would be found a kind of death that left
nothing to be desired in the way of refined torture.

And now she told him how he would die, painting it
to him, sometimes in her singing, ringing tones, again
in whispers close to his ear, like the tender murmurings
of love:

" Hope not," she whispered, " that it will be quick;
casting you from a rock or hanging you head down till
the blood soon rushes to your brain and death comes
gently. So merciful it will not be — after the beatings
that will mangle your back when Petepre pronounces
sentence. For when I disclose your violent deed he will
be seized with a sand-storm such as comes from the
mountains of the East, and his fury will rage and his
malice be unbounded. It is horrible to be given to the
crocodile, to lie bound and helpless in the reeds when

the devourer draws nigh and his wet belly glides over you, beginning his meal with shoulder or thigh so that your wild shrieks mingle with his satisfied gruntings as he feeds — for nobody will hear or heed. For I have heard when it happened to others, and felt a light pity, without much thought or realization, one's own flesh being safe. But now it is yourself and your flesh which the oncoming devourer nuzzles, beginning in this place or that, while you are fully conscious and would hold back the inhuman shriek that wrings itself from your breast — shriek not, beloved, for me, who would have kissed you where that wet-belly sets his teeth! — But perhaps there will be other kisses. Perhaps they will stretch my beautiful one upon his back on the ground, your hands and feet made fast with brazen clamps, and heap firewood on your body and light it, so that with tortures for which there is no name and you alone can know them, gasping and shrieking, while the others only look on, your body is consumed to charcoal by lingering flame. So may it be, beloved; or perhaps they will put you, living, in a pit, together with two great dogs, and cover it with beams and earth, and again no one thinks, nor yourself until it come to pass, what shall happen there below among you three. — Do you know of the punishment of the mortise and tenon? For being accused by me and thereupon condemned, you would be shrieking and praying for mercy with the iron rod in your eye and the door grinding your head whenever it pleased the avenger to pass through. These, then, are but a few of the punishments you are certain to find, if I give voice to my complaint, as I am in my last despair resolved to do; for you will not be able to make yourself white after my oath. Out of pity for yourself, Osarsiph, give me your wreath! "

" My friend and mistress," he answered her, " you are right, I shall not be able to make myself white if it please you so to blacken me before my master. But among the punishments with which you threaten me, Petepre must choose; he cannot visit me with all, but only with one, which limits his revenge and my suffering. And even so, my suffering can only comprise what is humanly possible; and whether those limits be small or great it cannot overpass them, for they are finite. Delight and suffering, both, you have painted to me as measureless, but you exaggerate, for with both one soon reaches the limits of human capacity. It is only the error which I should commit that would be measureless, if I destroyed myself in the sight of God the Lord, whom you do not know, so that you cannot tell what it is to be forsaken of God. Therefore, my child, can I not yield to your desire."

"Woe to that wisdom of yours! " she cried in her singing voice. " Woe to it! I, I am not wise. Unwise am I, out of my measureless longing for your flesh and blood, and I will do what I say! I am the loving Isis and my gaze is death. Take care, Osarsiph, take care! "

THE LADIES' PARTY

AH, how splendid she seemed, our Mut, standing before him and threatening him in her bell-like voice! And yet she was weak and helpless like a child, quite without regard for her dignity or her saga. She had of late begun

to confide her passion to all the world, and the misery
she suffered because of her young man. It had come to
this: that now not only Tabubu, the rubber-eater, and
Mekh-en-Weseht, the concubine, were initiated into her
love and longing, but also Renenutet, the wife of Amun's
overseer of bulls, as well as Neit-em-het, the wife of Pharaoh's head washerman, and Ahwere, spouse of Kakabu,
the scribe of the silver-houses, from the king's silver-
house; in short, all her friends, all the court, and half
the city. It was a distinct sign of her degeneration that
toward the end of the third year of her passion she told
everybody without restraint or embarrassment and im-
parted to all the world regardless that which in the beginning she had so proudly and shyly kept hidden in her
own bosom that she would sooner have died than confess it to the beloved himself or to anyone else. Yes, it
was not only the worthy Dudu who degenerates in this
story; Mut, the mistress, did too, so much that she lost
her manners and her self-control. She was a person
deeply afflicted and possessed, entirely beside herself,
no longer a denizen of the civilized world, and estranged
from its standards; a runner upon the mountains, ready
to offer her breasts to wild beasts; a garlanded, panting,
exulting swinger of the thyrsis. To what all did she not
finally descend? This is not the place to speak of the
magic she abased herself to practise with black Tabubu
—we shall come to that later. Here we must only note,
with mingled amazement and pity, that she prattled
everywhere of her love and unslaked longing, restrain-
ing herself before neither high nor low, so that soon
her affliction was the daily talk of all the household,
and the cooks as they stirred the pots and plucked the

fowls, the gate-keepers on their bench, said to each other:

" The mistress is keen on the young steward, but he won't hear to it. — What a state of things! "

For that is the form such subjects take in the heads and on the lips of ordinary folk, by virtue of the lamentable contradiction between the lover's own consciousness of his sacred, serious, painfully beautiful passion and the impression it makes on the detached observer, to whom its lack of purpose or power to conceal itself is a mockery and a scandal, like a drunken man on the street.

All the later versions of our story — with exception of the briefest but most prized — the Koran as well as the seventeen Persian songs, the poem of Firdausi the disillusioned, on which he spent his old age, and Dshami's late and subtle version, all of these, as well as countless renderings by pencil and brush, tell of the ladies' party which Potiphar's chief and true wife gave to the high society of No-Amun, to acquaint them with her suffering and its cause; to arouse sympathy and also envy in the bosoms of her sisters. For love, however unslaked, is not only a curse and a scourge but also a priceless treasure, which one cannot bear to keep hidden. The songs contain some errors and are guilty of superfluous variations and adornments which despite their sweetness and charm are a burden upon the simple truth. But as for the episode of the ladies' party, there they are in the right; and if again, for the sake of pleasing effect, they depart from the original form of the story, or even belie each other by their variations, yet the singers are not the inventors of this event, the story invented it, or rather it was the personal invention of Potiphar's wife, poor Eni, who made it up and put it into effect with a shrewdness which stands in the strangest though most realistic contradiction to her bemused state.

We who know the revelatory dream dreamed by Mut-em-enet at the beginning of the three years of her love can easily understand the connection between it and the ingenious, pathetic device she adopted to open the eyes of her friends. And the dream, which bears every mark of genuineness, is the best evidence for the historicity of the ladies' party and makes quite clear that only laconic brevity of style is responsible for its omission from our nearest and best-prized source.

As a prelude to the ladies' party Mut-em-enet fell ill: of that illness, in its nature not very well defined, which seizes all the young princes and kings' daughters in the fairy-stories when they love unhappily, and which regularly "mocks the skill of the most famous physicians." She sickened of it, according to all the rules, because it was the right and proper thing, and the right and proper thing is hard to resist; but also it was important to her (and seems in general to be a principal motive of all these illnesses of princes and kings' daughters) to attract attention, to put the world about her in a flutter of excitement, and to be *questioned*, this above all: to be importuned, as in a matter of life and death, and from all sides — for her changed appearance had for a long time now been the subject of genuine anxiety and question in her closer circle. She fell ill out of the urgency of her need to preoccupy the world with her affliction, with the bliss and torment of her love for Joseph. That there was not much more, literally and strictly speaking, in her illness than this is shown from the fact that when there was question of a ladies' party Mut could arise from her couch and play the hostess — and no wonder she could, for it was all part of the same plan.

So, then, she fell ill, seriously, if rather indeterminately, and lay abed. She was treated by two eminent doctors, one from Amun's book-house, who had previously been called to Mont-kaw, and another learned man from the temple; cared for by her sisters of the house of the secluded ones, Petepre's concubines; and visited by her friends of the order of Hathor and Amun's southern house of women. The lady Renenutet called, Neit-em-het, Ahwere and many others. Came too in her litter Nes-ba-met, head of the order, consort of the great Bekne-chons, " head priest of all the gods of Upper and Lower Egypt." And all of them, singly or by twos and threes, sat by her bed, mourned over and importuned her, in a flood of words, partly from their hearts but partly also in cold blood, out of pure convention or even envy.

" Eni with beloved voice when you sing," said they. " In the name of the Hidden One say what ails you, and how, naughty girl, can you so distress us? As the king lives, you are changed, for a long time now; all of us, in whose hearts you live, have seen the signs of fatigue, and alterations too, which — while doing no violence to your beauty — give us great concern. May there be no evil eye upon you! We have seen, and wept among ourselves to see how weariness overtook your body, and a decrease of flesh that attacked not all parts at once, for some are fuller while others have shrunk. Your cheeks, for instance, are gaunt, your eyes begin to stare, and suffering sits upon your much-praised sinuous mouth. We, your admirers, have seen all this and spoken of it with tears. But now your exhaustion has reached a point where you take to your bed and can neither eat nor drink, while your ailment mocks the doctors' art. Truly at this news we knew not where we were, so great was our alarm. We have besieged with questions the wise men from the book-house, Te-Hor and Pete-Bastet, your physicians, and they have answered they are almost at the end of their skill and will soon be helpless. They had only a few more remedies which might avail, for all those they have tried have been unavailing. It must be some great affliction that gnaws at you as a mouse will gnaw at the root of a tree so that it sickens. In Amun's name, our treasure, is it true, say, have you a gnawing sorrow? Tell it quickly to us who love you, before the accursed thing strikes at the root of sweet life itself! "

" Supposing," Eni answered in a faint voice, " that I had, what good could it do me to name it to you? All your kindness and sympathy could not free me from it, and in all likelihood nothing remains to me but to die."

" Then it is true," cried they, " it is really such a sorrow that is wearing you down? " And they expressed their shrill-voiced surprise: how could it be possible — a woman like her, belonging to the highest society, rich, enchantingly lovely, the envied of all others of her sex! What could she lack? What heart's desire was denied her? Mut's friends could simply not understand. They questioned her persistently; partly in the goodness of their hearts and partly out of sheer curiosity, envy, and love of excitement. For a long time she evaded their questions; in her feeble, hopeless tones she refused them all information, saying they could do her no good. But at last, very well, she said, she would answer them. She would answer them all together and make an occasion of it: she would give a ladies' party, very soon, and invite them all. She was very weak and without appetite, could scarcely take anything, at most a bird's liver and a little vegetable; but she would try to find strength to get up, so that she might reveal to her friends the cause of her disordered and altered state.

So said, so done. At the next quarter of the moon — it was not long before the new year and the great feast of Opet, on which day decisive events were to come to pass in Potiphar's house — Eni gave out invitations to that ladies' party in Petepre's house which has been so widely if not always so wisely celebrated in song. It was a large afternoon affair, and took on added lustre through the presence of Nes-ba-met, Beknechons's wife and first among the women of the harem. There was no lack of flowers or unguents, or of cool drinks, some of them intoxicating, some only refreshing; or of cakes of various sorts, crystallized fruits and spun-sugar sweetmeats, handed by young maidservants in charmingly exiguous costumes, with black braids hanging in their necks and veils shrouding their cheeks — a novel refinement which was much applauded. A delightful orchestra, of harpists, lute-players, and flautists in wide diaphanous garments revealing their embroidered girdles underneath, made music in the fountain court, where most of the ladies settled down informally, partly on chairs and stools among the laden tables, partly kneeling on gaily coloured mats. They also occupied the columned hall, from which the image of Atum-Re had been removed.

Mut's friends were graceful and exquisite to behold. Their flowing hair was anointed with perfumed oil from the crowns of their heads to where it finished off in a twisted fringe, through which peeped the golden disks of their ear-ornaments; their limbs were a lovely brown, their sparkling eyes reached to their temples, their little noses bespoke nothing but pride and high spirits. The patterns of their jewelled and faience necklaces and arm-rings, the spider-web linen that spanned their sweet bosoms and seemed woven of sunshine or moonbeams, were the very last word in elegance. They smelt of lotus flowers; they passed each other sweetmeats and chattered in high twittering voices, or else in deeper, rougher ones — for in this climate women sometimes have such voices; for instance, Nes-ba-met. They talked of the approaching feast of Opet, of the great procession of the holy Triad in their barks by water and land; of the reception of the god in the southern house of women, where they, the ladies, would dance and sing and shake their rattles in their character as sweet-voiced concubines of the god. The topic was both attractive and important; yet at this moment it only served to keep their tongues wagging and fill in the time until their hostess, Mut-em-enet, should give them answer and let them know the thrilling cause of her exhaustion.

She sat, a figure of suffering amongst them, beside the basin, smiling faintly with her tortured sinuous mouth and awaiting her moment. As in a dream, and after the pattern of a dream, she had made her arrangements to enlighten her friends; and she felt dreamlike certainty of their success. The moment arrived with the climax of the feast. Splendid fruits were standing ready in flower-trimmed baskets, fragrant golden spheres bursting with refreshing juice under their leathery skins. They were Indian blood-oranges, a great rarity; and beside them lay charming little knives that had handles inlaid with blue stones and highly polished bronze blades to which the hostess had given special attention. She had had them sharpened — to a pitch of sharpness, indeed, such as seldom any little knives had ever been brought before. They were of such a razor sharpness that a man might have shaved with them were his beard never so tough. But they required great care in their use, for even a moment of absent-mindedness or unsteadiness was sure to bring about an annoying injury. They had acquired an edge — a positively dangerous one, these little knives; one had the feeling that one only needed to come near the blade with a finger-tip for the blood to gush out. Were these all the preparations? By no means. There was a precious wine " from the port," sweet, fiery Cyprian wine, a dessert wine, to be served with the oranges; the charming cups of hammered gold and glazed and painted earthenware stood ready, and at a sign from the hostess were handed round in the fountain court and the pillared hall by dainty little maids who had nothing on but bright-coloured sashes. But who should pour this island wine into the cups? The little maids? No; the hostess had decreed that too little honour would thus be paid to her entertainment and her guests. She had arranged something else.

She beckoned again, and the golden apples, the exquisite little knives were passed. Both elicited cries of rapture: they praised the fruit, they praised the dainty tools — that is, they praised their daintiness, for with their chief property they were as yet unacquainted. They all set to at once to lay bare the sweet pulp; but soon their eyes were distracted from the task.

Again Mut-em-enet had beckoned, and he who now appeared on the scene was the cup-bearer, the pourer of the wine — it was Joseph. Yes, the lovesick woman had commanded him to this service, requesting, as his mistress, that he should himself serve the wine of Cyprus to her guests. She did not tell him of her other preparations, he did not know for what purpose of edification he was being used. It pained her, as we know, to deceive him and deliberately make such misuse of his appearance. But her heart was set on enlightening her friends and laying bare her feelings. So she said to him — just after he had once more, with all possible forbearance, refused to lie with her:

"Will you then, Osarsiph, at least do me a favour, and pour out the famous Alashian wine at my ladies' party day after tomorrow? In token of its excelling goodness, also in token that you love me a little, and lastly to show that I am after all somebody in this house, since he at its head serves me and my guests?"

"By all means, my mistress," he had answered. "That will I gladly do, and with the greatest pleasure, if it be one to you. For I am with body and soul at your command in every respect save that I sin with you."

So, then, Rachel's son, the young steward of Petepre, appeared suddenly among the ladies as they sat peeling in the court; in a fine white festal garment, with a coloured Mycenæan jug in his hands. He bowed, and began to move about, filling the cups. But all the ladies, those who had chanced to see him before as well as those who did not know him, forgot at the sight not only what they were doing but themselves as well, being lost in gazing at the cup-bearer. Then those wicked little knives accom-

plished their purpose and the ladies, all and sundry, cut
their fingers frightfully — without even being aware at
the time, for a cut from such an exceedingly sharp blade
is hardly perceptible, certainly not in the distracted state
of mind in which Eni's friends then were.

This oft-described scene has by some been thought to
be apocryphal, and not belonging to the story as it happened. But they are wrong; for it is the truth, and all
the probabilities speak for it. We must remember, on
the one hand, that this was the most beautiful youth
of his time and sphere; on the other, that these were the
sharpest little knives the world has ever seen — and we
shall understand that the thing could not happen otherwise — I mean with less shedding of blood — than as it
actually did. Eni's dreamlike certainty of the event and
its course was entirely justified. She sat there with her
suffering air, her brooding, sinister, masklike face and
sinuous mouth, and looked at the mischief she had
worked; the blood-bath, which at first no one saw but
herself, for all the ladies were gaping in self-forgotten
ardour after the youth as he slowly disappeared toward
the pillared hall, where, Mut knew, the scene would repeat itself. Only when the beloved form had disappeared
did she inquire of the ensuing stillness, in a voice of
malicious concern:

"My loves, what ever has happened to you all? What
are you doing? Your blood is flowing!"

It was a fearful sight. With some the nimble knife had
gone an inch deep in the flesh and the blood did not ooze,
it spouted. The little hands, the golden apples, were
drenched with the red liquid, it dyed the fresh white-
ness of the linen garments and soaked through into the

women's laps, making pools which dripped down on
the floor and their little feet. What an outcry, what
wails, what shrieking arose when Mut's hypocritical concern made them aware what had happened! Some of
them could not bear the sight of blood, especially their
own; they threatened to faint and had to be restored
with oil of wormwood and other pungent little phials
brought by the bustling maids. All the needful things
were done; the neat little maids dashed about with cloths
and basins, vinegar, lint, and linen bandages, until the
party looked more like a hospital ward than anything
else, in the pillared hall as well, whither Mut-em-enet
went for a moment to assure herself that blood was flowing there too. Renenutet, the wife of the overseer of
bulls, was among the more seriously wounded; they had
to quench the flow of blood by putting a tourniquet on
the wrist to shut off the circulation from the slowly paling
and yellowing little hand. Likewise Nes-ba-met, Beknechons's deep-voiced consort, had done herself considerable injury. They had to take off her outer garment, and
she was tended and reassured by two of the girted maids,
one black and one white, while she raved and raged in a
loud voice at everybody indiscriminately.

"Dearest Head Mother and all of you my dear
friends," said the hypocrite Mut, when order had somewhat been restored, "how could it happen that here in
my house you have done this to yourselves, and this red
episode has marred my party? To your hostess it is almost intolerable that it had to be in my house that it
happened — how is such a thing possible? One person,
or even two, might cut their fingers while peeling an
orange — but all of you at once, and some of you to the

bone! Such a thing has never happened before in the
world, and will probably be unique in the social life of
the two lands — at least, let us hope so! But comfort me,
my sweethearts, and tell me how ever it could happen! "

" Never mind," Nes-ba-met answered in her deep bass
for the rest of the women. "Do not think of it, Enti, for
everything is right now, at least nearly, even though red
Set has spoilt our afternoon frocks and some of us are
pale with blood-letting. Do not be upset. For your intentions were good, and as for the party, it is exclusive
in every respect. Yet after all it was pretty thoughtless
of you — the thing you did in the middle of it. I am
speaking quite frankly, and for all of us. Put yourself
in our place. You invited us to explain the cause of your
exhaustion, which mocks the best skill of the physicians;
we must wait for the revelation, and that makes us nervous, so that we hide our suspense by making conversation.
As you see, I am telling everything as it was, according
to the simple truth, speaking for us all and not mincing
matters. You served us with golden apples — very good,
very fine, even; Pharaoh himself does not have them
every day. But just as we are peeling them, there comes,
by your order, this young cup-bearer into our already
excited group — whoever he is, I suppose that he is your
young steward known on the land- and the water-ways as
Nefernefru; and it is mortifying for a lady to have to
agree with the people of the dams and the canals, and
with their judgment and taste, but really there can be
no question of disagreeing with them, for he is certainly
a picture of a young man from head to foot. In and for
itself it is something of a shock when a young man suddenly comes among a group of already nervous women,

even if he is less attractive than this one. So what could you expect but that we should tremble in all our limbs and have tears come in our eyes when such a young god appears on the scene and bends with his jug over our cups? You could not expect us to attend to what we were doing and take care not to cut our fingers! We have caused you much bustle and annoyance with this blood-letting, but the blame, dearest Eni with the lovely voice, is your own, for the trouble ensuing on your startling entertainment."

"Yes, yes!" cried Renenutet, wife of the overseer of bulls. "You must take the blame, my dear, for you have played us a fine trick and we shall all remember it — though not with anger, since we realize that you could not be affected by it, and hence thought nothing of it. But that is just it, my treasure, that you failed in tact and consideration, and so to yourself is due in all justice the awkwardness of this red episode. For naturally the total femininity of this whole gathering affects each single female in it and heightens her susceptibility to the uttermost! And then you elected to introduce a young man among us, and at what moment? Precisely when we were peeling our oranges! How could we help cutting ourselves? For it has to be just this cup-bearer who comes in, your young steward, a perfect young Adonis! I must say frankly that I was beside myself at the sight. I speak without shame, for this is an hour and these are circumstances when the mouth speaks from the fullness of the heart, and for once it seems quite right to say just what one thinks. I am a woman with a great deal of feeling for the masculine; you all know that besides my husband the director of bulls, who is in his best years, I know a certain young officer of the guard, and also there is a young priest of the temple of Khonsu who comes to my house. You all know these things without my telling you. But all that does not prevent me from being always on the alert, so to speak, for the masculine — it is easy for me to feel perfectly divine — but I have a special weakness for cup-bearers. There is always something of the god — or a darling of the gods — about a cup-bearer! I do not know what that is, probably it is because of his office and his motions. But this Refertem, this blue lotus, this honey youth, with his jug — ye gods, it was all over with me! I quite thought that I was seeing a god, and for sheer delight I did not know where I was. I was all eyes, and while I gazed I stabbed myself with the fruit-knife, deep into my flesh, and the blood ran in streams and I never felt it, in the state I was in. But that is not the whole of it: for now whenever I want to peel fruit in the future I am convinced that the image of your divine young cup-bearer will come up before me, the wretch, and I shall cut myself to the bone for losing myself in the sight of him, and can never eat any more fruit that must be peeled, though I am passionately fond of it. And all that you brought about, my treasure, with your heedlessness."

" Yes, yes! " all the ladies echoed her, the ones who had been in the pillared hall as well, for they had come out to the court while Nes-ba-met and Renenutet were speaking. " Yes, yes! " they cried all together, in voices some shrill and some deep. " The speakers have spoken as it was, we all nearly killed ourselves in our amazement at sight of this cup-bearer, and instead of telling us the cause of your illness, to which end we were invited, Eni, you have played us this trick!"

But now Mut-em-enet raised her voice to its full singing power and cried:

"Fools! I have not only told but showed it to you, the cause of my mortal weakness and all my misery! Then have some eye for me, as you were all eyes for him! You have seen him but the space of a few heart-beats and done yourselves harm in your distraction, so that you all are pale with the red distress the sight of him gave you. But I — I must or I may see him every day — and what can I do in my own distress, which is unending and infinite? I ask you. Where shall I turn? For this boy, you blind creatures, who saw him in vain, the steward and cup-bearer to my husband — he is my anguish and my death, he has brought me to my end with his eyes and mouth; for him alone, my sisters, my red blood gushes out in agony and I die if he quench it not. For you only cut your fingers at sight of him; but love for his beauty has cut me to the heart, and I bleed to death!" Thus she chanted till her voice failed and she fell back in her seat with convulsive sobs.

We can imagine the state of high feminine excitement into which this revelation flung the troop of Mut's friends. They behaved as Tabubu and Mekh-en-Weseht had done before them, in face of the great news that Mut had fallen in love. They treated the sufferer much as the other two had done: crowded round her, stroked and patted, congratulated, commiserated, in many-voiced high-strung prattle. But the looks which they exchanged, the words which they murmured to each other, had quite other meaning than sympathy. They were angry and disappointed that there was no more to it, and that all this pretentious affliction amounted to no more than falling in love with a servant. There was silent disapproval, and universal jealousy on the youth's account. But more than all, there was a certain dog-in-the-manger satisfaction that this was Mut, the proud and pure, the moon-chaste bride of Amun, who had been visited so to speak in her old age and afflicted in quite the most ordinary way, that she was pining for a handsome slave and did not even know how to keep it to herself but must helplessly expose her humiliation like a regular female, wailing: " What shall I do? " That pleased her friends, if also it did not escape them that all the self-exposure and publicity were at bottom the same old conceit, which made of the most ordinary occurrence, when it was Mut to whom it happened, an extraordinary and world-shaking event — and that annoyed them afresh.

But if all this spoke in the side glances which the ladies exchanged, yet their animation and pleasure in the sensation and the charming scandal in high life was sufficient to make them capable of heartfelt sympathy with their sister in distress, and of feminine solidarity; they crowded round her, embraced and petted her, and prattled loudly, expressing their views of the youth's good fortune in having been granted to rouse such feelings in the breast of his mistress.

" Yes, sweet Eni," they cried, " you have shown us and we understand that it is no small thing for a woman's heart to have to be able to see such a picture of a young god every day — no wonder that in the end you, too, fell victim! The lucky fellow! What no man has suc-

ceeded in, during all these years, has fallen to his youth:
he has actually stirred your senses. Certainly he was
not born to it — but that shows the simplicity of the heart,
which asks not after rank or station. He is no son of a
nome prince and neither officer nor councillor of state,
being only your husband's steward; but yet he has melted
your heart and that shall serve him for title; and that he
is a foreigner, an Asiatic youth and so-called Hebrew,
makes the affair still more piquant and gives it a cachet.
Dearest, we are so glad and relieved that your distress
and weariness has no worse cause than your feeling for
this beautiful youth. You will forgive us if we cease to
feel anxiety for you and begin to feel it for him; for
certainly the only ground here for fear is lest he may
go out of his head with the honour done him. Otherwise
the business seems to us quite simple."

" Ah," sobbed Mut, " if you only knew! But you know
nothing, and I knew that you would not, even after I
opened your eyes. For you have no notion how it stands
with him, or with the jealousy of the god to whom he belongs and whose wreath he wears; so that he is much too
good to stanch the blood of an Egyptian woman and his
soul has no ear for all my crying. Ah, how much better
you would do, my sisters, not to be anxious for his great
honour, but to devote all your concern to me, who am at
death's door with his religious compunctions! "

Then her friends insisted on learning more particulars
about these religious compunctions; they could not believe their ears when they heard that this servant was not
bursting with pride at the honour done him but was de-
nying himself to his mistress. The looks they then exchanged did betray some malice, some suggestion that

after all their Eni was too old for the beautiful youth,
and he simply made pious excuses because he felt no
desire; some of them flattered themselves that they would
be in better case with him. But in general they were
sincerely indignant at the foreign slave's recalcitrance;
particularly Nes-ba-met, the head priestess, took the
word, in her bass voice, and declared that from this point
of view the affair was scandalous and indeed not to be
borne.

" As a woman, dearest," said she, " I am on your side,
your affliction is mine. But there is a political aspect to
the thing too, it touches the state and the temple; and
this little upstart — you will pardon me, I know you
love him, but I call him so out of honest scorn — in his
obstinate refusal to pay you the tribute of his youth,
displays an insubordination dangerous to the kingdom;
it is as though some Baal-city of the Retenu or Phœnicia
were to set himself up against Amun and refuse the duties
which it owed. In that case there would be a punitive
expedition fitted out, to protect the honour of Amun, even
if it cost more than the tribute came to. In this light, my
dear, I view your affliction; and as soon as I get home
I will speak with my husband, who is the head of all the
priests of Upper and Lower Egypt, to tell him of this gross
case of Canaanitish insubordination and ask him what
measures he thinks proper to deal with the disorder."

She reached her conclusion amid more and even more
animated chatter from all the guests; and thus the ladies'
party at last broke up, which has become so famous and
is here related in the true and actual course of its events.
By it Mut-em-enet principally succeeded in making her
unhappy passion the talk of the town — a success at

which she herself, in her clearer moments, was probably horrified, yet at other times was capable, thanks to her increasing degeneration, of thinking of with a drunken satisfaction. For most infatuated people cannot believe that sufficient honour is shown their feelings unless they occupy the thoughts of all the world, if only to be mocked at and scorned. They must be known to the sparrows on the house-tops. Her friends now often made her sick-bed visits, singly or by twos and threes, to inquire after her state, to comfort her and give her advice; they foolishly passed over the actual though entirely peculiar circumstances, and the sufferer could only shrug her shoulders and reply:

" Ah, my children, you chatter and advise and understand nothing at all of this peculiar case." Then the ladies of Wese would be annoyed afresh, saying to each other: " If she thinks the matter is above our heads, and there is something quite peculiar about it, beyond any good counsel of ours, then she should hold her tongue and not tell us about the affair."

But someone else came in person, borne to Petepre's house between vanguard and rear-guard: the great Beknechons, Amun's first, whose wife had informed him of the story, and who was not minded to take it lightly, but rather to see it in view of the larger interests involved. The mighty shiny-pate and statesman of the church, wearing his arrogated leopard-skin, strode to and fro before her lion-footed chair, straining upward from his ribs and holding his chin in the air as he declared that all personal and merely moral considerations must be put aside in judging this situation. This might be regrettable on the ground of standards of conduct and the moral

order, but once begun, must be pursued to the end in the
light of loftier considerations. As a priest, a spiritual
guide, and guardian of religious order, and not least as
the friend and colleague of the good Petepre at court, he
was obliged to censure the attentions Mut dedicated to
this young man and oppose the desire he aroused in her.
But the recalcitrant bearing of this foreigner, his refusal
to pay tribute, was intolerable to the temple, which would
be obliged to insist that the matter be set right without
delay and to the glory of Amun. Therefore, he, Beknechons, quite without regard to what might be personally
desirable or blameworthy, must warn and admonish his
daughter Mut to exert all her powers to the utmost to
bring the rebellious youth to a fall — not for her own
satisfaction, even though that might come to pass, without his approval, but for that of the temple; if necessary
the backward youth could be brought to book by force.

It shows with depressing clarity how low Mut had
sunk that this spiritual admonishment and authorization
to sin did her soul good, that she could see in it a strength-
ening of her position with regard to the beloved one. To
this had she come, the woman who but late and conform-
ably with her stage of development had made her joy
and sorrow dependent upon the freedom of his living
soul, that now she found a desperate and distorted pleasure in the thought of having the object of her hot desire
produced by force before the temple authorities. Yes,
she was ripe for Tabubu's magic.

But the position of the Amun authorities was not unknown to Joseph either. For no crack or cranny was too
small for his faithful Bes-em-heb to crawl into, that he
might be present at the interview between Mut-em-enet

and Beknechons the great, hear the advice with dwarf-fine hearing, and bring it hot and hot to his patron and protégé. Joseph listened and was extraordinarily strengthened in his view that this was a trial of strength between the power of Amun and God the Lord, and that he might not let Him down, at any price whatsoever, no matter how ill the resolve might accord with the old Adam in him.

THE BITCH

So then it came about that Mut-em-inet the proud, in the degeneration worked by her passion, fell low indeed, letting herself in for a course of action which her natural refinement would only a little while before have rejected with disgust. She sank to the moral level of Tabubu the Kushite and combined with her to deal with the unclean; in other words, to make magic spells for the binding of her lover and sacrifice to a horrible nether-world deity whose name she did not even know or wish to know. Tabubu simply called her the bitch, and that was enough.

This nocturnal spectre, it seemed, was a perfect ghoul and fury; but the Negress promised to make her compliant by means of charms to the wishes of Mut the mistress, and Mut was fain to be content — on the understanding that she renounced her claims to the soul of her beloved and would be glad if she might but hold his body — a warm-blooded corpse, as it were — in her arms. Or not glad, precisely, but mournfully assuaged; for of course it is the body, the flesh alone, that can be conjured in this wise and delivered into anybody's arms, not the soul at all. One needed to be very inconsolable

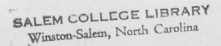

indeed to be consoled with that, and with the thought that love's craving and satisfaction is after all a matter for the flesh; in God's name, it was easier to dispense with the soul than the body, however mournful the satisfaction the body purveyed.

The state of Mut-em-inet's own body was responsible for her finally consenting to the rubber-eater's base proposals. She was fully aware of her witchlike state, and considered that the physical signs it had set upon her were proof that she belonged to the guild and was bound to act accordingly. We must remember that her new body was a result and product of love, a pathetic accentuation of her femininity. For witchery is at bottom nothing else than femininity raised to an exaggeratedly and illicitly alluring height; from which it follows not only that witchcraft is pre-eminently female, and male witches as good as never exist, but also that in it love plays a predominant part, is always the very centre of the activity, and love-magic, as its natural and preferred sphere, comprehends everything that can rightly be called magic.

I have earlier, with all due delicacy, suggested that something of the hag had entered into Mut's physical being; it probably contributed to her inclination and willingness to practise witchcraft, so that she now allowed Tabubu to set to work on the business of sacrificing and conjuring. For the deity whom they were to conjure was, according to the Negress, the personification of haggishness, a hag-god and hag-goddess combined, in whom one must envisage an embodiment and epitome of all possible repulsive connotations of the word " hag ": a being of the filthiest practices; in short, an arch-hag. Such deities there are and must be; for the world has sides that reek with blood and are stiff with foulness, seemingly very little fit to be deified. Yet these have just as much need as its more appealing sides of permanent representation and headship, of ghostly embodiment, so to speak. Thus it comes that the name and nature of the divine can enter into the horrible, and bitch and mistress be one; especially when it is the arch-bitch we are dealing with, having by right the characteristics of a mistress, in any case. Tabubu, when she referred to this embodiment of all filthiness and obscenity, actually called her " the gracious mistress bitch."

The black woman thought well to warn Mut that the nature and conduct of the proposed operations were quite outside the great lady's social sphere. She begged pardon of her refinement beforehand, and implored her for just this once to adjust herself to the tone of vulgarity because it was all that the gracious mistress bitch could understand, and without a certain indecency of speech there would be no dealing with her. The proceedings would not be very pleasant, she said — the ingredients for the conjuring were some of them most unappetizing; nor would there be a lack of imprecations and swaggering. The mistress must make up her mind to that and not take offence, or if she did she must conceal it. For this act of compulsion would differ from the religious services to which Mut was accustomed: it would be frightful, violent, and high-handed. Not even in intention did it proceed from the human side or in accordance with human tastes; but from the gross nature of the being they invoked, whom they summoned to their presence, the mistress-bitch, whose service could not be other than obscene, and whose character as arch-hag conditioned the form of the proceedings and their very low level of decency. After all, in Tabubu's opinion, if you were setting about to constrain a young man to a purely physical compliance with the demands of love, there could not be a very high tone to the business.

Mut paled and bit her lips. Partly from the shock to her conventions, partly also from hatred of the evil chance which forced the compulsion upon her as well as on him. Now that she had resolved, the baseness of her resolve was a wound in her thoughts. That is a very old human experience: that when a man is tempted to fall below his better self, his tempters, those who drag him down, alarm him and mock him when they have him safely below, by the insolence with which they suddenly speak of his new and unfamiliar state. Pride demands that he conceal his fear and bewilderment; that he answer them: " Let things be as they are, I knew what I did when I resolved to follow you." And in such wise did Mut express herself, taking up an attitude of defiance to a resolve originally foreign to her nature: the conjuring of her beloved by means of magic.

She had to be patient for several days. The black priestess needed to prepare her magic, for which not all the ingredients were to hand: rarities like the rudder of a wrecked ship, uncanninesses like wood from a gallows, rotting flesh, certain parts from the body of an executed criminal; most important of all, some hair from Joseph's head, which Tabubu had to procure by craft and bribery from the household barber-shop. Besides they had to wait for the full moon, for their work would be more fruitful if performed under the highest potency of that equivocal planet, which is feminine in reference to the sun, masculine in reference to the earth, and thanks to its double character guarantees a certain unity to the universe and can interpret between mortals and immortals. Besides Tabubu as priestess and the lady Mut as client, there would assist at the conjuration a Moorish acolyte and Mekh-en-Weseht, the concubine, as witness. The flat roof of the house of women was the theatre of operations.

Each day — whether feared or longed for, or fearfully longed for, with impatience and shame — comes on, at last, and becomes a day of one's life, bringing what it has to bring. So came on the day of Mut-em-inet's hopeful degradation, when in her bitter need she betrayed her station and embarked upon her unworthy course. She awaited each hour as she had awaited each day, conquering one by one. The sun sank, its glory faded, the earth was shrouded in darkness, and the moon, incredibly large, rose above the desert, substituting its borrowed lustre for that of the departed sovereign sun, and for substantial daylight the frail web of her painful, pallid magic. As slowly diminishing, she mounted to the zenith, and all was quiet, while in the house of Potiphar everybody lay with drawn-up knees and peaceful faces, sucking at the breasts of sleep; then the four women, alone in the house awake, with their mysterious feminine purposes, forgathered on the roof, where Tabubu and her assistant had already made the needful preparations.

Mut-em-inet, her white mantle round her shoulders, a blazing torch in her hand, hurried so fast up the steps which led from the fountain court to the low upper storey, and thence by a narrower one to the roof, that Mekh, the concubine, with her own torch, could not keep up with her. Eni began to run directly she quitted her bedroom, holding aloft her fiery torch, her head flung back, her eyes fixed, her mouth open, her garments caught up in one hand.

" Why run so, darling? " murmured Mekh. " You will be out of breath, I am afraid, you are stumbling; stop, go carefully with the torch! "

But Petepre's chief and true wife answered disconnectedly:

" I must run, I must run, I must storm these heights breathless, do not stop me, Mekh, the spirit commands me and so must it be, we must run! "

Panting and staring she swung the light above her head so that sparks of burning pitch flew off from the flax, and her breathless companion clutched in alarm at the whirling stick, to wrest it away. Mut would not suffer her, and the danger was the greater. They were now on the second stair, and Mut really did stumble when they came to grips, and would have fallen had not Mekh grasped her arm. The two women, thus embraced and flourishing their lights, staggered through the narrow door and out on the dark roof.

They were greeted by a wind and by the voice of the priestess, who took command from the first. She carried on the talk from that moment, without ever stopping for breath; and it was gross, domineering, bombastic, ever and again interrupted by the howling of jackals from the bleached desert on the east, yes, from farther away by the dull, shattering roar of a ranging lion. The wind blew from the west, from the sleeping city, and from the river, where the moon played in silver sparkles on the water; from the shore of the dead, and the mountains on that side. It was caught, panting, in the wind-chimneys

that faced the west, a sort of wooden roof designed to di-
vert cool air down into the house. There were also a few
cone-shaped grain-bins on the roof; but besides these
usual things were many more objects and preparations,
the properties for the performance. Among them certain
things on whose account it was well that the wind was
blowing: for on the floor and on tripods were pieces of
bluish putrid flesh, which would have stunk — and did
when the wind died down. The other objects for the dark
rite a blind man might have seen with inward eye, or a
person who, like Mut-em-inet, did not want to see anything, since then and thereafter she gazed diagonally upwards into space, with her mouth drawn down half open,
and staring eyes. For Tabubu described them all aloud.
She stood there black and naked to the waist, her head
a grey mass of tangled hair dishevelled by the wind;
girdled with a goatskin under her haglike breasts, as
was her young helper likewise; her loose mouth, in which
two lonely buck-teeth stood up, moved ceaselessly as she
shouted the name and use of each object, like a market-
woman crying her wares.

"There you are, woman!" she said as she gestured and
pointed, when her mistress staggered onto the roof.
"Welcome, scorned one, seeking protection, poor lan-
guisher, husk rejected of the stone, lovesick trull, come
to this hearth! Take what we give you! Take grains of
salt in your hand, hang laurel on your ear, crouch by the
hearth, where it flickers in the wind out of its hole; it
flickers for you, to your healing, poor soul, so far as
may be!

"I speak! I spoke, here above I spoke and said, as
priestess, before you came. Now I speak on, loudly and

grossly, for fine words avail not to wrestle with her, one must name things shameless by their names; wherefore I now name you aloud, supplicant, a fool for love and a trollop bewitched. Are you sitting with your salt in your fist, the laurel over your ear? And your companion, has she hers and is she, too, crouching by our altar? Up with us, then, for the sacrificial rite, priestess and minis- trant! For all is prepared for the meal, gifts and adorn- ments without flaw.

"Where is the table? It is where it is, facing the hearth, fittingly adorned with garlands and branches, twigs of ivy and blade of corn, that she loves whom we invoke, who approaches. Dark husk hiding the mealy kernel. Therefore it garlands the table and trims the stands whereon the tempting offering stinks to heaven. Does the rotting rudder lean at the table's side? It does. And on the other side what do we see? A beam from the cross whereon they raised the malefactor on high — in your honour, perverted one, who favours that which is rejected, and to allure you it leans beside the table. But do we offer you naught else of him who was hanged, no ear, no finger? Yea, the mouldering finger graces the table, with fine crumbs of bitumen and the gristly waxen ear from the miscreant's head, clammy with blood — all that so richly to your taste, may it bring you, unholy one! But the knots of hair that shine upon the offertory table, like in colour, they come not from the murderer's head but from other heads near and far, and we have them lying close together, may they be fragrant to you, if you will help, you on whom we call, you who come out of the night!

"Still, then, let no one budge! Ye who sit by the

hearth, keep your eyes on me, blench not, for no one can tell from which side she will creep up! I command silence for the offering. Put out this torch, wench. So. Where is the double-edged blade? To hand. And the cur? It lies on the floor, like a young hyena, with chains on its claws, with moist muzzle bound, that snuffs with such delight for every kind of filth. Give me first the bitumen. The ready priestess throws it in black crumbs on the flame, that its leaden qualmish smoke may curl up to your nostrils as incense, O mistress of the nether world! The drink-offerings now, the vases in right succession: water, cow's milk, and beer — I pour, I pour, I pour. My black feet stand in the liquid, the pool, the bubbling lake, while I perform the sacrifice and slay the dog — a loathsome rite, but it is not our choice, we only know that it is dear to you.

" Bring him on, then, the sniffling cur, the obscene beast, and slit his throat! Slit his belly and bathe your hands in the smoking entrails as they steam up into the cool moonlighted night. Smeared with blood, dripping with entrails, I hold them up to you, my hands, for I have made them in your image. I salute you, I invite you humbly to the sacrificial meal, O mistress of the hosts of night! Courteously we entreat you, solemnly we beg you, graciously share the meal, accept the flawless gifts! Does it please you to accept? For else know that the priestess will rise in strength against you, will seize you violently with bold practised clutch. Approach! Come springing from a noose, or from pressing hard the woman in labour as she groans; from the caresses of self-slain wives; come, blood-smeared one, from the haunting-place of corpses to gnaw their flesh! Come, lured thither

by your cankered lust of the impure, from unclean cling-
ings at the cross-roads where the malefactor lies.

"Do I know you, do you know yourself in these
my words? Do I wrestle nearer to you in your essence as
you are? Lo, I know you in your works and ways, your
unspeakable practices, your monstrous eating and drink-
ing, and all your bottomless lusts! Or shall I come to
you with closer grips and plainer, and my mouth forget
its last restraint, naming you as you are in all your swin-
ish essence? — Uttermost horror clepe I you, bitch and
strumpet, I rail at you, pus-eyed nightmare, rotten fungus,
slavering slut of hell. You that perch at home on gallows
where the criminal is flayed, squeaking and squalling
and slobbering as you gnaw the carrion bones! Last lust
of the hanged, wet-wombed receiver of his erected agony!
Yet weak with vice, unnerved and abject, quaking with
every breeze, starting at spectres, to all things of the
night a cowardly prey. Uttermost horror! Know I you?
Name I you? Have I you? See I you? Yes, it is she!
For lo, a cloud darkened the face of the moon and while
it was veiled she came. The dog that bays before the
house bayed louder, the blaze flared up from the hearth;
the handmaid there of her who invokes you writhes in a
fit. Where she bends her gaze, whither her eyes roll,
thence approaches the goddess.

"Sovereign, we greet you. Graciously be pleased; for
we have given of our best in gifts. If then the impure
offering appease you, help! If the unclean meal, aid us,
we pray! Help her, the despised and languishing! She
groans for love of a youth who will not as she will. Help
her, as you can, as you must, I have you in ban. Torment
him hither in the flesh, the reluctant one, till he come to

her on her bed, he knows not how, make smooth his neck
to her hands, let her once slake her longing with the
sharp smell of his youth, for which she yearns!

"Now the hairs, quickly, wench. The love-offering,
the burnt-offering, I now perform, in sight of the goddess.
Ah, the bright locks, from heads one near, one far, so
soft and shining! Waste matter from your bodies, I,
priestess, weave and wind, mingle and marry them in
my hands bloody from sacrifice, I knot and net, I twist
and tie; I let them fall into the flame, and flame consumes
them crackling. Why is the face of the suppliant one
writhen with horror and disgust? Is it the evil hornlike
smell of the burning offendeth your nostrils? 'Tis your
own substance, my delicate one, essence of your ardent
flesh — the odour of love! — Done! " she said abruptly.
" The worship has been well performed. May he please
you and relish you, your beautiful one! The mistress-
bitch blesses him to you, thanks to Tabubu's arts, which
are worth their hire."

And the low creature laid aside her lofty tone, stepped
back from her labours, wiped her nose with the back of
her hand, and put her blood-stained hands in a basin of
water to cleanse them. The moon shone out again. Mekh,
the concubine, came to after her faint.

" Is she still there? " she asked, shaking.

" Who? " asked Tabubu, scrubbing her hands like a
doctor after an operation. " The bitch? Calm yourself,
concubine, she has vanished again. She did not want to
come, she was enforced by my arts, because I know so
well how to get round her and compass her character so
tellingly in words. And she could do nothing here but
by my will, because I buried under the threshold a three-

fold spell against evil. But she will perform her task, no question of that. She received the offering, and likewise she is bound by the burnt-offering of the woven hair."

Mut-em-inet, the mistress, heaved a deep, audible sigh and rose from the hearth where she had crouched. In her white mantle, with the laurel still at her ear, she stood before the carrion flesh with her chin raised and her hands clasped beneath it. Since she had smelt the odour of burning hair, hers and Joseph's mingled, the corners of her half-open, masklike mouth had sagged more and more bitterly, as though weighted down; it was piteous to see, this mouth, with its stiff, tragic lips; to watch them move, as in her chanting voice she addressed her plea to the powers above:

" Hear me, ye purer spirits, who might have joyed me had ye smiled upon my love to Osarsiph the Ibrian youth; hear and see me, in my misery at this abasement, how anguish sits at my heart for the evil choice I must make, since no other remained to me, in my deep despair, to your mistress, sweet Osarsiph, my falcon! Ah, ye purer powers, how hard, how oppressive, how shameful is this renunciation of mine! For I have renounced his soul, when at last I yielded and was enforced to this making of magic. Your soul I renounced, Osarsiph, my beloved — and how hard, how bitter to love must this renunciation be! I have renounced your eyes, most anguishing of all, but I could no other, I was helpless and had no choice. When we embrace, thine eyes will be closed and dead, and only thy swelling lips will be mine — how often shall I kiss them, shamed in my bliss! For the breath of thy mouth is dearer than aught else; but more than all, more than aught else, my sun-youth, would have been the gaze of thy soul — and the lament for its loss welleth up from my depths. Hear, ye purer powers! From beside this hearth of the black arts, in the bitterness of my affliction I cry to you. Look upon me, a woman of high rank, driven by love to sink beneath it, that I must give my joy for lust, to enjoy if not the joy of his eyes at least the delight of his mouth! But woeful and evil it is to me, this renunciation, to me a daughter of a prince, I cannot but utter it aloud, ye higher powers, cannot but give it voice before I taste this conjured lust and enjoy a soulless bliss with his sweet body. Ye spirits, leave me my secret inmost prayer: let me hope that at the last the lust and joy may not quite part, so that if the lust be deep enough, love may blossom from it; that beneath my ardent kisses the dead boy's eyes may open and he may give me his gaze from his soul, so that perhaps after all the hard conditions of this magic art may not hold but be defeated. In my abasement, ye purer powers, leave me this silent secret hope; to you I raise my lament, deny me not the hope of this little defeat, this little, little triumph — "

And Mut-em-inet lifted her arms and with violent prolonged sobbing sank upon the breast of Mekh, the concubine, who led her from the roof.

NEW YEAR'S DAY

My audience must by now have reached the height of its impatience to hear what after all everybody already knows. The hour of satisfaction is at hand, the climax of the story, the chief hour of the feast, which has been since it first came to pass and related itself: the hour and day when Joseph, for three years Potiphar's head steward, for ten his property, just saved himself from the grossest error of his life, escaping from fiery temptation — though as it were with a black eye — and as a result completing a smaller cycle of his life, in that he went down again to the pit, by his own error, as he himself realized, and in punishment for behaviour so heedless, so provocative — almost, one might say, so wicked — that there was not much to choose between it and his earlier wrongdoing.

We are justified in drawing a parallel between his sin against Potiphar's wife and his earlier sin against his brothers. Once more he had gone too far, in his craving to make people " sit up "; once more the working of his charm, which it was his good right to employ, for his own enjoyment and for the honour and profit of his God, had been allowed to get beyond control, to degenerate into an actual danger. In his first life these workings had taken the negative form of hate; this time the immoderately positive and equally destructive form of passion. He had in his blindness given fuel to the flames of both; in the second case, misled by his own response to a woman's uncontrollable passion, he who stood in such need of instruction himself had tried to play the pedagogue. His conduct cried out for retribution, there is no doubt of that; but we cannot help smiling to see how the punishment which so justly overtook him was directed to the furtherance of a good fortune much greater and more brilliant than that which had been destroyed. The source of our amusement is the insight which these events afford into the mental processes of exalted spheres. Far

back in the very pre-beginnings of history, we have seen
that the fallibility of the creature man was a source of
dissatisfaction to certain circles. "What is man, that
Thou art mindful of him? " The question always hovered
on certain lips and was an embarrassment to the Creator,
who saw Himself driven to pay tribute to the "kingdom
of the stern " and let justice have its way — clearly less
of His own motion than under a moral pressure from
which He could not well escape. The present instance is
a delightful example of His dignified bowing to the storm,
while at the same time having His little game with the
austere and disgruntled ones, practising the art of healing where He chastened and making misfortune a fruitful
soil whence renewed good fortune should spring.

The day of decision, the turning-point, was the great
feast-day of the official New Year, the day of the beginning of the rise of the Nile and of Amun's visit to his
southern house of women. The official New Year, be it
noted; for the actual day when the sacred cycle closed,
the dog-star rose once more in the morning sky, and the
waters began to mount was by no means the same day.
In this respect disorder reigned in Egypt, where it was
otherwise so much detested. It did happen, through time,
men's lives, and kingly dynasties, that the actual New
Year coincided with the calendar; but only in one thousand four hundred and sixty years did this come to pass,
almost forty-eight generations must live without experience of it — which they did not mind at all, by comparison with other of life's manifold cares. The century in
which Joseph's Egyptian course was run was not vouchsafed the pleasure of beholding the beauty inherent in the
union of the actual and the formal; the children of Kemt

who then lived and laughed and wept beneath Egypt's sun simply knew no more than that the two did not coincide — and it mattered to them not at all. Not that they celebrated the New Year, Akhet, the rise of the Nile, at a time when actually they were in the middle of the harvest, Shemu. But they did so in the winter season, Peret, also called the time of the sowing; and if the children of Kemt saw nothing strange in that — for an irregularity which will go on for another thousand years is after all regularity of a sort — Joseph for his part did, he even found it comic, by reason of his inward detachment respecting the life and customs of the Egyptians. He kept the irregular feast, as he did all those of the nether land, with reservations, and with just that amount of indulgence which he considered justified from above in respect of his worldly participation. It is worth while to point out in passing, and is almost a cause of amazement, that a person having so much critical detachment from the sphere where he lived, and from activities to him fundamentally foolish, could yet take life seriously enough to achieve all that Joseph achieved, and accomplish all the good that he was destined to accomplish.

But whether a detached mind took it seriously or no, the day of the official rise of the Nile was celebrated in all Egypt, and especially in Nowet-Amun, the hundred-gated Wese, with a solemnity which we can only realize by comparing it with one of our own great national and popular festivals. The whole city was on its legs from early dawn, and its huge population, greatly exceeding a hundred thousand, as we know, was still further increased by hordes of country-folk from up-river and down, streaming in to celebrate Amun's great day in the god's own seat. They mingled among the citizens, open-mouthed, hopping on one leg, staring at the city's majestic sights, the glory of which made up to the betaxed and belaboured little peasantry for the grey poverty of the whole past year and strengthened their patriotism for the floggings of the one to come. In a sweating throng, their noses full of the odours of burnt fat, the fragrance from mountains of flowers, they filled the gay, canopied, alabaster-paven forecourts of the temples, which echoed with sacred chorals, glowed with colour, and were full to bursting with abundance of heaped-up food and drink of every sort and kind. There, this one day, they might fill their bellies at the expense of the god, or rather of the higher powers who robbed and exploited the whole year round but now smiled in extravagant generosity; they might, against their own better knowledge, lull themselves in the dream that it would always be thus, that with this feast the golden age of free beer and roast goose had dawned, and never again would the tax-gatherers come, accompanied by Nubians bearing palm rods to harass the little peasantry, but every day would be like the temple of Amun-Re, wherein they saw a drunken woman with flowing hair, spending her days in riotous living because she held the king of the gods.

By sunset all Wese was so drunk that it went reeling and bawling about the streets, committing all sorts of nuisances. But in the early morning and forenoon it was still fresh-eyed and well in hand; receptive to the splendours of Pharaoh's progress, when he drove out " to receive the office of his father," in the official phrase, and Amun moved in his famous procession on the Nile to Opet, to his southern house of women. The populace was all joyous reverence and pious zeal, untiringly it gazed upon the unfolding splendours of State and Church, which were calculated to lay up in the hearts of Wese's children and her guests a fresh supply of daily patience and proudly self-deluded devotion to the fatherland. This was accomplished nearly as efficiently in the present as in the old days when earlier kings came home booty-laden and triumphant from Nubian and Asiatic campaigns and perpetuated their victories in reliefs on the temple walls — victories which had made Egypt great, and were indeed the first beginning of the exploitations and floggings of the little peasants.

On high feast-days Pharaoh drove out wearing crown and gloves; he came out from his palace brilliant like the rising sun, and betook himself to his father's house, to behold his beauty; in his high swaying canopied carrying-chair, surrounded by ostrich-feather fans, enveloped in heavy clouds of fragrant smoke, which streamed back upon him from incense-bearers walking in front of his chair, their faces turned toward the good god. The voices of the reading priests were drowned in the jubilations of the throng, as they hopped on one leg and rejoiced. Drums and cornets preceded the procession, in which walked troops of Pharaoh's relations, dignitaries, unique and true friends of the king as well as just plain friends. Ranks of soldiers closed up the rear, with field badges, battle-axes, and throw-sticks. The life-time of Re to thee, the peace of Amun! But where should one stand — staring, swallowing dust, stretching one's neck — were it better here, or at Karnak beside Amun's house, aflutter with banners, whither everything would finally proceed? For the god himself came out today,

left the dim shrine in the farthest background of his mam-
moth tomb, behind all the forecourts, courts, and halls,
each one lower-ceiled and more silent than the last; and
moved, a strange, mis-shapen, squatting puppet, through
all his halls, each loftier and more brightly coloured, on
his bark adorned with the heads of rams, secluded in his
veil-shrouded chapel, which was borne by long poles on
the shoulders of four-and-twenty shiny-pates in starched
kilts. He too, among fans, in clouds of incense, went into
the light and the noise to meet his son.

The great event was the " flight of geese," a custom
dating from primitive times, the scene of which was the
beautiful meeting-place on the square before the temple.
What a lovely and joyous spot this was! Gay flags flut-
tered from gilded poles with the head-ornament of the
god on top. Mountains of flowers and fruits heaped the
offertory tables before the shrine of the holy Triad,
father, mother, and son; statues of Pharaoh's ancestors,
the kings of Upper and Lower Egypt, brought up by the
crew of the sun-bark, divided into four watches, were
here set up. Priests standing on golden pedestals above
the crowd, their faces turned to the four quarters of the
earth, released the wildfowl in four directions, to carry
to the gods of each the news that Horus, son of Osiris
and Eset, had set upon his head the white as well as the
red crown. For he that was conceived in death had once
chosen this form when he mounted the throne of the two
lands and the ceremony had been repeated through countless years, and lay and learned in their different ways
had drawn conclusions about the general or the individual destiny from the manner of flight.

After the flight of geese, Pharaoh performed many

beautiful mysteries and ceremonies on the square. He sacrificed before the images of the early kings. He cut with a golden sickle the sheaf of spelt handed him by a priest and laid the grain as an offering of praise and petition before his father. He burned the incense of the gods before him in a long-legged pan, while readers and choir-singers chanted out of their book-rolls. Then the majesty of this god seated itself in a chair and sat motionless to receive the congratulations of the court, expressed in quaint and high-sounding words or brought before him in the shape of letters couched in flowery, subtilizing phrases, from courtiers who were prevented from coming. They were read aloud, to the great entertainment of all who listened.

This was only the first act of the celebration, which went on from beauty to beauty. They went down to the Nile, the barks of the holy Triad swaying aloft on the shoulders of twenty-four shiny-pates each; and Pharaoh walked like a modest son on foot behind his father Amun's bark.

The whole crowd swarmed down to the river, thronging round the procession of the gods, led by Beknechons, the head priest, in his leopard-skin, just behind the trumpets and cornets. The incense rose, the music swelled, the fan-bearers fanned. Arrived at the shore, the sacred barks were put on three large ships, each more beautiful than the other, but the most indescribably beautiful of all was Amun's bark, made of cedar-wood which — it was said — the princes of the Retenu had had to fell in the cedar mountains and themselves pole across the river. Each ship was mounted in silver, and all of gold was the great heaven-throne in the centre and the flag-poles and

obelisks in front, adorned with serpent-crowns fore and
aft and furnished with all sorts of little emblematic soul-
figures and sacred symbols, most of which people would
not have known how to explain, from so remote a past had
they been handed down. The fact strengthened instead
of weakening the veneration they enjoyed.

The state ships conveying the great Triad were not
boats, but barges; not rowed, but towed by light galleys
and a crew from the shore, up the Nile toward the southern house of women. It was an honour to belong to these
crews, and a man so chosen reaped many practical benefits throughout the year. All Wese, save the dying and
the age-ridden — for the infants were carried on their
mothers' backs or at their breasts — in other words, a
mighty host, rolled like a wave along the bank with the
crews, accompanying the divine procession, and a procession in themselves. They were led by a servant of
Amun chanting hymns; soldiers of the god followed with
shields and throw-sticks; dressed-up Negroes came after,
greeted with roars of laughter from the crowd as they
danced and drummed, cut grimaces and made ribald
jokes. They knew they were held in contempt and so
played the fool even more than lay in their natures,
to flatter the grotesque conception the people had of
them. Temple musicians of both sexes shook castanets
and sistra; there were animals garlanded for the sacrifice, standard-bearers, war-chariots, lute-players, upper
priests with their retinues; burghers and peasants followed on, singing and clapping out the time with their
hands.

Rejoicing and exulting the train moved on to the pillared temple on the river, where the state ships tied up;

the sacred barks were hoisted to the shoulders of the bearers and carried in a new procession, to the sound of drums and long trumpets, to the glorious house of birth, received and met with curtsyings and contortings and waving of boughs by Amun's earthly concubines, the ladies of the order of Hathor, who now danced before their exalted spouse, the squatting swaddled little doll in his shrouded bark; in diaphanous garments, beating tambourines and singing in their universally beloved voices. This was the great New Year's reception in Amun's harem, a most regal spread, mountains of offerings in the shape of food and drink, unending genuflections and symbolic ceremonies, for the most part no longer understood by anybody, in the inmost, inner, and outer parts of the house of embrace and birth, in its rooms full of gay reliefs and inscriptions, its corridors of rose-granite papyrus-columns, silver-paved tent-halls, and courts of statuary where the populace might enter at will. The full gorgeousness of the New Year will be best appreciated if we realize that toward the end of the day the whole procession re-formed in the same splendour as before and went back by water and land to Karnak; and that in all the temples the fairs and feastings, the popular jollification and theatrical entertainments — in which masked priests performed scenes from the lives of the gods — went on without stopping through the evening. The whole great city swam in beer and bliss and belief in a carefree golden age. The crews which had towed the state barks, crowned with garlands, anointed with oil, and very drunk indeed, ranged through the streets and might do more or less what they liked, without let or hindrance.

THE EMPTY HOUSE

It was necessary to sketch in the scene of the feast of Opet, the official celebration of the rising of the Nile, in order to make clear to my readers the frame and setting of those events in the lives of individuals which form the climax of our tale. The bare sketch suffices to show that Petepre, the courtier, had his time very much taken up. He was a member of the immediate entourage of His Majesty Hor-in-the-Palace, who had this day more pontifical duties to perform than on any other of the highdays and holy-days in the year. And Petepre's place was among the nearest; that is, among the " unique " friends of the king. Yes, on this very morning he was raised to the rare and exalted rank and addressed in a manner which caused him the utmost gratification. The titular captain of the guard was away from home all day. Indeed, the whole household was away, the place was empty, like every other house in Wese; for, as I said, only cripples and the moribund remained at home. Among the last, indeed, were Huia and Tuia, the exalted parents in the upper storey; for they never went farther afield than the garden house on the mound, and seldom even as far as that. It was a miracle that they yet lived; for during the last ten years they had reckoned hourly on their passing, yet still tottered about, the old mole and the swamp-beaver, she with her blind slits of eyes, he with his beard of tarnished silver, together within the dark caul of their brother-sisterhood; perhaps because some aged people simply go on living and cannot find death, being powerless to die; perhaps because they were afraid of the king of the nether regions and the forty frightfully named ones, on account of the clumsy bribery of which they had once been guilty.

Huia and Tuia, then, had remained at home in their upper storey, together with the two stupid little maids who served them in succession to others grown in the course of time too unchildlike to wait on the exalted parents. Otherwise house and court were empty, like all others in Wese. Yet were they? No, for there was one other exception — single, but important. Mut-em-inet, Potiphar's wife, his chief and first, had stopped at home.

That must seem very strange to anyone with knowledge of the feast. She did not take part with her sisterhood, Amun's concubines, in the sacred service of the god; did not wear the horns and disk, nor in the narrow garment of Hathor undulate in the dance, nor raise her beloved voice to accompaniment of the silver rattle. She had made her excuses to the protectress of the order, Tiy, wife of the god; they were the same excuses which Rachel had once made a pretext what time she sat on the teraphim hidden in the camel bedding, and would not rise and stand before Laban. She had sent word that unfortunately she was unwell, meaning by the discreet phrase that unfortunately on this very day she found herself incapacitated. The exalted ladies had shown more understanding than Petepre, to whom she had said the same. For he, with a lack of feeling for human frailty, had been as obtuse as in his time the obtuse Laban. "How do you mean unwell?" he asked. "Have you toothache, or the vapours?" He used a silly medical expression current in high society to describe a hypochondriac state of health. And when she had finally gone into detail he had been unwilling to admit the excuse. "That doesn't count," he had said — very much, we will remember, as Laban in his time had done. "That is not an illness that anyone can see, or an excuse for staying away from the feast of the god. Some people would drag themselves to it half dead rather than stay away, but you want to remain at home on account of a simple and normal thing like that." "There does not need to be anything unnatural about an ailment, for it to attack us, my friend," she answered him. Then she gave him the choice of dispensing her either for the public feast or for the private entertainment at their own home in the evening, with which Petepre was to celebrate his promotion to the rank of " unique friend." It was impossible, she said, for her to attend at both. If she danced before the god she would be worn out by evening and have to absent herself from Petepre's feast.

In the end though in great annoyance he had had to agree to her saving her strength in the day-time in order to act as hostess in the evening. He was annoyed because he was suspicious — so much we can say with certainty. He did not like it. He did not feel easy in his mind at her remaining at home alone on the pretext that she was unwell; he was disturbed, he had a vague sense of apprehension — on the score of his own peace of mind and that of the household; and he came home earlier than necessary to the evening party, on his lips the usual question, outwardly confident, but inwardly anxious: " Is all well in the house? Is the mistress happy? " — this time to receive a frightful but secretly long-expected reply.

We have thus anticipated our story, because after all, in the words of Renenutet, wife of the chief overseer of

bulls, we know it already without being told; so that there
is no more suspense save in the matter of details. Neither
will it surprise anybody to hear that the thought of Joseph
had a share in Petepre's annoyance and disquiet; and that
he mentally connected the idea of his wife remaining at
home with the question of whether Joseph was doing the
same. We share his disquiet, and we too must, not without misgivings on the score of the seven reasons, inquire
of Joseph's doings on the day of the feast. Did he, in
fact, remain at home too?

He did not; it would have been quite impossible for
him, and strikingly inconsistent with his principles and
practice. The Egyptian Joseph, in this tenth year after
he had been snatched away into the land of the dead, was
now at seven-and-twenty Egyptian incarnate, in a social
if not in a spiritual sense; even his fleshly garment had
been for the last three years wholly Egyptian, the form
of him entirely occupied and informed by Egyptian substance. We know his attitude: with certain reservations
he adapted himself, became a child of Egypt and par-
taker in the Egyptian year, celebrating her heathen feasts,
sharing in her outlandish practices, in his tolerant, cos-
mopolitan way, if also with moderation and a certain
irony; confident that the man who had brought the calf
to this field would indulgently close his eyes to the sight.
Certainly the New Year's day, the great Amun-feast, was
a proper occasion to be affable, to live and let live; and
the son of Jacob went to it. Like everybody else here below, he was arrayed in feast-day garments and on foot
from early morn. Yes, he actually paid symbolic honour to the popular custom and drank a little more than
he needed; but only later in the day, for at first he had

to perform official duties. As the steward of a high dig-
nitary and title-bearer he walked in the suite of the king's
suite from the western house of the horizon to Amun's
great house and took ship thence to the Opet temple.
The return procession of the divine family was not quite
so formal, it was easy to withdraw from it; and Joseph
spent the day as thousands did, sauntering and sightseeing, visiting masses in the temples, sacrificial feasts, and
masques of the gods. He knew of course, that he must
be at home betimes, by late afternoon and before all
the other servants, to perform to his own satisfaction his
duties as head of the household and responsible overseer; to assure himself that in the long serving-room
(where once he had received from the scribe of the buffet
the refreshment prepared for Huia and Tuia) and in the
hall where the banquet was spread, everything was ready
and in order for the New Year's feast and the celebration
of Petepre's promotion.

He laid stress in his mind, and in his intentions, on
carrying out this supervision alone and undisturbed,
while the house was still empty and his subordinates not
yet returned from the feast. It seemed to him right and
proper so to do; and in support of his resolution he ex-
cogitated a set of sayings — in his own mind, for they
had never existed before, though he couched them in
the form of popular proverbs — such as: High estate,
golden weight; great honour, great onus; first to aspire,
last to retire — and other golden rules of the same kind.
He thought them out, and repeated them to himself, after
learning, during the water journey, that his mistress, being indisposed, was not taking part in the dances of the
order of Hathor but remaining at home alone. For be-

fore he knew this fact he had never thought of the jingles, nor persuaded himself that they were proverbs; nor had he realized what now became perfectly clear, that in the sense of these maxims it was imperative for him, the head of the house, to be at home before the rest of the staff, to see that all was in readiness.

He used that very word, in his mind, though even to him it was suggestive, and an inner voice warned him that he should refrain. Joseph, as an upright young man, did not deceive himself about the great and soul-shattering peril involved in following out his own maxims. It was a soul-shattering peril, yes; yet also it was a joyful opportunity — but for what? Yes, little whispering Bes, an opportunity to bring to an issue the affair of honour between God and Amun; to take the bull by the horns and in God's name to let matters come to a head here and now. This was the goal, this the great, soul-shattering opportunity; and everything else, frightened, whispering little Bes, is just nonsense and rubbish. " The servant still may sleep, the master watch must keep." Joseph, the young head steward, would cling to his proverb-wisdom, undeterred by either the futile croaking of his little friend or his mistress's artful indisposition.

We may gather from overhearing this much of what went on in his mind that there is no ground to feel assured of his safety. The original story, to be sure, long ago played itself out to the end, and what we here relate is only a repetition in the feast, a temple masque, as it were. Otherwise, out of sheer anxiety and concern, the sweat might be standing on our brows! But what is a repetition in the feast? It is the abrogation of the difference between was and is. When the story first told itself, there was, at this crisis in it, simply no ground whatever for thinking that its hero would come off with a black eye instead of losing his God and his all. Nor have we any better right to premature unconcern. The women as they buried the beautiful god in the cave wailed no less shrilly because the hour of his resurrection would come. For when they wailed he was dead and mangled; and to every hour of the feast as it comes on and is present is due its meed of tears and triumphing, of triumph and tears. Esau celebrated his great hour, swelling his chest and flinging out his legs, pathetic and comic to behold. His story had not yet reached the wailing and weeping stage. We are in like case: at this moment, reading Joseph's thoughts and hearing his jingling little rhymes, we are justified of the sweat that stands on our brows, and should not be justified if it did not so stand.

We shall be in even worse case if we return and see how matters stood in Potiphar's deserted house. The woman who remained there alone, who in this drama plays the part of the mother of sin, was ardently confiding in the feast-hour for a glowing realization of her hopes. Certainly she no less than Jacob's son was resolved to stake all on the issue; certainly she had every reason to await the bitter-blissful triumph of her passion, the hour of sweet and sinister fulfilment, when she should enfold her beloved in her arms. Were her hopes not confirmed from above and from below? She was empowered by the highest spiritual authority in the kingdom, the honour and sun-power of Amun were pledged to her support; but no less was she upheld by the powers of darkness, which by virtue of infernal magic she, daughter of a nome prince, had debased herself to conjure and to bind —

though in her breast still lingered hope that she might
evade the humiliating conditions they imposed. For in
her shrewd feminine mind she thought that after all love
made no such clear distinction between body and soul;
that by the sweet embraces of the flesh she would succeed
in wooing the soul of her beloved as well, and in uniting
lust with bliss. As we tell the tale, the wife of Potiphar
is — here and now, as well as in the then which has become the now — bound up with the event, and cannot
know what has not yet happened. But this she knows:
that Joseph will come to her in the empty house; with
all the burning passion of her soul she knows it. The
bitch-goddess will torment him hitherwards. In other
words, he will learn on the way that she is not taking
part in the feast, that she has remained alone in the silent
house. And the thought will grow in him to overmaster-
ing strength, that he must come back at a time when this
significant and extraordinary situation still obtains. The
bitch-goddess will give this thought power over him,
will make it guide his steps. Joseph, thinks Mut, knows
nothing about the bitch-goddess and Tabubu's vile arts;
he will think it is his own, that overwhelming impulse to
join Mut in the empty house; he will suppose that he is
irresistibly drawn to seek her out in her solitude. And
if he does, if he is convinced that thought and impulse
are his own, then will not the illusion become truth in
his soul, and thus the bitch have been defeated on her
own ground? A man will often say " I am urged " to do
so and so. But what is it that urges him, which he distin-
guishes from himself and makes responsible for his act?
Certainly it is only himself; himself, together with his
desire. Is there any difference between "I will " and

"Something within me wills"? Must we say "I will" in order to act? Does the act come from the will, or does not rather the will first show itself in the act? Joseph will come; and by his coming will realize that he willed to come, and why. But if he comes, if he hears the call of opportunity and heeds the call, then all is decided, Mut has triumphed, she will crown him with ivy and garlands of the vine!

Thus Potiphar's wife, and such the reasoning of her drunken, over-stimulated mind. Her eyes looked unnaturally large and quite as unnaturally bright, for she had applied quantities of black antimony to brows and lashes with her ivory pencil; and they looked out from it with a sinister look as of one possessed. And her mouth, as always, had no truck with her eyes: it was a sinuous, smiling, assured, and triumphant mouth. But her lips moved constantly in a slight sucking, chewing motion, for she was eating little balls of crushed incense mixed with honey, to sweeten her breath. She wore a garment of the thinnest royal linen, which revealed all her love-bewitched contours; from its folds, and from her hair, came a fragrance of fine cypress perfume. She was in the room reserved for her use in the master's house; on one side it adjoined the vestibule with the seven doors and the constellated pavement; on the other Petepre's northern pillared hall, where Joseph performed his reading service. But in one corner it gave on the banqueting-hall next the family dining-room; in this hall the evening feast was to be served, in honour of Petepre's new rank. Mut's door into the northern hall was open, likewise one of the doors thence into the banqueting-hall. Confident, expectant, she moved about in these rooms, solitary in the house save for the two exalted parents awaiting their end in the upper storey. Eni, their daughter-in-law, as she went to and fro, gave them a thought, and cast a glance upwards toward the painted ceiling from her jewelled, sinister, glittering eyes. Often she retired from hall and banqueting-room into the twilight of her private chamber, where the light fell from above through open-work stone panels. There she lay down, outstretched upon her diorite couch, and buried her face in the pillows. Cinnamon wood and myrrh burned in the incense stands, and their fragrant vapour curled out through the open doors into the dining- and banquet-halls.

So much for Mut, the enchantress.

To return to the departed son of Jacob: he came back, as we know, before any of the other members of the household. He came — and perhaps thereby became aware that he wanted to come, or was urged to come — which is the same thing. Circumstances had not prevented him from sticking to his duty and adhering to the view that it was right and proper for him to break off his sightseeing sooner than the others and give his attention to the house over which he was set. Though actually he had lingered longer than one might suppose, in the performance of a duty prescribed and postulated by so much proverbial wisdom. He did come back when the house was still empty; yet not so very long before the others, those of them, that is, who had not permission to stop in the city because they were needed that evening at home. Perhaps not longer than a winter hour, or even less — considering that in this latitude winter hours are so much shorter than summer ones.

He had spent a quite different day from Mut's: in sunlight and noise, in the lively hubbub of the pagan feast. Behind his lashes he still saw pictures of the magnificent processions, the masques, the bustling crowds. His Rachel-nose still smelled the burnt-sacrifices, the flowers, the emanations from all these hordes of human beings hot with hopping on one foot and excited with so much sensual gratification. His ears were still full of the sound of drums and horns, rhythmical hand-clapping, and the shouts of men intoxicated with hopeful fervour. He had eaten and drunk; without exaggerating his condition, I may say that he was in the frame of mind of a young man who is disposed to see in a threatened danger less a danger than an opportunity. He had a blue lotus-wreath on his head and a single blossom in his mouth. He twirled his fly-fan of white horsehair round on his wrist and sang as he went: " Blithe the servant, free from care, the master's eye is everywhere! " He actually thought that this was a line from some treasure of folk-wisdom, and that he had made up only the tune. So, as the day wore to its end, he reached his master's house, opened the gate of cast bronze, crossed the constellated pavement of the vestibule, and entered the beautiful banqueting-hall, where all was laid ready, in the most elegant refinement, for Petepre's party.

He had come home, Joseph, the young steward, to see that all was complete, and whether or no Khamat, scribe of the buffet, was deserving of a reproof. He moved about the pillared hall, among the chairs and little tables, the jars of wine in their holders, the buffets laden with pyramids of fruit and cakes. He looked to the lamps, the table of wreaths, floral necklaces, and unguent boxes; and rearranged the sideboard, making the little golden

beakers ring. He had spent awhile in these masterly re-
touchings, and made the beakers ring once or twice,
when he started; for he heard a voice, a singing, ringing
voice, calling him from some distance; calling the name
which he had taken in this land:

"Osarsiph!"

In all his life he never forgot that moment, when in
the empty house the sound of his name struck on his ear.
He stood with his fan under his arm and two golden
beakers in his hands. He was inspecting their polish and
certainly he had made them ring as he held them; he
listened, thinking he had not heard aright. Yet he must
have been mistaken, for he stood thus a long time listening, the two beakers in his hand, and there was no sound
for a long time. But at last it came again, that singing
voice echoed through the rooms:

"Osarsiph!"

"Here am I," he answered. His voice failed him for
hoarseness; he cleared his throat and said again:

"I hear."

Again there was a pause, and he waited motionless.
Then it came, singing and ringing:

"Is it you, Osarsiph, whom I hear in the hall, and
have you come home alone to the empty house?"

"As you say, mistress," he replied, setting back the
beakers in their place and going through the open door
into Petepre's northern hall, to speak into the adjoining
room.

"Yes, I am here, to see that things are in train in the
house. 'Much oversight to put all right' — you know the
proverb, and since my master has set me over the house
and knows no care save for the bread he eats, for he

has put all into my hands, keeping naught back, and will literally be no greater than I in this house — I have given the servants a little extra time to enjoy themselves, but thought best to resign the latter end of the day's pleasures and come home betimes. ' Harsh with thyself, to others merciful ' — as you know must be the rule. But I will not praise myself before you, and I am but little ahead of them, they may come at any moment, and Petepre too, the unique friend of the god, your husband and my noble master — "

The voice came ringing out of the twilit chamber: " And seeing after all that is in the house, will you not also, Osarsiph, see after me? Have you not heard that I remained alone and that I suffer? Cross over the threshold and come to me! "

" Gladly would I," Joseph replied, " and would cross the threshold and visit you, but there are many things here in the hall to attend to, and much still to arrange which needs me to cast my eye — "

But the voice sounded again:

" Come in to me. The mistress commands it."

And Joseph crossed the threshold and went in to her.

THE FATHER'S FACE

HERE our story loses its tongue. I mean our present version and repetition in the feast does so; for in the original, as it happened and told itself, it by no means lost its tongue; it went on, there in the twilit room, in an agitated exchange, a dialogue in the sense that both parties talked at once. I prefer, however, to draw over the scene the veil of delicacy and human feeling. For in that long-ago time it went on without witnesses, whereas here and today it is performed before a large audience — a decisive difference, as no one can deny, where a question of tact is involved. Joseph, particularly, was not silent; he could not be silent, but talked very volubly, almost breathlessly, bringing to bear all his wit and charm against the woman's desire, in the attempt to talk her out of it. But just here lies the reason why our story loses its tongue. For he became involved in a contradiction, or rather a contradiction presented itself, as he talked, most painfully affecting and troubling to human feeling: the contradiction between body and soul. Yes, as the woman, in words or by her silence, answered to what he said, his flesh stood up against his spirit, and in the midst of his most fluent and eloquent speech he became an ass. And what a shattering contradiction that is, what restraint it demands from the narrator: when eloquent wisdom is given the lie by the flesh and is manifest an ass!

He fled — for we know that he succeeded in flying — in the state and condition of the dead god; to the woman an aggravated occasion for despair and the raging fury of frustration. Her desire had discovered in him a manly readiness; and the forsaken woman alternately tore at and caressed the garment which he left in her hands — for we know that he left his garment behind him — in paroxysms of frantic agony, with loud outcries of exultation and anguish. The Egyptian woman's cry, repeated over and over again was: " *Me'eni nachtef!* I have seen his strength! "

Something enabled Joseph, in that uttermost extremity, to tear himself away and flee: that something was his father's face. He saw his father's face — all the

more detailed versions say so, and we may take it for
the truth. It is so: when, despite all his skill of tongues
he was almost lost, the face of his father appeared to
him. Jacob's image? Yes, certainly, Jacob's image. Not
an image of settled and personal lineaments which he saw
somewhere in the room. Rather he saw it in his mind and
with his mind's eye: an image of memory and admoni-
tion, the father's in a broad and general sense. For in it
Jacob's features mingled with Potiphar's fatherly traits,
there was something of the modest departed, Mont-kaw,
and over and above all these were other, mightier traits.
Out of bright, brown father-eyes with soft tear-sacs beneath them, it peered at Joseph in tender concern.

This it was which saved him. Or rather, he saved himself — for I would speak in the light of reason and give
credit where it is due, not to any spirit manifestation.
He saved himself, in that his spirit evoked the warning
image. In a situation only to be described as far gone,
with defeat very nigh, he tore himself away — to the
woman's intolerable anguish, as we must, in justly divided sympathy, admit — and it was fortunate that his
physical agility equalled his glibness of speech; for he
was able, one, two, three, to twist himself out of his
jacket — the " garment," his outer raiment — at which
she clutched in the abandon of her love, and to escape,
in not very stewardlike array, to the hall, the banqueting-
room, the vestibule.

Behind him, in her thwarted love she raved, half in
raptures — " *Me'eni nachtef!* " — but yet betrayed beyond bearing. She did frightful things with the garment
still warm with his body, which she held in her hands, the
precious hated object: covered it with kisses, drenched

it with tears, tore it with her teeth, trod it underfoot —
dealt with it, in short, much as the brethren had dealt with
the veil of the son at Dothan in the vale. " Beloved! "
she cried. " Whither do you go from me? Stay! O blissful boy! O shameless slave! Curses upon you! Death!
Treachery! Violence! Seize the miscreant! He has slain
my honour — help, help! Help for the mistress! A fiend
has attacked me! "

There we have it. Her thoughts — if we may speak
of thoughts where there was nothing but a whirlwind of
rage and tears — had brought her to the accusation with
which she had more than once threatened Joseph in the
fury of her desire, when she raised her lioness claws
against him: the murderous accusation that he had mon-
strously forgotten himself toward her, his mistress. The
wild recollection rose in the woman's mind, she flung
herself on it, shrieked it with all her strength — as one
hopes, by sheer voice-power, to lend truth to the untrue
— and our justifiable sympathy must make us rejoice
that the insulted woman found this outlet to her anguish,
that she could give it an expression, false, of course, yet
matching it in horror, which was calculated to enflame
all who heard, turn them into allies of her insulted state
and make them pant to avenge it. Her yells resounded.

There were already people in the vestibule. The sun
was setting, and most of Petepre's household had returned to house and courtyard. So it was good that the
fugitive had a little time and space to collect himself before he emerged. The servants stood rooted to the ground
with horror, hearing their mistress's cries; and though
the young steward came at a measured pace out of the
banqueting-hall and passed with composed mien among

them, it was as good as impossible not to connect the impaired state of his clothing with the shrieks that issued from the inner room. Joseph would have liked to gain his room, the special room of trust, to put himself to rights. But as there were servants in the way, and a craving to get out of doors took the upper hand, he crossed over to and through the open bronze door to the courtyard, which was full of the bustle of home-coming. Several litters were drawing up before the harem, containing the secondary wives; the chattering little creatures, under supervision of Nubian eunuchs and scribes of the house of the secluded, had been vouchsafed their glimpse of the feast and were now being returned to their gilded cage.

Whither should the fugitive flee with his black eye? Out through the gateway by which he once had entered? And thence? That he himself did not know, and was glad that he still had space before him in the courtyard and might move as though he were bound somewhither. Then he felt his clothing twitched; and Bes-em-heb, the little dwarf, piped up at him, his face all crumpled with his grief: " Ravaged the field — burnt by the bull — oh, ashes, ashes! Osarsiph, Osarsiph! " They stood halfway between the main house and the gateway in the outer wall. Joseph turned, the little man hanging to his coat. The sound of the woman's voice came over to him, the voice of the mistress. The white figure stood at the top of the house steps, surrounded by a crowd which poured after her out of the hall. She stretched out her arm, and men followed it running with arms likewise outstretched in his direction. They seized him and brought him back among the courtyard folk running up before the house:

gate- and door-keepers, artisans, stablemen, gardeners,
cooks, and silver-aproned waiters. The weeping midget
clung to his coat and was borne along too.

And Potiphar's wife addressed to her husband's servants thus gathered before and behind her in the courtyard that well-known speech which at all times has been
counted against her by all men; which even I, despite
all I have done for Mut-em-inet's saga and her cause, cannot fail to condemn. Not on account of its untruth, which
might pass as the garment of the truth; but on account
of the demagogy which she did not scorn to use to rouse
the people.

" Egyptians! " she cried. " Children of Kemt! Sons
of the river and the black earth! " — What did she mean
by that? They were just ordinary people, and at the time
nearly all of them a little drunk. Their Egyptian birth
as children of Hapi — in so far as it was a fact, for there
were among them Moors from Kush and people with
Chaldæan names — was a native merit: they had nothing to do with it nor did it help them in the least if they
neglected their duties, for their backs were bruised with
thick leather straps well laid on, regardless of whose
children they were. And now all at once their birth,
which had been very much in the background and had
no practical value for the individual, was brought to their
notice with flattering emphasis — because it could be
used to rouse their sense of honour, unite them in a common pride, and make them pant with fury against someone who had to be destroyed. Her challenge bewildered
them. Yet it had its effect, combined with that of the
good barley beer.

" Egyptian brothers! " — They were her brothers all

at once; it went through and through them, they found it thrilling. " Behold me, your mistress and mother, Petepre's chief and true wife! See me as I sit upon the threshold of this house — we know each other well, you and I! " — " We," and " each other "! They swallowed it down, this was a good day for the lower classes! — " But likewise know you this Hebrew youth, standing here half naked on this great day in the calendar, lacking his upper garment, because I have it in my hands. Do you recognize him, who was set as steward above the children of the land and over the house of one great in the two lands? He came down out of his wretched country to Egypt, Osiris' beautiful garden, the throne of Re, the horizon of the good spirit. They brought this stranger to us into this house " — " us " again! — " to mock us, and bring shame upon us. For this frightful thing has happened: I sat alone in my *kemenate*, alone in the house, for I was unwell and was dispensed from appearing before Amun and kept the empty house alone. Then the abandoned one, the Hebrew fiend, took advantage of my being alone and came in unto me that he might do his will with me and bring me to shame — the servant would lie with the mistress! " — she screamed the words — " lie with me to enforce me! But I cried with a loud voice, when he would have done it and have shamed me for his servant-lust; I ask you, Egyptian brothers, have ye heard me cry out with all my strength, in evidence that I repulsed him and defended myself to the utmost, as the law demands? Ye have heard it. But when he too heard it, the abandoned one, that I lifted up my voice and cried, then his boldness failed him and he struggled out of his outer garment, which I have here as evidence and would hold him by it that ye might seize him, and fled away from me with his evil purpose un- accomplished and got him out, so that I stand here pure before you, thanks to my outcry. But he, who was set over you all and over this house, he stands there in his shame, who will be seized of his deed, and judgment shall come upon him as soon as the master, my husband, comes home. Put the clog on him."

This was Mut's speech — it was not only untruthful but provocative. And Potiphar's household stood there stupefied and helpless; they had already been not too clear-headed, with all the free temple beer they had had, and now they were completely dazed. They had heard, all of them, that the mistress was infatuated with the handsome young steward and he denied her. And now suddenly it turned out that he had laid hands on the mistress and tried to do her violence. It made their heads go round, what with the beer and what with the mistress's tale; they could not make it rhyme, and all of them were fond of the young steward. Certainly the mistress had cried out, they had all heard her, and they knew the law: it was evidence of a woman's innocence if she cried out when she was attacked. And she had the steward's garment in her hands; it really looked as though she held it as a forfeit when he tore himself away; but he himself stood there with his head sunk on his chest and said not a word.

" Why are you hesitating? " they heard a strong manly voice saying — the voice of Dudu, the gentleman dwarf, who stood among them in a stiffly starched feast-day skirt. " Do you not hear the mistress, that she has been so cruelly insulted and nearly brought to shame, and she commands that the clog be brought and laid upon the Hebrew slave? Here it is, I have brought it with me. For when I heard her lawful outcry I knew where we were and at what o'clock, and quickly fetched the tools out of the whipping-room, to have them at hand. Here they are. Stop gaping, and fetter his lustful hands — bind up this infamous slave, bought long ago on the advice of the shallow against that of the sound; for long enough has he played the master and been set over us who are true-born! By the obelisk! He shall be brought to the house of retribution and death! "

It was Dudu's great hour and he savoured it to the full. And two of the servants took the clog out of his hand and put it on, while little Shepses-Bes whimpered in a way that made the rest of the crowd titter. It was a spindle-shaped block of wood with a slit in it, which could open and shut, holding the culprit's hands helplessly in the narrow hole, weighed down by the heavy wood.

" Fling him in the kennel! " commanded Mut, with a frightful sob. Then she crouched on the step where she was, in front of the open door, and laid Joseph's garment down beside her.

" Here I will sit," she said in her chanting voice that rang across the darkening courtyard, " on the threshold of this house, with the accusing garment by my side. Withdraw from me, all of you, and let no one advise me to go in, that I suffer no harm from my thin garb in the cool of the evening. I shall be deaf to such pleas, for here will I sit beside my forfeit until Petepre drives in and I receive atonement for my monstrous wrong."

THE JUDGMENT

ALL hours are great, each in its own way, whether great
in pride or great in misery. Esau had his, when all went
well with him, and he boasted, throwing out his legs. But
when he flung out of the tent, crying: " Curse it! Curse
it! " and limped away, tears like hazel-nuts rolling from
his eyes, was the hour less great, less momentous for the
hairy one? So now: we are come to Petepre's feast-hour,
the most painful in his life, and at all times inwardly
anticipated by him: when he hunted birds, or the hippopotamus, or followed the desert chase; even when he read
his good old books, always that hour abode in the background of his thoughts, always he vaguely looked forward to it, ignorant only of its details — though these,
when it came, were largely in his hands. And as we shall
see, he shaped them nobly.

He rode in between torches, driven by Neternakht, his
charioteer; earlier, as I said, than the festivities required,
on account of his premonitions. It was a home-coming
like many others, when each time he had felt dread in
his heart — but this time the dread was to be realized.
" Is all well in the house? Is the mistress happy? " Just
that she is not: the mistress sits, a figure of tragedy, on
your threshold, and your helpful cup-bearer lies fettered
in the kennel.

So, then, this was the form which the reality took.
Well, let us deal with it. He had already, from some distance, seen that Mut, his wife, somehow frightful to behold, sat beside the door of his house. Yet as he dis-
mounted from his gala chariot he threw out the usual

questions — this time they remained unanswered. The grooms hung their heads and were silent. Yes, yes, it was all just as he had always expected, though of course the hour might hold its minor surprises. The car was led away; the crowd drew back into the torch-lighted courtyard; he moved, that Reuben-tower of tender flesh, with his fan and symbol of office in his hand, toward the steps; he mounted them to where she crouched.

"What am I to think of this scene, my dear friend?" he asked, with courtesy and circumspection. "You sit thinly clad in so exposed a place, and beside you is something I am at a loss to understand."

"So it is," answered she. "Yet your words are pale and weak to describe a reality so much more frightful and violent than you paint it. But what you say is true: here I sit, and have that beside me of which you shall soon have frightful understanding."

"Aid me to reach it," he replied.

"I sit here," she said, "awaiting your judgment upon the direst crime ever known in the two lands or probably in all the kingdoms."

He made a sign with his fingers to ward off evil and waited, composedly.

"He came," she chanted, "the Hebrew servant whom you brought to us, he came to me to mock me. I begged you in the hall that sunset evening, I embraced your knees that you might send away the stranger, from whom I boded no good. In vain; the slave was too dear to you and I went away unconsoled. But now the wretch came upon me and would have his lust of me in your empty house, being in manly readiness for the act. You do not believe, you cannot comprehend this abomination? Then see this sign and interpret as you must. Stronger than the word is the sign; in it is nothing to interpret or to doubt, for it speaks the absolute language of fact. Behold! Is this robe your slave's robe? Examine it well, for I am clean before you by this sign. For when I cried out as the wretch assailed me, he was afraid and fled from me, but I held him by his garment and in his fright he left it in my hand. The evidence of his shocking crime — here I hold it before your eyes, the evidence of his flight and of my crying. For if he had not fled I had not his garment; if I had not shrieked he had not fled. Moreover all your household are witness that I shrieked — ask all the people!"

Petepre stood silent, his head bent. Then he gave a sigh and said:

"That is a very sad affair."

"Sad?" she repeated, stormily.

"I said, very sad," he answered. "It is even frightful; I would seek a yet stronger word, but that I may gather from what you say that, thanks to your presence of mind and legal knowledge, the issue was favourable and things did not come to the worst."

"You seek no word to describe the shameless slave?"

"He is a shameless slave. As the whole affair is a matter of his behaviour, the words I used apply above all to him. And this evil thing must confront me, on this evening of all evenings, the evening of the great day of my elevation to the rank of unique friend, when I come home to celebrate Pharaoh's goodness and grace with a little evening party, to which the guests will soon be coming. You will agree that it is hard."

"Petepre! Have you no human heart in your breast?"

" Why do you ask? "

"Because in this hour of nameless horror you can speak of your new court title and how you will celebrate it."

" I did so but to bring the nameless horror of the hour into sharpest contrast with the homage of the day and set it off the more. It lies in the nature of the nameless that one may not directly speak of it, but only express it by indirection."

" No, Petepre, you have no human feeling! "

" My love, I will tell you something: there are situations in which one welcomes a certain lack of feeling for the sake of the injured as well as of the situation itself, which may be better dealt with in the absence of too much human feeling. What is now to be done, in this dreadful and very sad affair, which mars the day of my own promotion? It must be dealt with and dispatched without delay; for in the first place I quite understand that you will not stir from this spot, where it is impossible you should remain, until you have satisfaction for the unspeakable annoyance you have suffered. But in the second place, everything must be put right before my guests arrive, and that will be soon. Therefore I must hold domestic court without delay, and the trial, praise to the Hidden One, will be brief, for your word, my friend, has sole validity and none other comes into question, so that judgment can be rendered speedily. — Where is Osarsiph? "

" In the kennel."

"I thought as much. Let him be brought before me. Have the exalted parents summoned from the upper storey, even though they may sleep. Let the household assemble before my seat, which I will have set up here, where the mistress sits, that I may raise her after I have given judgment."

His orders were quickly carried out; the only obstacle to them being that at first Huia and Tuia, the brother-sister pair, refused to appear. They had heard of the trouble from their spindle-armed child-servants; these, with mouths like funnels, had poured out the course of events below, and the frightened old folk, like their sin-offered son the courtier of the sun, found that they had always been prepared for something of the sort. Now they were afraid and would not come, because the trial seemed to promise them a foretaste of the judgment in the lower regions and they felt too weak-headed to mar-shal their arguments in their own justification, further than the phrase: " We meant it for the best." They sent word that they were near to death and not equal to at-tending a domestic court. But their son, the master, grew angry, stamped his foot, and ordered that they be helped downstairs, just as they were. If they were on the point of dying, then the fitting place was where their daughter-in-law sat accusing and demanding justice.

So then they came down, on the arms of their child-maids, old Huia's silver beard wagging and his head aquiver; old Tuia with a frightened smile lifting her blank white face, with its slits of eyes, as though she were seeking something. They were placed beside Petepre's judgment seat, where they sat distractedly babbling: " We meant well." After a while they became quiet. Mut the mistress crouched, with her token and forfeit beside her, next the footstool of the throne, behind which a Moor in a red coat waved a tall fan. Torch-bearers lighted up the group. The courtyard, too, was lighted up with torches, and the household, save those on holiday, were gathered there. And they brought Joseph in his fetters before the judgment seat, with little Sa'anch-Wen-nofer-and-so-forth, who had not let go his skirt; likewise Dudu, pompous and secure in the hope that his great hour was mounting from better to best. The two dwarfs stood there, on the culprit's either side.

Petepre raised his refined voice and spoke rapidly and formally:

" We shall hold a court here, but we are in haste. — I summon thee, Ibis-headed One, who wrotest the laws for men, white ape beside the scale; thee, goddess Ma'at, who representest truth, in adornment of ostrich-feathers. The offering we owe you will be offered later, I stand warrant and it is as good as done. Now the hour presses. I pronounce justice for this house which is mine, and thus I pronounce."

He had said this while holding up his hands. Now he took an easier position in a corner of the lofty chair, supported his elbow, and lightly moved his little hand over the chair-arm as he went on:

" Notwithstanding the host of precautions taken in this house to oppose evil, despite all the words and maxims which should make it invulnerable to harm, yet affliction has succeeded in entering in and breaking for a time the charm which preserved it in peace and tender mutual consideration. Very sad and frightful is all this, there are no other words; so much the more that the evil must come to a head on the very day when Pharaoh's love and grace vouchsafed to honour me with the rank and splendid title of unique friend; one would think that on such

a day I must needs be met with courtesy and congratulations from all sides, instead of the frightful news that the
order of my house stands tottering. But be that as it may.
That beautiful order has for long been gnawed at by
affliction, and evil has slipped through the protecting
guards, to break in and bring about that which stands
written, that the rich shall be poor and the poor rich and
the temples desolate. For long, I say, has evil consumed
in secret, hidden from most, but not from the eye of the
master, who is father and mother to the house, for his
glance is like the moonbeam which makes the cow to conceive, and the breath of his words like the wind which
bears the pollen from bough to bough in sign of divine
fruitfulness. And as from the lap of his presentness all
beginning and prospering flow as the honey from the
comb, so naught escapes his oversight; however hidden
to the many, to his eye it lies open. Let this occasion
teach it. For I know the legend that follows my name:
that I take upon myself nothing on earth save that I eat
and drink. That is but gossip and negligible. Know that
I know all; and if the fear of the master and the dread of
his all-seeing eye come strengthened anew out of this
distress, upon which I sit in judgment, then one may say
that despite all its deep sadness it had its good side."

He carried to his nose a little handled malachite scent-
bottle, which hung on a chain over his jewelled collar;
after refreshing himself he went on:

" Thus were long known unto me the ways by which
evil penetrated into this house. And also to me were
known the ways of those who in their arrogance and spite,
out of envy and hatred, nourished it and prepared its
paths — and not only this but even first gave it entrance

that it might glide in past all the good words and charms. These traitorous powers stand before my seat, in the dwarfish person of my former guardian of the wardrobe and jewel-caskets, called Dudu. He himself has had to confess to me all his malice and how he opened the way for the consuming evil. Upon him may judgment fall! Far be it from me to deprive him of the virility which the sun-lord was once minded to unite with his puny form. I will not touch it. They shall cut out the traitor's tongue. — Half his tongue," he corrected himself, waving his hand with a movement of disgust as Dudu set up a loud wail. " But," he added, " as I am used to having my clothing and precious stones in charge of a dwarf, and it is not desirable that my habits should suffer from this misfortune, I will name the other dwarf of my house, Sa'ankh-Wen-nofer-Neteruhotep-em-per-Amun, as scribe of the wardrobe, and he shall from now on preside over my coffers."

Little Bes, the nose in his wrinkled face all cinnamon-red from weeping for Joseph, jumped for joy. But Mut, the mistress, raised her head to Petepre's chair and murmured through her teeth:

" What judgments are these, my husband? They touch but the margin of things, they are but trivial. What shall I think of your judgment and how shall I raise myself from this place, if you so judge? "

" Patience! " he answered her as softly, bending down from his seat. " For here each will in his turn have justice and judgment, and his guilt will overtake the culprit. Sit quietly! You will soon be able to rise from your sitting, as satisfied as though you had yourself been judge. I judge for you, my love — though without admixture of all too human feeling — and you may rejoice! For were feeling and its violence to pronounce the judgment, there might be no end to the remorse."

After he had so whispered to her he sat up straight again and spoke:

"Take your courage in your hands, Osarsiph, my former steward, for now I come to you, and you too shall hear my judgment, for which perhaps you have long anxiously waited — to sharpen your punishment I have prolonged your suspense. For I think to lay hold on you roughly and assign you bitter punishment — aside from that growing out of your own heart. For three beasts with ugly names follow at your heels; they are called, if I remember aright, shame, guilt, and mocking laughter. And these, it is easy to see, have brought you before my seat, your head bent and your eyes cast down — as I am not now for the first time aware, for I have kept my secret eye upon you during the torture of the time of waiting I have chosen to inflict. You stand, your head bowed low, your hands in fetters, and utter no word. For how should you speak, since you are not asked to justify yourself, and it is the mistress who witnesses against you, with her own word, which is unimpeachable and of itself would call down judgment; yet there is also the evidence of your upper garment to shame you, and the irrefutable language of things speaks of your presumption, which at last has brought you so far that you have raised your hand against the mistress, and when she would hold you to a reckoning, you are driven to leave your garment in her hand. I ask you, what sense it could have to speak in your own defence against the mistress's word and the plain language of things?"

Joseph was silent, bowing his head even lower than before.

"Obviously none," Petepre answered himself. "You must be dumb, as the sheep before its shearers is dumb — naught else remains for you to do, however glib of tongue and pleasing of speech you are. But thanks to the god of your tribe, that Baal or Adon who is probably like to the setting sun in power, for he preserved you in all your presumption that it came not to the uttermost with your rebellion, but rather thrust you out of your coat — thanks to him, I say, for else you had been at this hour thrown to the crocodile, or your part had been the slow death by fire, if not the torture of the door and the rod. But there can be no talk of such punishments. For you were preserved from the worst and I am not in a position to inflict them. But doubt not that I am minded none the less to handle you roughly; take then your sentence, after your lengthened-out suspense: For I will cast you in prison, where lie the prisoners of the king, at Zawi-Re, the island fortress in the river; not to me any longer you shall belong, but to Pharaoh, and shall be a slave of the king. I will give you into the hand of the master of the jail, a man with whom one does not jest; of whom moreover one may think that he will not be deceived by your beneficent-seeming ways; so that at least in the beginning he will be hard on you. Moreover I will write to the official and advise him of your affair and shall know how to speak of you to him. To this place of atonement, where no laughter is, you shall be taken tomorrow by boat and see my face no more, after those long and pleasant years when you could be near me, fill my cup, and read to me from the good old books. That may well be painful for you, I should not wonder if your downcast eyes were full of tears. Be that as it may, tomorrow you shall be brought to that place of durance. You need not go back to the kennel. That punishment you have already borne, it shall rather be Dudu who shall spend the night there until tomorrow they cut off half his tongue. But you may sleep in your wonted place, the special room of trust, which for this night shall be called the special room of custody before punishment. Also, since you wear fetters, it is but just that Dudu wear them too, if there is another set. If there is but one, Dudu shall wear it. — I have spoken. The trial is ended. Let each one go to his post for the reception of the guests."

No one will be surprised to hear that after such a judgment as this, all those on the court fell on their faces and raised up their hands, crying out the name of their mild and wise lord. Joseph too fell down, in gratitude; even Huia and Tuia, supported by their little maids, did honour on their faces to their son; and as for Mut-em-inet, the mistress, she made no exception; but was seen to bow over the footstool of the judgment seat and hide her face upon her husband's feet.

"My friend," said he, "there is no reason for thanks. I rejoice if I have succeeded in satisfying you in this affliction and have showed myself loving with my power. We may now go into the banqueting-hall and celebrate my feast. For since you have wisely kept the house all day, you have spared your strength for the evening."

So then Joseph went down a second time to the prison and the pit. The story of his rising again out of this hole to a still higher life may be the subject of future lays.

THE PRINCIPAL WORKS OF

THOMAS MANN

FIRST EDITIONS IN GERMAN

DER KLEINE HERR FRIEDEMANN
(Little Herr Friedemann). *Tales*
Berlin, S. Fischer Verlag. 1898

BUDDENBROOKS
Two volumes. Novel
Berlin, S. Fischer Verlag. 1901

TRISTAN
Contains Tonio Kröger. *Tales*
Berlin, S. Fischer Verlag. 1903

FIORENZA
Drama
Berlin, S. Fischer Verlag. 1905

KÖNIGLICHE HOHEIT
(Royal Highness). *Novel*
Berlin, S. Fischer Verlag. 1909

DER TOD IN VENEDIG
(Death in Venice). *Short novel*
Berlin, S. Fischer Verlag. 1913

DAS WUNDERKIND
(The Infant Prodigy). *Tales*
Berlin, S. Fischer Verlag. 1914

BETRACHTUNGEN EINES UNPOLITISCHEN
Autobiographical reflections
Berlin, S. Fischer Verlag. 1918

HERR UND HUND
(A Man and His Dog). Idyll
Contains also Gesang vom Kindchen, *an idyll in verse*
Berlin, S. Fischer Verlag. 1919

WÄLSUNGENBLUT
München, Phantasus-Verlag. 1921

BEKENNTNISSE DES HOCHSTAPLERS FELIX KRULL
Stuttgart, Deutsche Verlags-Anst.

BEMÜHUNGEN
Essays
Berlin, S. Fischer Verlag. 1922

REDE UND ANTWORT
Essays
Berlin, S. Fischer Verlag. 1922

DER ZAUBERBERG
(The Magic Mountain). Two volumes. Novel
Berlin, S. Fischer Verlag. 1924

UNORDNUNG UND FRÜHES LEID
(Disorder and Early Sorrow). Short novel
Berlin, S. Fischer Verlag. 1926

KINO
(Romanfragment)
Berlin, S. Fischer Verlag. 1926

PARISER RECHENSCHAFT
Berlin, S. Fischer Verlag. 1926

DEUTSCHE ANSPRACHE
Ein Appell an d. Vernunft
Berlin, S. Fischer Verlag. 1930

DIE FORDERUNG DES TAGES
Berlin, S. Fischer Verlag. 1930

MARIO UND DER ZAUBERER
(Mario and the Magician). *Short novel*
Berlin, S. Fischer Verlag. 1930

GOETHE ALS REPRÄSENTANT DES BÜRGERLICHEN ZEITALTERS
Berlin, S. Fischer Verlag. 1932

JOSEPH UND SEINE BRÜDER
(Joseph and His Brothers). *I. Die Geschichten Jaakobs. 1933. II. Der junge Joseph. 1934. III. Joseph in Ägypten. 1936. Novel*
I, II, Berlin, S. Fischer Verlag. III, Vienna, Bermann-Fischer Verlag

LEIDEN UND GRÖSSE DER MEISTER
Essays
Berlin, S. Fischer Verlag. 1935

FREUD UND DIE ZUKUNFT
Lecture
Vienna, Bermann-Fischer Verlag. 1936

EIN BRIEFWECHSEL
(An Exchange of Letters)
Zürich, Dr. Oprecht & Helbling AG. 1937

AMERICAN EDITIONS IN TRANSLATION
ALFRED A. KNOPF, NEW YORK

ROYAL HIGHNESS: A NOVEL OF GERMAN COURT LIFE
Translated by A. Cecil Curtis. 1916 (out of print)

BUDDENBROOKS
Translated by H. T. Lowe-Porter. 1924

DEATH IN VENICE AND OTHER STORIES*
Translated by Kenneth Burke. 1925. Contains translations of *Der Tod in Venedig, Tristan,* and *Tonio Kröger* (out of print)

THE MAGIC MOUNTAIN
Translated by H. T. Lowe-Porter. 1927. Two volumes

* Now included, in translations by H. T. Lowe-Porter, in *Stories of Three Decades.*

CHILDREN AND FOOLS
Translated by Herman George Scheffauer. 1928. Nine stories, including
translations of *Der kleine Herr Friedemann* and *Unordnung
und frühes Leid* (out of print)*

THREE ESSAYS
Translated by H. T. Lowe-Porter. 1929
Contains translations of *Friedrich und die grosse Koalition* from *Rede
und Antwort,* and of *Goethe und Tolstoi* and *Okkulte Erlebnisse*
from *Bemühungen*

EARLY SORROW
Translated by Herman George Scheffauer. 1930 (out of print)*

A MAN AND HIS DOG
Translated by Herman George Scheffauer. 1930 (out of print)*

DEATH IN VENICE
A new translation by H. T. Lowe-Porter, with an Introduction by
Ludwig Lewisohn. 1930 *

MARIO AND THE MAGICIAN
Translated by H. T. Lowe-Porter. 1931 (out of print)*

PAST MASTERS AND OTHER PAPERS
Translated by H. T. Lowe-Porter. 1933
Thirteen essays (out of print)

JOSEPH AND HIS BROTHERS
*I. Joseph and His Brothers. 1934. II. Young Joseph. 1935.
III (two volumes). Joseph in Egypt. 1938*
Translated by H. T. Lowe-Porter

STORIES OF THREE DECADES
Translated by H. T. Lowe-Porter. 1936
Contains all of Thomas Mann's fiction except the long novels

AN EXCHANGE OF LETTERS
Translated by H. T. Lowe-Porter. 1937

FREUD, GOETHE, WAGNER
Translated by H. T. Lowe-Porter, Rita Matthias-Reil, and Marie
Hottinger Mackie. 1937
Three essays

* Now included, in translations by H. T. Lowe-Porter, in *Stories of
Three Decades.*

A NOTE ON THE TYPE IN WHICH THIS BOOK IS SET

This book is composed on the Linotype in Bodoni, so called after Giambattista Bodoni (1740–1813), son of a printer of Piedmont. After gaining experience and fame as superintendent of the Press of the Propaganda in Rome, Bodoni became in 1766 the head of the ducal printing house at Parma, which he soon made the foremost of its kind in Europe. His Manuale Tipografico, *completed by his widow in 1818, contains 279 pages of specimens of types, including alphabets of about thirty foreign languages. His editions of Greek, Latin, Italian, and French classics, especially his Homer, are celebrated for their typography. In type-designing he was an innovator, making his new faces rounder, wider, and lighter, with greater openness and delicacy. His types were rather too rigidly perfect in detail, the thick lines contrasting sharply with the thin wiry lines. It was this feature, doubtless, that caused William Morris's condemnation of the Bodoni types as "swelteringly hideous." Bodoni Book, as reproduced by the Linotype Company, is a modern version based, not upon any one of Bodoni's fonts, but upon a composite conception of the Bodoni manner, designed to avoid the details stigmatized as bad by typographical experts and to secure the pleasing and effective results of which the Bodoni types are capable.*

THIS BOOK WAS COMPOSED, PRINTED, AND BOUND BY THE PLIMPTON PRESS, NORWOOD, MASS. THE PAPER WAS MADE BY CURTIS & BROTHER, NEWARK, DEL.